KUBIAK'S DAUGHTER

KUBIAK'S DAUGHTER

•

Stephen Lindley

AVALON BOOKS
NEW YORK

Lin

All the characters in this book are fictitious,
and any resemblance to actual persons,
living or dead, is purely coincidental.
Published by Thomas Bouregy & Co., Inc.
160 Madison Avenue, New York, NY 10016

Library of Congress Cataloging-in-Publication Data

Lindley, Stephen.
Kubiak's daughter / Stephen Lindley.
p. cm.
ISBN 0-8034-9808-X (acid-free paper)
I. Title.

PS3612.I53275K83 2006
813'.6—dc22

2006018078

PRINTED IN THE UNITED STATES OF AMERICA
ON ACID-FREE PAPER
BY HADDON CRAFTSMEN, BLOOMSBURG, PENNSYLVANIA

Chapter One

Four years hadn't changed Baumgarten. He was weathered no more by prison than by life in general. Kubiak had agreed to meet him in Union Station's food court, and that was where he had found him waiting, standing smack dab in its center in front of The Snuggery at a waist-high table the diameter of a bicycle's tire. His shoulders were hunched, and he wore the face of a dog left too long tied to a tree.

It was Friday afternoon; the railroad station was busy. Kubiak looked at the faces crowded in the clutter of tables around them, each advertising a better time than he was having. Though he and Baumgarten had talked of convenience, Kubiak had agreed to this meeting place because of its easy egress, a quick glance at the watch followed by an apology and one step backward into the flow of commuters. It certainly offered no other amenities. If he had to wait for a train he would have chosen somewhere else to do so. This was the cusp of the Loop, after all, where a two block hike in any direction offered the same priced drink in a comfortably lit leather booth, a lower ceiling, maybe even a piano playing in the corner farthest from the windows.

"That all you're going to eat?" Baumgarten asked, gesturing at the soft pretzel in front of Kubiak. He had to speak up over the din.

"Like I said, Paul, I'm in a bit of a hurry." The choice of food had been as deliberate as that of the place. Baumgarten wanted him anchored. A soft pretzel and a beer were all Kubiak was offering.

"You promised me an hour."

"I have to meet my wife."

"That's not fair." Baumgarten's voice perpetually carried a trace of lament. When he whined, he was unbearable. "You know, I could have caught a whole other train if I'd known you'd be this late. Do you realize how long it takes me just to get down here?"

"I'm sorry. I have no choice. It's our daughter's birthday. We're having a little party for her tonight. Just the family."

"Right. No choice." Baumgarten sulked, pulled a cold rib from the paper boat in front of him, gnawed its meat into the spaces between his teeth. "I always forget you have family, Kubiak. Why is that?"

Kubiak said nothing. There was a clock over The Snuggery's bar, and its minute hand glowed neon bright as it dipped down toward the half hour.

The day had been reserved to act on promises made. Kubiak had planned his schedule so meticulously he had guaranteed its collapse. Still, Baumgarten seemed to have forgotten Kubiak was doing him a favor by reserving any time for him at all.

"So, how old is she?"

"Who?"

"Your daughter. Come on, Kubiak."

"She's twenty-two. Twenty-three. No." Odd, but he hadn't given Maria's age a thought. Silently, he counted backwards. "Twenty-five."

"Twenty-five years old," Baumgarten snorted. "And you still throw her little birthday parties?"

Kubiak shot Baumgarten his first curious look since they had met. Baumgarten shrugged his friendless, bachelor's shoulders.

"Birthday or no," he said, "what I've got to offer you I can't explain in a lousy fifteen minutes."

Kubiak lifted his beer, drank a third of it in one gulp. He might as well have turned over an hourglass.

"All right, dammit." Baumgarten looked over both shoulders, then leaned slightly forward. "I hear you're retired these days. Must be sweet."

"Sweet as hell. Is that our little secret?"

"What I mean is, you cops are like the military. Put in your time fast and get out while you still got your teeth and a couple of years of you-know-what in you."

Baumgarten made an obscene gesture with his fist and forearm. The leer that accompanied it only made it even more revolting.

"Two years, huh."

"You still bother to keep up with the news now that you don't have to, Kubiak? Go through the papers at all?"

"My wife reads me the comics over soft eggs every morning. Just before my sponge bath."

"That's too bad, because she wouldn't have found this story in the comics. Maybe it didn't even make the Chicago papers. It happened up by me."

"Waukegan?"

"No. Out by the Chain of Lakes."

"High turnover at the parole board, Paul? They're giving you a longer leash on your ankle bracelet."

Baumgarten's eyes flashed. "You're not so funny when you try to be, Kubiak. You want to put away the stopwatch, I'll listen to your jokes."

Kubiak hadn't expected the outburst. Baumgarten's glare immediately softened. He must have mistaken the look of surprise on Kubiak's face for anger, and he retreated to his rack of ribs. *Like a child forced to eat his peas,* Kubiak thought. He let him take his time, concentrating on ignoring the sudden interest of a pinch-faced woman at the nearest table.

"This has nothing to do with me, by the way," Baumgarten finally said, not looking up from his food. "Except that there are some people who have asked me for my help and I've promised them I'd do what I could for them."

"Why would you do that?"

"Why? Come on, Kubiak. Some of us have a heart."

"Some. Who are these people, and why would they need your help?"

"They're acquaintances of mine, that's all. And it isn't my help—hey, I'm trying to tell a story here."

"Well, you're doing a lousy job of it. Just start at the beginning and make it quick."

Baumgarten took a deep breath, then exhaled. "Okay, there's this guy. He got himself killed, shot to death, out by the Chain. Everybody knows who killed him, but there isn't anybody willing to do a thing about it. Except now, me, and maybe you." He looked up, waited.

"That's it?"

"You wanted me to make it quick."

"So, who is this guy? Another one of your acquaintances?"

"No. I never even met him."

"But you read about him in the papers. If it was murder, why aren't the police acting on it?"

"They're saying it was a suicide."

"You're claiming it wasn't. You have any proof?"

"If I did, I wouldn't be bothering you, would I? But I have a load of facts that contradict themselves. And a lawyer who's already taken up the case."

"You've got all that, you should be having this conversation with the Lake County Sheriff's Department."

"I would be, except for one problem."

"What's that?"

"They're the ones who killed him."

Kubiak drummed his fingers lightly on the side of his plastic cup, and watched the beer's bubbles break loose and float upwards. So, that was it. He looked back up at the neon clock, fully aware of the dramatic glare Baumgarten was holding for effect. He even glanced back at the pinch-faced woman to see if she was still interested in the conversation. She wasn't.

Chain of Lakes. The county sheriff's department. A pursuit ending in suicide. Kubiak remembered the incident, it having occurred only a month or so ago. The details were coming back to him, but he was stuck on searching for the name of the dead man, a drifter who had spent his life using up his luck before being taken in by an elderly couple known for their charitable ways. The lowlife had repaid their kindness by shooting them each in the head, then stealing their car. He didn't get far in it, winding up sandwiched in a slow speed police pursuit where he determined the simplest exit from the situation would be a bullet in his own skull.

Jack something. That was it.

"Jack Mackay."

Baumgarten wiped barbeque sauce from his fingertips with his tiny, stiff paper napkin, then brought the napkin to his lips.

"Along with the comics, your wife likes to read you the obituaries too."

"Just plain morbid is what she is. Might not have made the Chicago papers? What are you working on me here, Paul? Are you really unaware of the amount of coverage Mackay's death managed in the *Tribune* and *Sun Times*?"

"Big deal. A couple of columns of print and sixty seconds on the ten o'clock news. A man's been murdered, he deserves a little more than that, don't you think?"

"Most get less. And Mackay wasn't murdered. He blew his own brains out his car window when he ran out of road."

"He was shot three times, Kubiak."

"So, the first two didn't take."

"One bullet went through his cheek. The other they found in his leg. I don't care how good you are at messing things up, you don't attempt suicide by blowing out your lips and kneecaps."

"He was in a moving car on a rural road, juggling a wheel and a gun with takedown lights flashing in his eyes. You try it sometime. In fact—"

"Right. Thanks. You believe everything you hear, buddy? Or just what your fellow cops tell you?"

Kubiak drained his beer, pulled his wallet out of his back pocket. The first gesture brought concern to Baumgarten's eyes, the second near panic.

"Five minutes. Hey, Kubiak."

"I'm sorry." Kubiak tossed a ten dollar bill onto the table. "If it makes you feel any better, your calling me buddy is only half the reason I'm leaving. And no, if any cop I ever knew were to tell me you would ride all the way down here from Waukegan on some noble mission to bring honor to Jack Mackay's name, I wouldn't believe a word of it. So, you see where it's my lack of trust that trips me up, not vice versa."

"All right. Wait. One minute. One minute, good lord, what kind of schedule do you keep?"

"One minute."

"It's not only for him I'm here. You know that. We both know that." Baumgarten managed a weak smile. "It's for us."

"You and him?"

"Me and you."

Kubiak turned toward the flow of commuters. Baumgarten reached across the table and grasped his sleeve.

"What's wrong with you? You act like I'm trying to sell you something sour when all I'm doing is offering you some quick money."

"I was afraid you might be."

"I know better than to toss anything illegal at you, Kubiak. All this is, it's a one hundred percent legitimate supplement to your retirement income. What's wrong with that?"

"Nothing. I prefer my free time, is all."

"Two days work, max, paying upward of, maybe, fifty to a hundred thousand, depending? How much free time do you need?"

"A hundred thousand legal for two days of work? Who's writing the checks, the Sultan of Brunei?"

Baumgarten released Kubiak's sleeve, rested his elbows on the table. "You criminal justice types ought to cross the hallway every so often to get a feel of the size of the pockets sweating it out in the civil courts."

"So, that's it. Mackay's family is filing a suit. Against who, exactly?"

"Well, that depends. There are details that run this way and that, the way details in any case do. It might depend on what you find out."

"Why me?"

"You're a cop."

"Was."

"You were a cop. Cops talk to cops."

"I was Cook County, they're Lake. I don't even know how those boys think."

"Well, you're the only cop I ever talked to who I didn't have to, so my recruiting options are sort of limited."

"You expect me to go up there and buddy up to the sheriff's department, those fellow cops whose every word I believe, in order to extract information that will cause them to be hanged by some lawyer low enough on the food chain to hire you to hire me?"

"Not necessarily. Let's say you find something that helps clear them. You wouldn't mind that, would you?"

"No. Except that I wouldn't be making any money."

Baumgarten shrugged. "The perils of working on spec, buddy. But then, that's where the incentive comes in. The more you get . . ." He smiled that ugly smile of his again, tapped his index finger against his ear, then rubbed it against his thumb. "The more you get."

It wasn't the smile that upset Kubiak, nor his being called buddy again. It was that Baumgarten had let go of his sleeve, yet he was still standing here, ready to open up his mouth and continue arguing until . . . Until what? Until he felt totally justified in turning down Baumgarten's offer? Or, until the little man's arguments changed his mind?

Without offering another word, he turned into the

crowd and let it aim him toward the nearest exit. Baumgarten called out to him, then was gone. However, as Kubiak turned the corner toward the escalators, Baumgarten was back with him, stuffing his wallet back into his pants pocket. Kubiak realized he must have run back to the table for the ten dollar bill.

"I'm only asking you for two days," Baumgarten said as he tried to keep in step. "You owe me that much."

"I don't owe you anything."

"Four years in Stateville? What's that worth? You testified against me."

"I testified to evidence. You were the one who left a full set of prints on just about everything you came across. How long have you been out now?"

"Nearly six months. Why?"

"You might want to keep from pissing off county sheriffs and concentrate on staying out."

"Well, that's what I'm trying to do here, make an honest—Hey!"

Kubiak had taken the stairs. Baumgarten had tried his luck beside him on the escalator and found his movement blocked by the thick of bodies. In seconds, Kubiak was a dozen steps ahead of him and gaining ground.

"I'm the one trying to do what's right here, Kubiak," Baumgarten shouted, leaning far over the rubber handrail. "While you're running to meet your wife so you can plan your pretty, pink birthday parties for your little Maria, I'm the guy . . . he was shot three times, Kubiak. Three times. You think just because it was a guy like Jack Mackay that makes it all right? You think it can't happen to someone like me, or you? You think it can't happen to, even that pretty, pink daughter of yours?"

Kubiak was already on ground level, then was through

the doors and out into the late August afternoon glare of the street. Over his shoulder, an empty cab was screaming along the curb working a right lane pass. Though he had only a dozen blocks' walk to Marshall Field's, he took the cab's arrival as a sign and shot up his arm, quickly climbed in, and left Paul Baumgarten far behind.

Still, Baumgarten's parting shot stayed with him. Funny. If it had come from anyone else, Kubiak might almost have considered it something of a threat.

Chapter Two

She was one of only two people left in the Walnut Room, and the other person was her waiter, a young man who was making a bad job of looking busy. She sat at a two-top near the windows that looked out onto State Street seven stories below, reading an oversized paperback which advertised its tedium in the abstract, muted browns on its front cover and load of type on the back.

The fountain dominating the restaurant had been turned off. Kubiak's footsteps on the carpet fell silent as he crossed the empty room. As he approached Denise's table, she closed her book and stuffed it into her handbag. He hadn't seen her look up.

"Do I have time to sit?" he asked, once he had.

"Of course. Where have you been?"

"Refusing favors." He gestured toward the waiter. "Why hasn't he opened one of these windows and tossed you out yet?"

"I knew you'd be late, so I tipped him an extra twenty. Now I suppose he feels he has to stay and look after me."

She smiled and waved to the young man. He beamed back at her.

"I gave a kid a tip like that once. All I remember is his goofy grin disappearing around the nearest corner."

"I hope you've had lunch."

Kubiak surveyed the table's rich dessert remnants, and could only imagine the meal leading into them.

"I had a pretzel."

"A pretzel?"

"And a beer."

"Oh, so that's it." She slung her handbag over her shoulder and stood to leave. Kubiak followed. They rode the elevator down one flight to the sixth floor, wound their way through the maze of aisles. Eventually, Denise slowed in a section filled with porcelain, lingering amid the silver, and finally seemed to end her run surrounded by crystal figurines. Kubiak, his hands in his pockets, watched her study each piece.

"So?" she asked after some time. "What do you think?"

"I think you might have managed this just as well without me."

She fixed him with the same critical eye she'd had aimed at the figurines, mercifully let her point die there, and shifted her glare back to the merchandise. He sighed, turned his attention to a glass case holding some of the larger crystal pieces, inspected a wide-based crystal castle with a glass archer in one of its towers, and wondered if the artist considered the possibility of a market for his product or just chiseled away at his fancy. On the shelf below the crystal castle was a glass eskimo fishing through a hole in an ice floe. Beside that was an explorer hiking up the side of a crystal cliff that was covered with tiny, glass pine trees. Kubiak bent and squinted at the miniature price tag looped around one of the trees on the cliff, grunted at the four figures and change printed on it.

He straightened, suddenly feeling uncomfortably close to the clutter of precariously placed crystal, tucked in his elbows, wandered over nearer the towels, found himself at the gallery of the building's north light well. He leaned over the rail, looked down at the people on the busy ground floor. He watched a woman three floors down try on a coat, saw some bored salesclerks sharing a quiet joke. He thought of the clerks standing on that same floor day after day, wondered if they were on duty the day Jack Mackay pumped the fatal bullet into his skull, and if they were sharing a joke as he was desperately maneuvering some sideroads only a few miles upstate, looking for an option other than suicide. And, he wondered what bits of high drama might be going on just now. Somewhere in the Chicago metropolitan area a squad car was being dispatched at just this second while the shoppers continued to stream past him on the ground floor. He looked up at the floors above him, experienced a slight sense of vertigo, turned away from the well and back toward his wife.

"What do you remember of that Jack Mackay story in the news?" he asked her.

"Who?"

"About a month ago. The drifter up north who murdered that old couple who took him in."

"The one who shot himself," she said, moving slowly toward him. She held two large, dimpled copper fish figurines at arms' length, and was busy examining their subtle differences. "In his car. Only, he wasn't a drifter, was he? I thought he was a relative of theirs. A nephew or something."

"No, I don't think so. I thought they took him in strictly out of kindness."

"What are you saying, Kubiak, that you can't take in a nephew strictly out of kindness?"

"No, I suppose you can do anything you please. But as I remember it, the whole lesson of the story was that those poor geezers were known for being a soft touch, and that's what got them killed—taking in strangers."

"Really. Well, the story I recall had a different lesson," Denise said.

"Oh. That being?"

"How about, when being pursued by half of the local police department, it's wise to do in self before self is done in."

"I'm sorry," Kubiak said. "Was that supposed to be Confucius or Charlie Chan?"

"Neither. Just a voice in what's-his-name's head."

"Jack Mackay."

"Right. Why are we having this discussion, anyway?"

"Because, believe it or not, there are people who believe Mackay didn't do in self, but had self done in."

"What people?"

"I don't know."

"Well, what's their point?"

"It's one hell of a point."

"What I mean is, is it justice they're after, or who it was dispensing justice?"

"In this case, it was either the perpetrator or the police, neither of whose job it is to dispense justice."

"I don't understand, Kubiak. If Mackay did shoot himself, I don't know what more can be done to him without digging up his bones. And if it was the police who shot him, what reason would they have to lie? They were chasing down an armed murderer, and had every excuse imaginable to use deadly force. Either way, all anyone cares about is that the whole mess closed itself out on that rural road. If anything, Mackay has managed to redeem himself by saving the taxpayers the cost of a trial."

"Provided he was guilty in the first place."

"Did you ever think for a moment he wasn't?"

Kubiak said nothing.

"Anyway, what does any of this have to do with you?"

"Nothing whatsoever."

"In that case, what's your opinion of this?" She held out one of the copper fish.

"I wouldn't want to run into the mad child who took to pounding on it. What is it, a serving tray?"

"It's art, Kubiak. It hangs on the wall."

Kubiak took the fish, examined it, turned it over. Its price tag read a mere hundred dollars, so he handed the fish back to her and told her he thought Maria would love it.

Denise had driven the Ford downtown, which was just as well, as she naturally would have refused to close an afternoon at Field's with a run on the 151 bus, and if Kubiak was going to sit in rush hour traffic on Lake Shore Drive he'd prefer not to do so in a cab. They exited at Belmont just after 4:30. Kubiak dropped his wife at the front entrance of Park Tower, then swung around the corner to the entrance of the building's underground parking garage. He parked the Ford, and rode the elevator back up to the seventh floor.

Denise had started a pot of soup cooking earlier in the day. The smell of it hit Kubiak hard as he entered the condo, harder than it should have, which he attributed to nothing more than the type of head-spinning effect the rich aroma of simmering stock might have on any man who'd had nothing all day but beer and pretzels. The shopping bag holding the copper fish sat on the dining room table next to the mail and Denise's keys. He didn't see her; the living room was empty, as was the kitchen. He turned into the hallway and saw that the bathroom door was shut, heard the muffled whir of the exhaust fan on the other side of it, and felt a sense of relief as disconcerting as the feeling he'd had on entering the apartment. This time the feeling didn't pass, but followed him into the back bedroom where the aroma of the soup was more subtle. He sat on the chair by the bed, intending to take off his shoes.

It had been a long time since there had been homemade soup on the Kubiak household's stovetop; vegetable soup had always been Maria's favorite. That cursed olfactory gland. Serving as the strongest of the senses, it had carried Kubiak not through the condo tonight, but had taken him back to the old house on the west side in which he'd spent half his life, the home he had walked into every evening after work, a home not only filled with the smells of a real family dinner, but busy with his wife and daughter smack in the middle of whatever was occupying them on any particular day. That feeling he'd had on passing the closed bathroom door was an aching not to greet the wife he had just moments before let out of the car in front of the building, but to see her as he had before, to come home to her like all those nights when the sounds, scents and traces of her and Maria filled those hollow doorways of the old house.

After all, that was why he and Denise had moved into this condo in the first place, wasn't it? It wasn't because they longed for less space or needed to view Lake Michigan from the plate glass window in their front room. It was to escape those dark, hollow doorways that had become so silent since Maria had married David Hollinger and moved away.

Kubiak bent over and undid his shoelaces. Well, he would be getting his dose of family in an hour or so. He wondered just what he was going to wear tonight for the occasion, whether a tie would be too much. He smiled and thought of Baumgarten again, and the look of genuine puzzlement on his face when they were discussing the birthday party. The poor, lonely bastard. Maybe Kubiak shouldn't have treated him in such a short manner. Hell, maybe he should have invited him to the party tonight. He could imagine Denise's reaction to that.

The bedroom door opened and his wife entered, startling him.

"Are you all right?"

"No," he answered after a moment. "Do I need a tie or not?"

"You shut the bedroom door."

So he had. Well, he had been walking through the old house, after all. Couldn't have little Maria see her father removing his pants.

"Promise me that if I fall back in my chair and start drooling halfway through dinner you'll whisk me off to a proper home."

"I swear, the party won't even skip a beat." She bent over and kissed the top of his head, she was *that* excited about the evening. "I wouldn't bother with a tie. You know how David is. He might take it as an affront."

Kubiak watched his wife change her clothes, listened to her talk, let his mind empty of Baumgarten and Jack Mackay and to become filled with the coming evening. He shaved for the second time that day. He tended the roast in the oven, admired the cake from the bakery on Addison. He helped spread the silly, paper party decorations around the front room, lit candles while Denise set the dining room table.

Maria and David were to arrive at seven. Just before the hour, Kubiak mixed two vodka gimlets and handed one to Denise. She took a sip from the glass, set it down, and went about her business.

By 7:30, Kubiak had mixed himself a second gimlet and was working on the cheese and crackers. At eight o'-clock, he asked Denise if she would like another drink. She only shook her head.

8:30; Kubiak switched to beer. He had picked at the roast while Denise wasn't looking.

"Do you think we should call them?" she asked.

"It's Friday night. She got caught up with the crowd from her work. We're not the only people in the world who celebrate birthdays."

The phone rang at 9:15. Kubiak couldn't have beaten Denise to the receiver if he'd jumped for it. Listening to her half of the conversation, he inferred Hollinger was on the other end of the line with excuses.

"Well, is she all right? Did you call the doctor? No, I don't suppose . . . no. No, don't wake her. Of course, I understand. I wish you'd called sooner, I would have told her not to even make the effort. . . . Is there anything you need, Kubiak and I could run over—well, just to drop off her gift. . . . No, of course, I understand. Tomorrow. Or Sunday. Of course. I understand."

She hung up, stared at the phone for a long time, finally looked over at Kubiak, waited to get a feel of whose side he was on.

"I liked the part about wishing he had called sooner," he said.

"She has the stomach flu."

Funny time of time of year for that, he thought, but he said nothing.

"They would have called earlier, except that Maria really thought she'd be up to it if she just rested a bit."

"Of course. I understand."

"She's still asleep. I didn't want to . . . oh, shut up, Kubiak. Damn you, anyway."

She moved off to the kitchen. He stared at the thin, neatly wrapped box holding the fish which sat on the buffet table in the foyer. There was the sound of the oven door, then Denise's voice. "It's just as well. The roast is ruined. Just ruined. We'll have them over another night, is all. As soon as she's feeling better. That's all there is to it."

They ate in silence. Neither of them bothered to clean up the party decorations or extinguish the candles. If the meat was tough or tender Kubiak couldn't tell as he chewed while trying not to watch his wife work so hard at finishing what little food she had spooned onto her plate.

"Do you think . . . ?" she ventured at one point. "Say we just run over there for a minute. To drop off the gift."

Kubiak had only to send her the same glare she had given him in Field's, knowing that even if he agreed, she would talk herself into using better sense before the dishes were put away.

"People do catch the flu," he said.

Denise only grunted.

"The way I figure it, though," he continued, taking a long sip of water to wash the beef out of his mouth, "her office-mates dragged the birthday girl out for a long Friday lunch. A little food, a lot of drinks, before you know it, the afternoon is shot. As I remember it, that calls for more drinks."

"Maria never inherited your taste for liquor, Kubiak."

"No. If she had, she'd be here right now, rosy cheeks and all. Instead, they had to roll the poor, little amateur into a cab. By the time she finally lurched through her front door, she had already decided she needed to rest a while, just until the room stopped spinning, and she's still passed out. I'm sure David would have loved to have provided you with details, only he's smarter than that."

Denise stood abruptly and carried her plate to the kitchen. Kubiak offered to clean up after the meal. She gave him no reply, so he went to the front room, leaving her to her work. He did put away the party decorations, as he was afraid that effort might bring to tears this mother who wanted nothing more, but nothing less, at this moment, than to touch the forehead of her sleeping daughter to assure herself that she was safe asleep, as she had done for most of the past twenty-five years.

But then, it had been twenty-five years. And this mother had taken Kubiak shopping not for a rock and roll poster or a stuffed animal, but for a copper fish figurine only a grown woman could discern was a piece of art rather than a jello mold, a grown woman who could be trusted to take her own temperature and who, besides, had a husband to take care of her.

Kubiak would have liked to have sat Denise down and convince her of as much, but he knew better than to try tonight. So, he turned on the television and vacantly watched the shapes move and chatter about until they put him to sleep.

He woke just before five, stiff from sitting in the chair

all night, wondering if Denise had bothered to try to wake him. He turned off the television, opened the curtains, and watched the first gray of morning grow flat over the lake. However, the midnight dark that remained in the apartment affected his thoughts, filling him with that vague sense of lonely fear one feels only in the middle of the night. The silent phone sat on the table close by.

He drifted off to sleep again, waking when he heard Denise moving around the back of the apartment. The room was light now. The mantle clock read 6:30 on a Saturday morning.

Well, to hell with it, he thought. He picked up the phone and dialed his daughter's number.

Four long rings, followed by Maria's voice on the answering machine message. He hung up, phoned again, waited through the rings and the message. At the beep, he placed the receiver back in the cradle.

Chapter Three

Kubiak couldn't remember the last time he had ridden the El on a Saturday morning. The city always felt different on weekends, but today it felt downright foreign. As familiar as he was with the Howard line, he twice caught himself peering through the window at the streets below to reassure himself he hadn't boarded the wrong train. The faces sharing the rocking CTA car with him were an unfamiliar type; he couldn't guess where they were coming from or what their immediate business might be. And while he had been prepared to wait some extra time on the platform for the train, even the ride between the stops seemed longer, the car, itself, grittier.

Shrinking lonely into his bit of space on the plastic seat, he kept thinking back to Baumgarten and the not-quite threat the man had called out from the top of Union Station's escalator. The more Kubiak reflected upon it, the more certain he was that Baumgarten had used Maria's name. There was no reason he should have known that.

'I always forget you have family, Kubiak,' Baumgarten had said just a few minutes earlier. 'Why is that?'

Well, to begin with, handing out names of your immediate family to ex-cons put away on your testimony was something you just didn't do. Maybe Kubiak had become lazy in the short time since he had retired; maybe he had slipped because he considered Baumgarten almost comically harmless. But all morning he'd been running their short conversation through his head, trying to put each statement into sequence, recall how every phrase had been put, and he couldn't remember delivering his daughter's name. That didn't mean he hadn't. After all, he was the one who had brought up the subject of her birthday. And what reason would Baumgarten have to claim no memory of his family if he could pull Maria's name out of his head? He didn't have a reason. Only . . .

Only, at this point nothing short of the sight of Maria or the sound of her voice would put Kubiak's mind at ease.

He'd left the Ford with Denise, as she was the one waiting beside the phone in case there actually was an emergency. Kubiak was carrying their daughter's birthday gift under his arm, a sad excuse to cover an early morning visit bound to cause embarrassment. Though it had been carefully wrapped, the box was thin, and the nose of the copper fish was already pressing against a tiny rip in the paper, causing Kubiak to hold the package more closely than its contents warranted.

The train pulled into the Morse El stop. Kubiak took the stairs down to the street, weaved past the slouching young men in nylon jackets gathered in front of the corner convenience store, one of the few businesses on the block not locked empty behind soaped windows or rusted gates.

He avoided their eyes and they left him alone, and two blocks later he was walking along the quiet of Greenleaf Street with its old trees and once grand stone buildings.

Maria and David rented a top floor apartment in a brick three-story planted smack dab between the El tracks and the lake. Having arrived from Wisconsin with everything they owned packed into a U-Haul trailer, they had chosen the apartment because of an opportunity to finish out the nine months remaining on a sublet, though they had just signed a lease for another year. This morning, the shades in the windows were up, the curtains drawn. Neither David's truck nor Maria's car was parked anywhere along the block.

Kubiak rang the buzzer, waited, rang again, and had just turned to make his way to the back stairs when the downstairs buzzer sounded. He caught the door at the last instant, was rounding to the base of the staircase when the gray head of the lady on the second floor peered over the bannister above him.

"Hello, Mr. Kubiak. I hope you don't mind."

"Mind?"

"My ringing you in."

Kubiak had met Maria's downstairs neighbor three or four times, but he couldn't remember her name. Maria referred to her as Mrs. Ears. David's name for her wasn't as kind.

"It's the bleed," she said, quieter now, as he approached her landing. Her eyes were interested in the package under his arm.

"Bleed."

"In the intercom system. This old wiring, we all get a dose of everyone else's visitors. Makes you jump if you're not expecting company, that's for sure."

Kubiak nodded as he passed her. He certainly hadn't woken her this morning. She was neatly dressed, fully made up. He reached the third floor landing and pounded on the door.

"They're not home," she called up.

"I suppose not, though I have known David to sleep in." He pounded again.

"Oh, haven't we, though." She giggled. "I'm sure I would have heard him come home last night. You know how he is with his stomping about."

"Not really."

"Like the Frankenstein monster. Not that I mind, I mean. It's just the way he walks, and these old floorboards. Except that the hours he keeps, lounging about on the beach all day, every day, playing checkers with the riffraff. Then, he's up all night. Sometimes I lay in bed staring at the plaster in the ceiling, waiting for it to rain down on my head."

Kubiak stared down at her, pictured her with blankets pulled up to her nose, glaring into the dark. She asked him if he wanted to come in for coffee, and he agreed.

She was as nervous about his company as she was grateful for it. She sat him in her dining room. From the clatter she made in the kitchen, Kubiak imagined her emerging with a full silver service, but she brought him only a gray mug, along with a sugar bowl caked around its rim.

"It's his youth, of course," Kubiak said, and when she gave him a puzzled look he added, "the way they walk down a hallway, might as well be doing calisthenics from the sound of it. I remember Maria—"

"Oh, she's quiet as a mouse. You must be so proud."

The coffee was burnt.

"I was trying to get hold of David last night," he said. "I hope my phoning didn't keep you up."

"Oh, no." After a moment, she added "I thought they were with you last night. For Maria's birthday."

"No."

"I could have sworn she told me—"

"Not last night. I wonder how I could have missed David. You didn't hear him stomping about at all?"

She shook her head, eyes slightly narrowed, sorting this new information.

"What about during the day?" he asked. "Oh, I don't imagine you were home."

"No, I was."

"You were?"

"Yes."

"Are you sure?"

"Yes. Yes, I was here all day."

"I only ask because UPS was supposed to deliver a package."

She glanced at the gift box, which he had placed on her dining room table. The head of the fish had ripped through the wrapping and was now entirely exposed. Its dead eye stared back at her.

"I'm sorry, but I don't remember a package being delivered. I would have heard—"

"Of course. The bleed."

"Besides, when no one's home, the mailmen all know to leave any packages with me."

"Well, then I'm sure either David or Maria must have been home to accept it."

"No. I told you, Maria was gone all day. She never even came home from work. I thought she was with you, celebrating her birthday. I'm absolutely sure she told me—"

"David, then."

She shook her head, exhaled sharply through her nose. "I'm sorry, Mr. Kubiak, but I know for a fact Mr. Hollinger hasn't been home since . . ." Her eyes narrowed again. "Since Thursday night. When he left with that friend of yours." She sat back triumphantly. "So you see, that package couldn't possibly have been delivered. Not possibly."

Kubiak sipped his bitter coffee. He didn't know Hollinger had any acquaintances in Chicago, much less one the two of them shared.

"Which friend would that be?" he asked, working to keep his voice flat.

"Why, the one you introduced to him, of course."

Of course.

"Yes, but I've introduced him to so many people."

"I'm sorry. I don't remember his name."

"But you've met him."

She nodded. "One day last week, when Mr. Hollinger wasn't home."

"You buzzed him in."

She nodded, now nervous again, afraid she might have done something wrong.

"You offered him coffee."

"I had seen him with Mr. Hollinger before, and he said he was going to wait for him, and it was so hot outside—"

"And he was the one who told you I'd introduced him to David."

"Yes."

"What else did he say?"

"Nothing, really."

"Was he about my age? Some gray hair?"

"No. A little younger, with dark hair. Somewhere in

age between you and Mr. Hollinger. It's hard for me to tell sometimes. But he acted older. He wasn't a very happy person, that's for sure. He slumped. Like the weight of the world was on his shoulders. I told him he should stand up straight, but that only seemed to make him even sadder."

"I don't suppose he told you where he lives?"

"Why, yes." She brightened. "Waukegan. I remember, because I told him everyone I ever knew from Waukegan moved out of there years ago. At least that gave him a chuckle, though I can't imagine why."

"Mind if I use your phone?"

The request took her by surprise, but she led Kubiak to the kitchen wall phone, then hovered nearby, pretending to move things about the cabinets. The phone was dark yellow, lacquered with everything she had ever cooked. Kubiak dialed up Crawford's direct line at 3510 South Michigan, figuring the lieutenant would be at his desk despite the fact that it was Saturday, and he was right.

"Kubiak? Two years out of the department, and you still don't sleep in on Saturdays?"

"There's no need to put up defenses, Crawford. All I need from you this time is an address."

"Whose?"

"An ex . . ." He turned his back to Mrs. Ears. "A fellow, shouldn't be too hard to find, a Paul Baumgarten." Kubiak spelled it. "Out of Waukegan."

"What's it about?"

"Nothing. Personal matter."

"Then, look him up in the phone book, same as anybody else."

"He hasn't been at his present address long enough to be listed, but it should be in your computer. His previous residence was with the state of Illinois."

"Baumgarten," Crawford muttered. Kubiak could picture the phone's receiver tucked against his shoulder as his hands worked the keyboard. "What put him away?"

"B and E."

"How long ago?"

"Four years. Five, maybe."

"If you could only be as much help to me as I am to you. Seriously, Kubiak, what is this?"

"Seriously, Crawford. The man asked me for a favor, I turned him down, now I want to get back in touch with him."

"What kind of favor?"

"Something about a job."

"And you changed your mind. You're a sucker, Kubiak. I hope you give him glowing references, he empties the safe, and you get sued. I can't find him. Give me a couple of minutes. Are you home?"

Kubiak read the number off the phone, hung up, and asked his hostess for another cup of coffee. As he drank, she tried to make conversation, but he was short and sullen, no longer caring to be polite for the sake of his daughter and son-in-law. He was imagining her sitting at this same table with Baumgarten last week, over the same gray mugs of bad coffee, the two of them hitting it off splendidly as any pair of busy hens, when the phone rang. She handed it to Kubiak.

Crawford gave him an address on Genesee Street. "You familiar with Waukegan? It's right downtown. Who lives in downtown Waukegan?"

"I don't think Baumgarten owns a car. He has to stay close to public transit."

"Well, he's also only a couple of blocks from the Lake County Courthouse and the sheriff's department. I suppose that puts him within walking distance of everywhere he needs to be. I'd be interested to find out what kind of record they've got on him."

"I'll ask him when I see him. Thanks, Crawford, I owe you another lunch."

Mrs. Ears offered Kubiak a curt good riddance, and watched through her window as he began his hike west to the Rogers Park Metra station. He would have liked to have gone back for the Ford, but he didn't want to face Denise's questions holding only the answers he had so far.

Luckily, he was climbing up to the station platform just as the northbound train was arriving. The car was nearly empty, the air conditioning frigid. Kubiak bought his ticket from the conductor, sat back, and watched the city landscape give way to the neat, deliberate ostentation of the north suburbs. Forty-five minutes later, all of that was behind him as well, and he was staring out at the lake and the smattering of old industry lounging filthy along its shore.

Waukegan was the last stop. The few riders left exited the train and walked toward the parking lot or climbed into waiting cars, leaving Kubiak alone in front of the station, looking up at the city's sad skyline: the abandoned News Sun building, a two-story concrete parking lot, and an old hotel that, years ago, had been converted into cheap apartments. He picked a timetable out of a plastic rack. It told him he had just two hours to catch the next train back or spend half his afternoon here.

A glance down at the Chicago arrival times stopped him short. He flipped back to the Metra line listings to make certain he had read it correctly, muttered a curse, pocketed the timetable, and began his walk up to Washington Street.

Saturday. Downtown Waukegan was deserted, eerily

so. He passed no one, saw not a single moving car, as he made his way to Genesee Street and turned south. He found the address he was looking for over the doorway of a flat, two-story brick building that held a half dozen units. The front door was propped open. A boy about seven or eight years old was playing a game of echo alone, in the dark lobby. He stopped when he saw Kubiak. Kubiak offered him a nod; the boy did not move.

Baumgarten's name was scrawled, in ink, on the wall over his mailbox. Kubiak took the stone staircase to the second floor, grit scraping the soles of his shoes. The hallway walls were stained from leaking water, and the door frame to Baumgarten's apartment was so warped, there was a good half inch of space next to the door's latch.

Kubiak bent to examine the lock. It wasn't much, set to automatically lock the door when it shut. He imagined there was a stronger bolt that turned from the inside so Baumgarten could at least sleep soundly.

When he was home.

He straightened with a grunt, slipped the copper fish out of what was left of its packaging, and aimed its tail at the space between the lock and the jamb. Then, sensing something behind him, he turned to see that the kid from the lobby had followed him upstairs.

"It's okay," he said to the silent boy. "The guy's a good friend of mine. I introduce him to everybody."

The lock broke free on the third thrust without making too much noise, and the door swung open. The apartment was as Kubiak had expected: small, poorly furnished, musty . . . and empty of Baumgarten. Long empty, from the looks of things.

His glance down at the train schedule caused him to guess as much. The Union Pacific North Line on which he had just ridden emptied into the Ogilvie Transportation Center in downtown Chicago, the old Northwestern Station. Yet, when Kubiak had agreed to see Baumgarten at the end of his train line, the man had made an appointment to meet him in Union Station. Convenient if you're riding some other Metra line, but not if you're coming down from Waukegan.

Ogilvie had its own share of food courts. It's where they should have met. Chances were Baumgarten had come in by train, all right, but like Kubiak, hadn't given a thought as to which line was supposed to end where, and had simply named the station in which he always arrived. This meant he had been living somewhere other than Waukegan for some time.

Kubiak searched the closet and dresser drawers, found them empty, then sat on the edge of the bed with the fish in his lap. He had bent its tail considerably. It wouldn't bend back.

"Fine," he said to himself. "So now everyone's disappeared."

The child was still there, standing in the doorway, staring in at him. The boy's expression never changed. It showed a dulled kind of curiosity, as though he had already seen too much. Kubiak imagined he had.

"What do you think?" he asked, holding out the fish. "Nothing a little more pounding wouldn't fix. Damaged goods. I don't want it. Go ahead."

The boy didn't move.

"Take it. It's to make Jello in. Your mother must make Jello. Everybody's mother makes Jello."

The boy looked over his shoulder, then disappeared from the doorway. Kubiak listened to his footsteps pounding quickly down the stairway, then heard a door slam. Then, silence. Suddenly, the apartment felt suffocating.

No, Kubiak supposed the kid couldn't bring this little three-figure gift home to his mother. His adventures were his own. She would ask him a dozen questions, and his secrets would have to be shared. Fresh rules might be laid down upon him, tighter boundaries. Not much of a trade at all.

Kubiak left without knocking on any doors. He would find no Mrs. Ears here. Arriving at the train station, he still had an hour to kill, so he walked down to the edge of the lake. He held the fish, discus-like, at his side, coiled back, and threw it as far as he could into the water. He watched it bob on the surface, and keep bobbing. For a moment, he thought the damn thing was actually going to float back to him, but then a wave broke over its lip. It listed, and finally, thankfully, sank out of sight.

Chapter Four

"Good lord, Kubiak, what took you half the day?"

He had expected the question, but not the nonchalant manner in which Denise asked it. The way she was acting, he'd have thought that the party was right back on.

She hadn't even met him at the door. He had found her in the kitchen, working up a large salad. Maurice, the hallway dog, was keeping her company. Kubiak hadn't seen him in over a month. The golden retriever made the entire apartment building his home. No one knew where he had come from, whether his owner had moved away and left him, or if he had simply wandered into the building one day and had taken a liking to the place. The condo association had long ago given up on the feasibility of eviction, and Maurice wandered the halls with impunity, staying with whoever offered him respite, sometimes for as little as an hour, sometimes for as long as a week.

Denise had put a bowl in the corner, and he had been lying beside it. When Kubiak entered, the dog got up to greet him. Maurice's tail was wagging; Denise was busy at the sink; the room was warm, as the oven was burning again, baking something that smelled of sugar and apples.

Indeed, the party was right back on.

"Where is she?" he asked.

"She's asleep."

"You mean she's here?"

"Yes. Don't look so shocked. It's her birthday weekend, remember? She had a rough night, but she'll be fine."

So, it was a birthday weekend now. He turned toward the hallway. Denise grabbed his arm.

"Let her be. She needs to rest."

"It's two o'clock in the afternoon."

"I gave her a valium."

"Valium? For her flu? I'd hate to know what you'd prescribe for pneumonia. Where's Hollinger?"

"With you all day, I thought. He wasn't home?"

"No."

"Too bad. I would have liked to hear his side of the story."

"Which story?"

"The same story." She rinsed her knife, dried her hands. "The same argument. Maria wants him to get a job; David would prefer to make his million first."

"I thought she was over that."

"You don't get over that, Kubiak."

"Wait a minute. Just before his business in Wisconsin went sour, wasn't it you and Maria trying to sell me on the virtue of self-enterprise?"

"That was when he was her boyfriend. Now he's her husband."

"Oh. That's how it works." Kubiak picked a plum tomato out of the salad. "So, they were fighting last night."

"All night, from the sounds of things."

"She tell you where this argument took place?"

"What do you mean? At home, of course."

The sounds of things, indeed.

"What did she say when you asked her why she wasn't answering her phone this morning?"

"She stayed on the couch all night. She couldn't sleep, so she went out for a walk early, had some breakfast at a coffee shop, didn't want to go home again, so she came here."

"What time was that?"

"When she left? Or, when she arrived here? What are you getting at, anyway? Say, if David wasn't home, what did you do with Maria's gift?"

"Oh, that. I had this idea I might drop it with a neighbor."

"Well, that wasn't very smart. What are we going to give her tonight?"

"How about a good whipping?"

"Kubiak, can't you please just let her be? The poor girl's a mess."

He turned back into the hallway. The door to the guest room was closed. Kubiak knocked lightly, received no answer, then opened the door slowly. The room was dark. As the dim light from the hallway spread across the guest bed, the blankets stirred. He entered the room, shut the door behind him, and crossed to the window.

"Do you mind?" he asked, opening the blinds to deflect the light and keep it from landing directly on the bed. Still, Maria held her open palm in front of her face. Her dark hair was all over the pillows, even as she arranged them to prop up her head.

The simple joy of seeing one's daughter wake. It had been so long, Kubiak had let the memory of it slip. He bent and kissed her forehead, then sat at the foot of the bed.

Maurice had entered the room with him. After examining the corners of the room, the dog moved to Maria's face and pressed his muzzle against her cheek.

"Hey, Maurice, you old thing," she said. "You come to wish me a happy birthday?"

"Happy birthday from us both," Kubiak said.

She offered him a weak smile. Her eyes were glassy from the Valium, maybe from lack of sleep, or maybe tears.

Her blue jeans lay neatly folded on the chair by the window, a gray T-shirt draped over them.

A minute passed.

"Your mother and I bought you a fish."

"A fish?"

"Not a live fish. It was a mold of a fish. A fish sculpture."

"Oh. That's nice. Thank you."

"You're welcome."

"But aren't you spoiling the surprise?"

"Well, the surprise is, I threw it in the lake."

"Oh."

"I'm sorry."

"I thought you said it wasn't a real fish."

"It wasn't. I could have thrown it into a Dumpster. The lake just happened to be there."

"The lake is like that."

"The only reason I'm bringing this up is I wanted to tell you before you found out about it later. From anyone else."

"Meaning, from Mother."

"I wanted to explain that I didn't do it out of anger, or spite, or anything of that sort. I just developed a strong dislike for the thing. And then I got to thinking, what if you were to hang it in a prominent place, where I'd have to stare at it every time I came over to visit? I decided it might be better to give you a gift certificate. Or cash."

"Okay. Well, thanks twice, I guess."

"So, I don't suppose David will be joining us tonight."

"No, I don't suppose he will."

"Your mother tells me you two had a fight."

"I'd rather not talk about David, if you don't mind."

"I understand. Any idea where he might be?"

"No. And I couldn't care less."

She was lying. Her eyes, working now to avoid his, were too nervous to fabricate a show of animosity.

Kubiak stood and opened the door to the room's small closet.

"You didn't think to pack a bag?" he asked.

"I only planned to go out for breakfast. It didn't seem necessary."

"What about a jacket?"

"It's August, Dad."

"I tried phoning you early this morning. What time did you leave your apartment?"

"I don't know. Earlier than early, it would seem."

"I mean, was the sun up?"

"Maybe. Just barely, if that."

"August or not, there was a chill in the air at dawn. The wind was coming off the lake. All you were wearing was this T-shirt?"

She laughed, but still wouldn't look directly at him. "I'm sorry. I know I should have worn my mittens, but I was in a hurry to get out of there."

"Your apartment?"

"Yes."

"So, you left David there."

"Yes."

"But if he was there, why didn't he answer the phone?"

A pause.

"I don't know. You'll have to ask him. Now, can we please talk about something else? It's my birthday, for pete's sake. That's my birthday wish."

"Your birthday was yesterday."

"Right. Sorry I couldn't be here to blow out my candles, but I had a touch of the flu, remember?"

"That's what David said when he called last night. Funny, him being the one to phone in the excuses. I mean, it would make sense if you were sick. But with the two of you right in the thick of an all-night slugfest, for him to make the gallant effort of phoning your parents so you can save face . . ."

"David's a better liar than I am, that's all."

"Don't sell yourself short."

Maria lay still, arms crossed, her face aimed at the wall. When she finally spoke, her tone was cold.

"Do you want to know the real reason I didn't call last night? Do you, really? Fine. It's that I was afraid you might be the one to answer the phone. Does that frighten you? It should. With Mother, I only would have had to reassure her I'd be all right, and that would be the end of it, all she needed to know. But you . . ." She turned to stare directly at Kubiak. Her voice rose, and kept rising. "Listen to yourself, interrogating me like I'm some sort of suspect, tiptoeing into every question so you can trip me up with my answers. I'm not the subject of an investigation, dammit, I'm your daughter. And I came here, dragged myself here through this frigid August morning, jacketless and mittenless, hoping to find just a few hours of peace and quiet, a safe haven, and instead, I have to listen to your insinuations and your accusations—"

There was a knock on the door followed immediately by Denise's entrance into the room. Kubiak wondered how long she had been listening at the door.

"Everything okay?"

"No," Maria told her. "Everything's anything but. Now, if it's not too much to ask, I'd like to be left alone so I can get dressed before anybody else waltzes in here."

They were both glaring at Kubiak. Even Maurice, made nervous by the shouting, had moved between Kubiak and his daughter. Kubiak left the room, and closed the door behind him, leaving him alone in the hallway. He went to the bedroom, transferred some small bills from his dresser drawer to his wallet, and was just exiting the apartment when Denise emerged from the guestroom.

"Where are you going?"

"Jimmy Dee's. To get a drink before dinner."

"You can have a drink right here."

"Not that kind of drink. I have to brace myself for any more birthday wishes."

Jimmy Dee's was strictly neighborhood, a nothing of an entrance a half block off Belmont under an old sign that could offer respite only if lit on the darkest of nights. Kubiak had discovered it a month or two after moving into the condo and had been coming in twice a week ever since.

The bartender, three hundred and fifty pounds of squeeze and maneuver, also happened to be named Jimmy. Because of that, he was often thought to be the owner and he put little effort into correcting the mistake. He might have been thirty, might have been fifty, nobody asked, and his breathing was labored. Some days a tank of oxygen was behind the bar with him; today, it wasn't.

Kubiak sat on a stool at the end of the bar and ordered a vodka tonic. On the television, the Cubs were trying to rally out of a two-run deficit in the bottom of the sixth. When Patterson struck out to end the inning, Jimmy shuffled over to keep Kubiak from feeling lonely. He asked how his wife and daughter were, and Kubiak said they were never better.

"Your daughter's birthday, right? How was the party?"

"Not over yet."

"That's great. You getting along any better with your son-in-law?"

"Sure. Right now, I'd say I'm probably the best friend he's got."

"That's great."

The Cubs lost the game by one run. Playing with the lime in his third vodka, Kubiak considered those angry words Maria had hurled at him, wondered if she might not have a point. After all, he had ridden all the way up to Waukegan concerned with nothing other than her safety. But when she was delivered, unscathed, to the sweet comfort of his guest bedroom, suddenly his concern was trumped by his curiosity. She was right. In his pursuit of whatever truth she was keeping from him, he had treated her less like a daughter and more like the subject of an investigation.

He was running her arguments against his through his head when Jimmy's bulk appeared in front of him again.

"It's your wife on the line. You here?"

"I had better be."

Kubiak had to stretch over the bar to get the receiver to his ear.

"If this is about the beef being ruined, it's not my fault," he told her. "You could have called me home anytime."

"I'm afraid dinner's on hold." There was an almost imperceptible strain beneath Denise's controlled voice. "Your friend Crawford is here."

"Crawford? What does he want?"

"You. Something about David's truck, he won't tell me. There are two other policemen with him."

"What kind of policemen?"

There was a muffle as she cupped the mouthpiece. "Detectives." Another muffle. "Lake County detectives."

"They've told you nothing?"

"No."

"You know that if David was hurt they would have said so right off."

"I realize that."

"You tell them anything?"

"Of course not."

"Good. I'll be right there. Try to get Crawford drinking. If he has one, make it all booze, whatever it is."

"You want me to add any of my flu medicine?"

"No. I want him talking, not lapsing into a coma."

Jimmy traded the tab for the phone.

"Everything okay?" he asked.

"Sure. Just some unexpected guests, is all."

"That's great. Give the birthday girl a smack on the kisser from me, huh?"

"Don't tempt me."

Chapter Five

Kubiak found them in the front room, quiet voices that went silent upon his entrance. Denise was sitting, back straight, in the chair by the window, Maurice on the floor beside her. Crawford's six-foot frame was slumped in the recliner. Unless he was taking his scotch in a teacup these days, he had refused Denise's offer. The two detectives were on the couch. The heavier one wore wire-rimmed glasses and was in uniform; the other had a moustache as dark as his eyes.

Crawford introduced them with the aim of his chin. The uniformed man was Dunning, the man with the moustache Strom. Both rose to a crouch to shake Kubiak's hand. There was no sign of Maria, and the door to the guestroom was shut. Evidently, Denise had had the good sense to keep her stashed away.

When no one said anything, Kubiak went to the bar, hoping Crawford might follow. He would have liked a minute or two alone with him to find out just where things stood and why. He had no doubt Crawford was just as anxious to set him straight, either for old time's sake or to get in a jab or two of his own, depending on his mood and whether he had volunteered to come up here to run interference for an old friend or had been dragged up by these Lake County detectives because of his acquaintance with Kubiak.

Crawford didn't move from the recliner, which meant the rules of this evening's game were being set by Strom and Dunning. Kubiak took his time mixing himself a drink, and finally broke the silence. "So, you wanted to see me about my son-in-law's truck."

Dunning cleared his throat with a cough. "When was the last time you saw Mr. Hollinger?"

"Funny you should ask that." Kubiak moved beside Denise's chair, gently squeezed her shoulder. "He was supposed to be here last night, but he never showed up."

"Oh?" Dunning looked to Strom, who didn't return the glance. "Any idea where he was?"

"Yes. At home, in Rogers Park, with our daughter."

"You know that for a fact."

"I phoned them there twice. And Denise spoke with David on the phone, as well, after Maria was in bed."

Dunning took his pen from his pocket. "What time were these phone calls made to your son-in-law?"

"I don't know. What does any of this have to do with finding whoever stole his truck?"

Another glance at Strom. A bad habit. Kubiak guessed the two detectives weren't accustomed to working together or Strom would have done something about it.

"I'm not aware that his truck was reported stolen, sir," Dunning said flatly.

"Well, it wouldn't be, would it? I mean, he never drives it except when he has to move it from one parking spot to the next in order to keep it from being towed. We told him six months ago to sell that old thing, didn't we, darling?"

"David's from Wisconsin," Denise said, working off Kubiak's cue. "You just can't convince him he'll never find a use for a Jeep Cherokee in East Rogers Park."

"So," Kubiak added. "Where did it turn up?"

Dunning tucked his pen back into his pocket. "What makes you so certain the truck was stolen?"

"I'm not. Maybe David lent it to someone. But seeing as how you're not telling me anything, I'm left to make my own assumptions."

"You might try simply answering my questions, Mister Kubiak."

Crawford sat up in his chair. "Let me save you some time, Dunning. Kubiak, you sure you don't want to take a seat?"

"I'm fine."

"First off, you know Lake County wouldn't send two detectives down here about a stolen truck."

"I'm aware of that. I imagine whoever took it got involved in some sort of trouble."

"Some sort. You ever locate that friend of yours in Waukegan?"

"No."

"Too bad. You should have checked in at the coroner's office. You were just a few blocks away."

In his peripheral vision, Kubiak saw Denise shift her weight slightly. His eyes busy reading the faces of the three men, he could only hope she wasn't mimicking Dunning's bad habit. Only Strom's gaze kept darting from Kubiak to his wife and back.

"You're telling me Baumgarten's dead? When?"

"Last night."

"Where?"

"They found him just outside of Mundelein, behind a shack in an auto salvage yard."

Dunning cleared his throat. Crawford ignored him and continued. "About twenty yards from your son-in-law's truck. You want to make one of your assumptions about what he was doing there?"

"No, thanks. If these guys got to him first, I suppose you'll tell me he was just looking for a quiet place to pump some bullets into his cheeks and kneecaps."

Dunning's eyes narrowed. "Oh, you're funny, Mister Kubiak."

"Try me sometime when you're not sitting in my front room interrogating me about my son-in-law's possible involvement in a homicide. I can be downright hilarious."

Strom spoke for the first time. His voice was a controlled monotone. Kubiak couldn't tell if that was natural or if he was keeping it in check.

"Detective Dunning didn't say anything about a homicide, Mister Kubiak."

"No, but if Lake County wouldn't send two detectives down here about a stolen truck, why would they bother themselves over a guy who wandered behind a junkyard shack to die quietly of natural causes?"

"If it's any comfort to you," Strom said, "Baumgarten's body wasn't discovered by us. And he wasn't shot."

"So, what did him in? Knife?"

"Nope," Crawford said. "Claw hammer."

Dunning cleared his throat again. "Lieutenant, I don't see the need to bother Mr. Kubiak with details."

"On the contrary," Kubiak said. "More than one blow?"

"I'll say. I saw the photos. Poor bastard, I suppose it beats being swung at with a hatchet, but . . ."

"So, whoever did it was either very angry or pretty darned incompetent."

"He got the job done well enough."

"Who found him?"

"A group of kids, teenage girls. They were cruising Route 176 a little after midnight, saw the truck's dome light on, pulled into the dark salvage yard on a thrill."

"I got a teenage daughter," Dunning interrupted. "I wouldn't want her to see what those poor girls stumbled onto."

"I thought you said he was discovered behind a shack. Who was in the truck?"

"Nobody. The door was open, is all."

"Which door?"

"What does it matter which door?"

"Come on, Crawford. It all matters."

Crawford shrugged, looked to Strom, who remained silent for a moment, then muttered, "passenger."

"How did the girls know to go behind the shack?"

Crawford spoke again. "You pound a man to a pulp with a claw hammer, Kubiak, you tend to make a mess. They followed the bloody trail."

"Brave girls."

"More foolish, I think."

"So, Baumgarten was attacked in the truck."

"Yes, but at some point the attacker yanked him out. I would imagine to get a better windup. He dragged him behind the shack, finished him off there."

"All that damage, you're sure it's Baumgarten?"

A nod. "Prints match."

"Lift any off the truck?"

"Nope."

“The door that was left open, was it the one Baumgarten was dragged through?”

“Okay, hold on.” It came as a bark, and came from Dunning, who rose up an inch from the couch and settled back in again after a filthy glare aimed at Crawford. “Let’s get off this tangent where we got on. Yes, Baumgarten was dragged through the truck’s passenger side door, the reason being he was sitting on the passenger side of the truck. He wouldn’t be behind the wheel, would he? Because it wasn’t his truck. It’s your son-in-law’s truck. Which brings me back to my original question: When was the last time you saw David Hollinger?”

Kubiak sipped his drink. He could feel Denise’s eyes boring into him. She would be wanting an explanation of who Baumgarten was and why Kubiak had been looking for him.

“David had nothing to do with this,” he said. “He’s not capable of that kind of brutality. Besides, if you couldn’t find any prints on the truck’s steering wheel or console, it’s more than likely they were wiped off, and David would have no reason to go to that trouble seeing as how it was his truck in the first place.”

“In that case, you’ll want to do everything you can to help us find Mr. Hollinger as quickly as possible.”

“I would, but I don’t know where he is.”

“Could you tell us where your daughter is, then?”

Kubiak hesitated only a split second, but it was long enough for Denise to step in.

“She was here,” she said. “All day. She just left.”

“When?”

“Maybe an hour before you got here.”

“She say where she was going?”

“No.”

"She say where she's been?"

Kubiak interrupted. "Aside from where David is now, which neither my wife nor I know, what is it you're looking for from us?"

Dunning sighed. "Mr. Kubiak, what does Mr. Hollinger do for a living?"

"He's self-employed. Why?"

"Doing what, exactly?"

"He's a real estate speculator."

"And what, exactly, does a real estate speculator do to make a living? To pay his rent, I mean."

"He speculates. On real estate. What does his line of work have to do with this?"

Crawford leaned forward. "You told me this morning, on the phone, that you had a job offer for Baumgarten but that you couldn't find him. We know now why you couldn't find him. We'd like to know what the job was all about."

"First of all," Kubiak said, "I never said anything about a job offer for Baumgarten."

"Don't give me that. I was on the other end of the line, remember? I know what I heard."

"What you think you heard. If I had known it was a party line I never would have dialed the number."

"I was curious about Baumgarten's record. I told you that at the time. I phoned Lake County, mentioned his name, set off some alarms. So, here I wind up, on my Saturday night, thanks to another favor for you, old buddy."

"You should have joined me at Jimmy Dee's instead, old buddy. I was preparing lessons on curiosity."

"Get serious, Kubiak. Open up. You could do worse than Strom and Dunning, here."

"Sorry, boys." Kubiak addressed the detectives on the

couch. "I actually had a soft spot for Baumgarten, and I'd like to do whatever I can to help you put away the bastard who caved in his sad head, but when it comes to your questions about my son-in-law I'm going to have to keep quiet until I talk to him."

"Are you so sure it's your son-in-law you're worried about?"

The question came from Strom, delivered in the same, cold monotone.

"Meaning what?" Kubiak asked.

"Well, let's see. David Hollinger has only lived in this state for about six months now, whereas you've had an ongoing relationship with Baumgarten going on a number of years."

"Ongoing relationship. Is that what that was?"

"You claim you believe Mr. Hollinger was in his apartment last night, but the phone call you made to Lieutenant Crawford this morning was from the home of your son-in-law's downstairs neighbor. She told us that she had explained to you that Mr. Hollinger hadn't been home for a number of days. She also told us he had disappeared with Baumgarten, and that it was you who had introduced the two of them to each other. And, she said that you were concerned about a package that was supposed to have been delivered to your son-in-law, and that you were carrying a box containing some sort of decorative plate shaped like a fish.

"Lieutenant Crawford then called you back at that number and gave you Baumgarten's address. An hour or so later, Baumgarten's apartment was broken into. A kid in the building gave us a pretty decent description of the man who did it, and told us he had offered him a decorative plate. Shaped like a fish."

That was the end of Strom's speech. Crawford waited a beat before adding, "Let's cut the crap, Kubiak. Just tell us what it was you were looking to find in Baumgarten's apartment, and what exactly is this business the two of you were involved in."

Kubiak finished what was left in his glass. As choosing that precise moment to turn and mix himself a fresh drink would have sent all the wrong signals, he stayed put. It was unfortunate Baumgarten wasn't still alive to hear this. The idea of Kubiak's being charged with breaking and entering, into, of all places, his apartment, might have actually put a smile on his sorry face.

He addressed Strom. "I'd have to be pretty stupid to phone Crawford and offer up Baumgarten's name if I were involved in any type of activity with the man that might, in any way, put me on the spot."

"Not if you were already on the spot," Strom said. "Granted, it might have been a desperate act. But if you're wound up tight with Baumgarten and were aware that what was left of him was being carted out of that salvage yard this morning, you'd be pretty desperate to start putting space between you and him."

"By telling a cop I'm looking for him on the day he turns up dead?"

"By beginning to set up the case that you're on the outside looking in. You can't find Baumgarten, haven't seen him for days. The phone call is the indication of your innocence. I didn't say it was smart. I said it was desperate."

Denise stood. Kubiak, right beside her, hadn't expected the movement and nearly dropped his empty glass.

"I'm sorry, Detective Strom," she said. "I've known Kubiak to be a lot of things, but desperate was never one of them. Seeing as how I, at least, have been as cooperative as

I could possibly be, would you let me know, now, if you're going to arrest my husband tonight? Our dinner's warming."

Only Crawford attempted a smile, and he had to rearrange himself in the chair before he could manage that much. "I don't think that's necessary," he said, missing the glare Strom shot his way.

Kubiak didn't miss it. He touched his wife's arm.

"You can't get rid of me that easily, darling. If they were to take me in now, I'd just shut up, call our lawyer, and be home before the ten o'clock news. This way, they can keep any charge they have hanging over my head and pick me up whenever they feel the need to."

"In that case," Denise said, addressing her guests, "seeing as how you gentlemen are beginning to get insulting, I have to insist that you leave now. Please."

Crawford was the first one up, then Strom. Dunning sat for another few seconds, looking as though he had missed a turn in the conversation, then joined them.

Denise left Kubiak and Maurice to see them to the door. Crawford tried to linger, but Strom would have none of it and was the last one out. Halfway through the doorway, he turned back to Kubiak.

"Nice place," he said. "Lake view. What did it cost you, if you don't mind my asking."

"The farm. And then some."

"You worked latent prints, put in your minimum. Must be a nice gig, Cook County. What am I doing wrong?"

"I'm already working up the list."

Kubiak shut the door in his face, turned the bolt, felt the relief of having locked the wolves out of the cabin. The feeling vanished when he turned and faced his wife.

"Who's Baumgarten?" she asked.

He mixed himself another drink and related Friday's

meeting in Union Station, along with his conversation with Mrs. Ears and his trip to Waukegan.

"I don't understand," Denise said when he had finished. "How could David possibly fall in with a fellow like Baumgarten? And if they were acquaintances, why wouldn't Baumgarten have mentioned that when he was trying to convince you to work with him?"

"I don't know. I went up there this afternoon to find out."

"By breaking into Baumgarten's apartment?"

"That little kid picked a hell of a time to finally open up his mouth."

"What would possess you to do such a thing?"

"To tell you the truth, I didn't think anyone would mind. Aside from Strom, I don't think anyone does. If Baumgarten were alive, he'd certainly understand."

"You told Strom you'd call our lawyer. We don't have a lawyer."

"Well, it's high time we got one. While you go through the yellow pages, I'll be in the guest bedroom engaged in an interrogation I only wish Strom could see. This time, if you hear any shouting on the other side of the door, just turn up the stereo. By the way, you managed quite a job of staying cool knowing Maria was here the entire time, but you shouldn't have lied to Dunning about it."

"I didn't lie. You were the only one who lied, about David's being home last night."

"No. They asked me if I had any idea where he was. It was the only thing I could come up with, even if I knew it wasn't the right thing. And I was accurate about the phone calls last night; I only mentioned them in the wrong order. What do you mean, you didn't lie?"

Denise said nothing. Her hands were clasped in front of her waist.

"Where is she?" he asked.

"She got a phone call. From David."

"When?"

"Like I told your friends, an hour before they got here."

His friends.

"You let her go?"

"I didn't know."

"You didn't ask David where he was?"

"No. I knew they'd had a fight, and he called her here, and I handed her the phone."

"How did he sound?"

"Looking back, I'd say not too good. A little strung out. Maria didn't say much into the phone. When she hung up, she told me David was staying with friends and she was going to meet him, that everything was all right, and that she'd call us, if not tonight, some time tomorrow."

Kubiak could have used a good blow-up; he had felt one coming on since the middle of the previous evening. Still, he held himself in check. His wife had done nothing wrong, and was probably more primed to lash out at him than he was at her. He carried his drink over to the window.

"So," Denise said at his back. The slight tremor had returned to her voice. "You're the bloodhound." She feared the conversation's ending. "What do we do now?"

The streetlights were beginning to blink on along the drive. The horizon was dissipating into darkness.

"We eat dinner," he said. "Then, we go to bed."

"If you're trying to make a joke, Kubiak, it's not funny."

"There are cops from two counties out there right now looking for David and Maria. There's no reason we shouldn't let them do the job for us. After all, it's not as if David actually is guilty of murdering Baumgarten." He glanced back at Denise, saw the look on her face. "Well, Maria certainly isn't. And the minute the police pick up her or David, she's bound to call us to get her a lawyer. Or bond money."

A thought flashed into Kubiak's mind. He wondered which of the two of them Maria would want on the other end of the line of that phone call. It was a vain, trivial thought, and he forced it to pass.

"What if it isn't the police who find her?" Denise asked. "It was Baumgarten with David two nights ago, and look where he is now."

Kubiak turned from the window, led his wife gently into the kitchen as he explained the unlikeliness of anything of that sort happening to their daughter. She tensed under his touch, wary of his consolation, and he knew better than to say anything he wasn't already telling himself. He said that Hollinger must have sent Maria to their condo in order to make certain she was safe, and that he wouldn't have called her back if he thought she might be in danger. They were holed up somewhere, as Maria had said, probably with friends.

"You know most of her friends," he said. "Say you were to call them tonight, one after the next, ask after her, and get a read on their tone? It might put us a step ahead of the Stroms and Dunnings running around out there. We have call waiting, and have to stay by the phone, anyway. After you're done, we'll sit down together and go through some possibilities."

It wasn't much, but it was what Denise needed, and she agreed. As for dinner, neither of them wanted a repeat of the previous evening, so Kubiak suggested one of Denise's phone calls be to Ritzi's Pizza on Clark. While she was on the phone, he sealed up the birthday meal for another date, telling her that if they continued to celebrate Maria's birthday much longer the two of them would starve to death. She didn't laugh, but continued to dial up numbers, and he absently listened to her voice in the background while he considered where he would concentrate his efforts tomorrow morning if that phone didn't ring before then.

When she was finished, she handed him the list of friends and gave him her impressions. He quizzed her, and it quickly became apparent to both of them that they had nothing but guesses. Still, they stayed up talking, over an open pizza box, one lamp burning, well into the night.

Chapter Six

They had first met David Hollinger at the Drake Hotel. "Nothing too fancy," Maria had told them, as if there was anything that wasn't fancy about the Drake. "Just a late lunch at the Coq d'Or. And David insists on paying. It's our idea, after all."

The idea, of course, had been all Maria's. Hollinger wouldn't have been able to find the Coq d'Or without a guidebook, while it was just the sort of place where Maria and her mother or her friends could waste an afternoon lingering over coffee and cigarettes without looking too much like princesses.

"Maybe he'll ask for salted butter," Kubiak said to Denise while they waited for their daughter and her boyfriend to arrive. "Just so I won't have to."

Outside, the winter sun was reflecting against the snow. Inside, it might have been any time of day, any time of year. For that matter, it might have been any year at all.

"Did I mention I've always considered salted butter the first hurdle for any of Maria's suitors? This Hollinger manages to demand it before I do, I'll not only give him a big, Wisconsin bear hug, but I'll take to calling him son immediately."

"Go ahead, Kubiak. Let it out of your system before they get here."

"Oh, I have plenty of time. She wouldn't take the chance of arriving before us and ruining the drama of their entrance."

And it was an entrance, Maria's arm in Hollinger's, the two of them beaming as though they had just discovered a cure for depression and didn't know who to tell about it first. Kubiak had to admit Hollinger could fill a suit, and the level of general enthusiasm the young man carried with him couldn't have been faked for their sake. He showed no sign of being ill at ease in a dining room the caliber of the Coq d'Or, though he had been dating Maria for a number of months so he probably had had a chance to acclimate to that type of environment.

A few years older than Maria, he had met her in Madison where she was going to college. He wasn't a student.

"I was renovating some student housing I bought a stake in last summer, walked into a bar with nothing on my mind but finding an ice cold beer, and there she was."

"Funny," Kubiak said. "That's exactly how I met her mother. She was sitting in a tavern, just having a couple of snorts by her lonesome—"

"I wasn't alone," Maria protested. "I was with friends."

Denise asked Hollinger if he renovated houses for a living. He laughed and shook his head.

"Don't get me wrong, it's fine work, only a little claustrophobic for my taste. I only entered into the investment in order to get hold of the cash for the project I'm involved in now. Maria hasn't told you all about it?"

"She mentioned something."

Hollinger began animatedly describing the resort in northern Wisconsin that he and his partner were opening, his fingertips tracing maps on the tablecloth. Nothing big, just a few cabins to begin with. But the possibilities. . . .

He was interrupted by lunch, saved the end of his sales pitch for Kubiak's ear when they were outside the restaurant. As the four of them walked, wind-whipped, along the noisy, crowded Michigan Avenue sidewalk, he described the tiny section of paradise he was creating in Wisconsin's north woods.

"You have to see it, Mr. Kubiak. Seriously, I can't wait to show you."

Kubiak was afraid the young man was going to stuff them all into his Jeep right then and head north to do just that.

Kubiak had seen the property, and he believed the resort might have had a chance had it not been for the woes David's partner had created. Hollinger, by now his son-in-law, had walked out of the deal with a reasonable amount of cash, but no fortune. When nothing else panned out up north, Maria, homesick, talked him into giving Chicago a try. That had been nine months ago.

It was an unusually cool August morning. The wind was coming off the lake. Kubiak, standing at the edge of the empty beach, stared out at the white foam of the breaking waves. A lone jogger pounded past him. Farther back, on Sheridan, a distant car's horn sounded. Two blocks beyond that sat Maria and David's empty apartment.

So what had this ambitious, young real estate speculator been up to over the past nine months? According to Mrs. Ears, he spent his days loafing about on the beach playing checkers. Well, Hollinger was anything but lazy, and Kubiak had never known him to bring up the game of checkers. But he could imagine his son-in-law being drawn to this lakefront where, though he was just a hundred yards from the congested streets of Rogers Park, he could gaze out at the horizon with the city silent at his back, probably with the same look on his face that Kubiak had seen when the two of them had looked out together at Lake Superior while standing on Hollinger's few acres of a dream in northern Wisconsin.

Loyola Park's snack stand had yet to open for the day. A thin, weathered screen door in the back accessed a tiny kitchen from which came the sounds of morning prep work. Kubiak pounded on it, and then pounded on it some more. Finally, the wary face of a round man in a dirty T-shirt appeared on the other side of the screen.

He refused to unlock the flimsy door, shook his head at the photograph of Hollinger which Kubiak held up to him.

"You telling me you've never seen this man before?"

Another head shake. His eyes showed only disinterest.

"He's been hanging around this park all summer long."

"So? A lot of people like that. Too many people."

"And you wouldn't recognize a single one of them?"

"I work on a beach. I got better things to look at than faces."

"Too bad I left the picture of his rear end at home on my coffee table."

The man's eyes narrowed, the first emotion he had shown. "I ain't that way."

"Police talk to you yet?"

"Why? They about to?"

"Probably." So, Mrs. Ears hadn't mentioned Hollinger's habits to Strom and Dunning. "You wouldn't prefer to save yourself the trouble?"

"I got no trouble. I sell hamburgers and popsicles. I got nothing to say to anybody."

"You're in this shack from sunup to sundown, seven days a week. You must talk to somebody."

"Only myself. I got no time to make friends. I'm too busy."

"It's worth five hundred to you if I find this guy."

"I don't need five hundred. I make a living here."

"Anybody else work here who might be a little friendlier?"

"Nobody but me, that's all."

And then he was gone, back to his lonely, deliberate kitchen work. Kubiak turned away, tucked the photograph back into his jacket pocket. There were others on the beach. As the man had said, too many like that. Loyola Park, like any public gathering place, had its regulars, its tight club who considered the park their own private space, who huddled together against strangers and discussed their own business in whispers. Those types missed little of what went on around them. Come noon, they would be impossible to single out among the scores of others here on any August day. It was only now, early in the day, under a cold sky bearing a harsh wind, that Kubiak would be able to find them.

The park ran only two blocks north, but stretched south well past Pratt. South was the direction Kubiak took, walking along the concrete breaker wall between the grass and sand, the park to his right, the beach to his left. The beach was an easy read, naked except for the white lifeguard towers, the guards' old rowboats chained to their bases, listing in the sand. The park was a little more difficult, its trees holding back the light.

Another jogger passed him, this one offering Kubiak a

guarded nod. The area around the squat, brick building that housed the public restrooms appeared to be empty; Kubiak wondered what he might discover inside, decided against finding out. Beyond the restrooms, two men dressed in winter clothes stood hunched over the smoking coals of one of the park's grills. As Kubiak approached, one slipped the bottle he was holding into his coat pocket, then turned slightly away.

Behind them, farther back in the trees, the figure of another man, dressed just as heavily except for his bare feet, lay asleep, curled into a ball. The perils of sleeping in, because he was missing the party. The bottle might even have been his.

To Kubiak's left, an older woman stood thin and alone at the water's edge practicing her tai chi. She stopped, grew visibly nervous as he crossed the beach toward her, relaxed only slightly when he showed her the photograph of Hollinger. She told Kubiak she was on the beach only in the early morning, expressed her regrets, and wished him the best.

Kubiak continued south. Just past the tennis courts, he saw a group of four or five men gathered around some tiny, stone tables under a cluster of trees. The area in which they stood was so shaded at this hour he nearly missed them. He lingered a moment, until he was certain they were aware of his presence, then made his way up the slight incline toward them.

They were five men, all in their twenties or early thirties, and they performed the usual too-casual-to-be-innocent shuffle as he neared. One remained seated; two stood behind the seated man, feet planted apart. The remaining two wandered a few yards back. Hands in their pockets, both wearing pants baggy enough to flap in the breeze, they toed the grass and occasionally muttered something only each other could hear.

The seated man was the calmest and most square-jawed of the bunch. His palms rested flat on the table. Ingrained into the tabletop was a black and white tiled checkerboard. The tops of the other tables held the same tiled checkerboards. Kubiak stopped at the table nearest the group, nodded a greeting, but received no acknowledgement. He smiled, looked up at the sky, then sat down, interlacing his fingers over his belly and breathing the air in deeply.

"Cold morning," he said, and waited for a reply that didn't come. "You won't catch me swimming on a day like this, no sir." Another pause. "Water ought to be warm, though, this late in the summer. Might do a little wading, what do you think?"

One of the men standing behind the square-jawed man glanced back over his right shoulder. He kept bouncing up on the balls of his feet. After a minute, Kubiak made a move as if he were about to get up, but only swung around on the seat and began to remove his shoes and socks. One of the grass-toers giggled.

"I don't suppose any of you gentlemen brought the checkers with you today?" Kubiak asked, rolling up the cuffs of his pants. "No? I didn't know the park offered this amenity, and thank goodness you were here or I never would have spotted these checkerboards. I've always liked checkers, though. Always preferred it to chess. I suppose you're wondering why."

Nothing.

"Well, I'll tell you. First of all, there's the time element. I'm not the kind of fellow who likes to waste time, mine or anybody else's, and if you get two people who know what they're doing, a game of chess can last about forever. Then, there's what I call the covert operations factor. You see, checkers only move one way, straightforward. But these chess pieces, every one moves in a different direction. And you spend all your time trying to maneuver these pieces in this sneaky, behind the back manner that your opponent won't see until it's too late for him. Well, I just don't see why two friends would want to sit on either side of a board doing that sort of—"

"Why don't you just get the hell out of here?"

It was Square-jaw, of course. He still had not moved. The man behind him looked over his right shoulder again. The two grass-toers moved closer.

"Yes," Kubiak continued. "I was going to touch on the aspect of subtlety, but I see I don't have to. Like I said, I never would have found this place without you, so I think I owe you a favor. I suppose you like money." He straightened until he was sitting upright. As he did, he slipped his hand into his pants pocket, came out with a fifty dollar bill which he held out just slightly over his head. It fluttered madly in the wind off the lake, a flag, a tiny, green flag, and Kubiak might have had them all singing the star spangled banner for the way they were staring at it.

He let the bill go. The wind carried it up ten feet over their heads and back toward the buildings' courtyards along Morse. One of the grass-toers let out a yelp and bounded after it.

"A resourceful little guy, isn't he?" Kubiak said to the remaining four. "I don't doubt he'll catch it eventually. But then, he's not smart enough to know you won't let him keep it. Besides, I've got ten more of those for you if you'd like to earn them. And I won't make you chase after them."

"What do you want, crazy man?" Square-jaw asked.

"I'm looking for David."

Again, nothing.

"You know David. He's usually right here. . . Wait, I have a picture of him somewhere."

Kubiak patted his pockets, then extracted the photograph of Hollinger. Square-jaw squinted at it.

"What's he to you?"

"I'm sorry. That's . . . private business. Besides, do you really care?"

"I don't know this guy."

"Then maybe you know someone who does, and you can put me in touch with that person. You manage that much, you'll still get the full five hundred. The fifty is a bonus when you pry it from your buddy's fist."

"What's to stop me from taking it from you right now?"

"Well, let's see. You look pretty comfortable here in this little hamlet of a spot you've made for yourself in the park. You rob me here, you'll probably have to relocate for some period of time, and all your friends would miss you terribly. Besides, you could take everything I have on me and still wind up a hundred or so short of what I'm offering."

Square-jaw scowled at the photograph of Hollinger. "Like I said, I don't know this guy."

"Fine. But in case somebody introduces you to him this afternoon, here's how you can get in touch with me," Kubiak said, scribbling his phone number onto a piece of paper. "If my secretary answers, leave a message. I promise to get back to you by this evening."

He offered the piece of paper to Square-jaw, who hesitated only a second before he took it.

The man behind him looked over his shoulder yet

again. This time, he didn't turn back. Kubiak followed his gaze. Fifty yards or so back, a thick, red-haired man in jeans and a denim shirt had been making his way down from Morse into the park, but had stopped. The grass-toer who had gone after the fifty was beside him, talking animatedly. Red was staring down at Kubiak.

"I'd call me as soon as you can if I were you," Kubiak said. "This offer is open to everyone on this beach, first come, first served. I fully expect to be handing over that money to someone before this day is—"

But now they were all staring up toward Morse. Red turned and headed toward wherever he had come from. He walked quickly, in the stilted manner of a heavy man.

One of the men standing next to Kubiak uttered a curse. Then they were all up and away, even Square-jaw, though he moved deliberately slower than the others.

"Who's your buddy?" Kubiak called out after him. "Ask him if he's heard what happened to Paul Baumgarten Friday night. If he claims he doesn't know, maybe you'd better make it your business to find out."

But Square-jaw never turned back. Alone again, Kubiak debated following them, but decided against it. After all, the point of this exercise was to make them want to come to Kubiak, not run from him. He put on his socks and shoes, continued down through the park. Though he came across no one as promising as the group of men by the checkerboards, by the time he returned to his car he was two hundred and fifty dollars poorer.

And all the way back along the beach, he was thinking of the words Denise had used last night when referring to Baumgarten: How could David possibly fall in with a fellow like that?

Chapter Seven

Sunday morning, the auto salvage yard was as empty as it must have been when Baumgarten and his companion had rolled into it in Hollinger's truck Friday night. Kubiak turned in off of Route 176. Gravel crunched under his tires as he braked to a stop.

He left the Contour running, and didn't bother to close the driver's door when he got out.

Whatever was worth salvaging was penned in a giant lot behind chain link and razor wire. Everything else littered the open front lot, about fifty square yards. A two-bay garage with a one-desk office was butted up against the fence. The shack behind which Baumgarten was found dead looked to be nothing more than a tool shed. Only it remained surrounded by sagging, yellow police ribbon.

Kubiak went behind the shed where wide splashes of dried blood had yet to be cleaned off of the aluminum. This indeed was the spot where he would have dragged the dying Baumgarten in order to finish him off, as it was the one area outside of the fence that was out of sight of the road. Crawford figured the killer dragged him here to get a better windup on his swings with the hammer. Kubiak wondered if maybe Baumgarten had been able to crawl out of the truck, or even simply manage to get the door open in a desperate attempt to draw attention from passing traffic.

But then, the killer hadn't bothered to close the passenger door, had he? The burning dome light was what had drawn the teenage girls into the lot that night. Maybe he was in a hurry to get away once his job was finished. But in what, a waiting car? On foot?

Kubiak walked back to the road. Traffic raced by on the two-lane strip at fifty miles per hour. Nothing in either direction but farmers' fields and industrial parks. He had passed a motel a couple of miles back. Not too far to hike if the rest of your life depended on your getting home and washing up. Of course, it was something the cops would be checking out, if they hadn't already.

He returned to the Ford, thought of what a horridly dark, lonely place this salvage yard must have seemed when Baumgarten's companion pulled in here. He wondered what the man might have said to convince Baumgarten that this was the perfect spot to stop for a minute, maybe to talk business, maybe to meet someone else to talk business.

He wondered whether Baumgarten had been sitting nonchalantly, as nonchalantly as poor Paul Baumgarten could sit, oblivious to all that was about to take place when that hammer landed its first blow, or if he had been sweating all along the ride down black, rural Route 176.

Kubiak pulled out of the yard, drove into Mundelein,

found a gas station, and asked directions to the library. Ordinarily, his next stop would have been the Lake County Sheriff's Department, but he could picture the look on Strom's or Dunning's face if he were to waltz in today to ask questions.

The library was larger than he had expected, a neat, brick building with just enough curves and eaves to give it character. On Sundays it didn't open until noon, and he waited in the freshly paved parking lot, keeping his distance from the handful of kids and old folks waiting with him, not only because he was the only person between the ages of eighteen and sixty-five who wasn't there to chaperone a group of gradeschoolers, but because out here, on this flat land of schoolyards and mowed lawns near the Wisconsin border and far from the city, Kubiak always felt like a foreigner on the verge of being branded as such. Every facet of the area seemed designed to make brutally clear it held no place for him. Even the sky looked different, hanging lower, close and clean over everything, so that each building, each fencepost and flagpole, stood stark and alone against it.

Finally, the doors opened. A friendly, young girl at the front desk directed him upstairs to an even friendlier, younger girl who aimed him toward the back issue periodicals. Kubiak chose the North Lake County edition of the suburban newspaper, gathered five stacks dated from mid May to late June, sat down and began to go through them looking for Mackay's name.

He found it in the paper dated Wednesday, May 30th, four paragraphs on page one beside a photograph of the car in which Mackay shot himself. The story continued on page seven, though it ran only another paragraph or two, the usual abbreviated who, what, where, and when, without a hint of why.

Round Lake Beach police had responded to a 911 call from the residence of Jerald and Bernice Wheeler at just after 7 A.M. on Tuesday. They found the front door of the house open, entered and discovered Mrs. Wheeler in her housecoat, face-down on the kitchen floor, having been shot once in the back of the head. Old Jerald was in the bedroom in his pajamas, wedged between the bed and the wall. It had taken two bullets to finish him off, one to the chest, another through his left eye. The phone's receiver was laying in his lap.

The police found the garage empty, so dispatchers put out a description of the couple's Honda Civic. Within minutes, a Lake County cruiser spotted the car driving erratically at high speed northbound on Route 83. As more police vehicles joined in the pursuit, the Civic slowed, and eventually turned onto a succession of narrow rural roads. The chase finally ended when the Civic rolled into a ditch where the driver, Jack Mackay, died of a self-inflicted gunshot wound to the head.

Mackay had been living with the Wheelers for the past year. The twenty-four-year-old had been employed by Jerald Wheeler at the lumberyard the man owned, and had a record of arrests for drug possession and multiple DUI's. When he took himself and the Wheelers out, Mackay was on probation for an assault on a bartender in an Antioch tavern.

The remainder of the article was focused on neighbors and coworkers expressing sorrow, along with their esteem for the Wheelers and disdain for Mackay. One person was even quoted describing Mackay as a loner who "kept pretty much to himself."

"Imagine that," Kubiak muttered as he moved on to Thursday's paper.

There was little there, but Friday's held the dissenting opinion. Jack's mother, Robin Mackay, was weighing in. Relegated to page four was a photograph of her with her daughter, Kimberly, in the living room of their Round Lake apartment. A forty-something woman standing beside a seated twenty-something amidst a clutter of mismatched furniture, they were both blond, grim-faced, and hard-looking, with a lot of dark under their eyes.

Of course, the son of the former and brother of the latter had shot himself to death just two days before the picture was taken, and Kubiak doubted the photographer had asked them to say cheese. Kimberly was holding a framed eight-by-ten photograph of Jack in her lap. He, at least, was grinning from ear to ear. Because of its size, most of the detail in the snapshot of him was lost in the newsprint's grain, but its point was clear: there was more to this happy, neatly dressed young man than had so far been reported by the press or the police.

The relatives were putting forth the version of the story Baumgarten had given Kubiak: Jack Mackay was no angel, but he deserved better than to be assassinated by the county police in lieu of a trial. They claimed the police had had it out for young Jack ever since he was picked up in front of the local high school for possession of marijuana the very week after the family had moved to Round Lake Beach from Chicago. They saw a vendetta behind each subsequent arrest, viewed the final confrontation as a convenient excuse for murder.

Their case centered on the fact that Mackay was shot three times, a point dismissed by a certain Detective Richard Strom of the Lake County Sheriff's Department, who had been one of the officers involved in the pursuit. He told the reporter the same thing Kubiak had told

Baumgarten, that the handgun, a .38 caliber Smith & Wesson, registered to Jerald Wheeler, could very easily have discharged accidentally into Mackay's leg during the high speed part of the chase or later, while Mackay was maneuvering over the rough terrain of the back roads onto which he had turned. In fact, he added, the pain resulting from the gunshot might have been the reason Mackay swerved into the ditch and determined to kill himself rather than surrender to the police. As to the second bullet going through his cheek, Strom pointed out that the fatal shot was aimed into Mackay's brain through his mouth; a botched first attempt at suicide in such a manner, in a moving car, was hardly out of the question.

A cold reply to a mother's accusation, but Kubiak could imagine Strom stating it in his deliberate monotone. He flipped through the front sections of all of June's papers, then went through July's as well as August's, but found only two more short articles related to the killings. One was a recap after the police investigation determined the case a murder/suicide; the other was the obituary for the Wheelers, he a loving husband, father, and Korean War veteran, she a loving wife and mother, survived by a son, Thomas Wheeler, also of Round Lake Beach.

Funny. It was the first Kubiak had heard of him. He copied down all the names, including those of the reporter and the funeral home, along with whatever addresses had been printed, thanked the young lady parked in front of the periodicals, and went back to his car.

He had picked up a map of Lake County at the gas station. On it, he located the street on which the Wheelers had lived, then headed north, past farmers' fields and scattered housing tracts, some new, most sunken and weathered. He was at his destination, a narrow block of old ranch houses on the south end of Round Lake Beach, in under twenty minutes. The Wheelers' home was distinguished from the rest only by the red, white, and blue FOR SALE sign driven into the center of its front lawn.

Kubiak parked and walked up the gravel drive. The garage was detached, set back behind the house. He peered through its sole, filthy window, noted that their car, in which Mackay had shot himself, had not found its way home. He turned to the house's side door, tested it, found it locked, was looking through its window into the home's kitchen trying to guess where Mrs. Wheeler's body might have lain when a voice behind him asked, "Can I help you?"

He pulled back just far enough to see the man's reflection in the window: sixty-something, faded work shirt, hands in his pockets.

"No, thanks. I think I'm doing fine. Unless you've got a key to this door."

"You looking to buy?"

"Just looking. You a neighbor?"

The man pointed to the house behind them. He used his entire arm in the gesture.

"How's the neighborhood?"

"Neighborhood's fine."

Kubiak grunted, moved around to the front of the house. The man followed, maintaining a few yards distance between them.

"How'd you hear about the place?" the man asked.

"Newspaper." The front window looked into a living room not unlike the one in which Mrs. Mackay and her daughter had had their picture taken. Kubiak stepped over a bush, onto the landing, and tested that door, which was locked as well. "You follow everybody around, or just people who go about peeping in windows?"

"Keeping an eye on the house, is all."

"A little late for that, don't you think?"

The man's face turned sour. His hands came out of his pockets.

Kubiak continued. "Who's handling the estate, the son?"

A long pause, then, "That's right."

"I understand he lives around here. I'd like to talk to him."

"The realtor's number is on the sign."

"I don't want to talk to a realtor, I want to talk to Thomas. I can get his address, anyway. You'll just be saving us time, doing us all a favor. Like keeping an eye on everybody's house."

A longer pause. "I couldn't give you his address if I knew it, which I don't."

"Fine, then." Kubiak started back to his car. "Keep up the surveillance. Anybody comes around actually wants to buy this thing, try not to scare them away."

"Tommy wouldn't be home when you got there, anyway," the man called after him.

"Oh?"

"Not on a Sunday afternoon. You going to stop and listen to what I'm telling you or not?"

"Nope."

The man glared as Kubiak climbed into the Contour, waited until the engine was running before calling out, "Sundays he'd be at the Legion, watching the Packers."

Kubiak waved as he drove off. He imagined that if he lingered another few minutes he would have the directions to the Legion as well, but determined he would prefer to take his chances finding it on his own, and so he did, just a dozen blocks away in a run-down area that, a half century ago, might have been the town's center.

Open to the public, the drinking quarters of the American Legion Hall was like any country tavern, maybe a little smaller, with a little more knotted pine on its walls. It had a satellite dish, and a twenty-seven inch TV hanging in each corner, one displaying the pre-season Bears game, the other three tuned to the Green Bay Packers.

Kubiak missed Tom Wheeler on his first glance and wound up sitting on the wrong side of the U-shaped bar. When the bartender asked if Tommy wanted another beer, the man who shoved his empty bottle into the rail was easily a decade younger than Kubiak would have guessed. A year or two short of thirty, he was the youngest man in a room of nothing but men, and he sat slumped over his beer, concentrating on the Wisconsin game, though he would occasionally call out some inside joke or a comment to another patron, provoking a chorus of hoarse chuckles.

The bartender was the type who liked to save his barstools for the regulars, so Kubiak concentrated on the veterans on either side of him. Two rounds of drinks and a quarter of football later, he knew everyone's name, and the last surviving Wheeler in Round Lake Beach had moved onto the stool beside him.

"So," Tommy said, "you're the guy who looks at houses he doesn't want to buy."

"You get your news off the wire."

Tommy lifted his cellular phone two inches off the bartop, let it roll off his fingers and drop back down.

"Andy even gave me your license plate number."

"He doesn't miss much."

"Andy Shultz was a good friend of my folks," he said, his eyes on the television. "I don't know. I hardly said two words to the man when they were alive. Now, he's calling me three times a day. We spent half of yesterday morning together putting the storm windows onto that place. I don't know."

He turned to Kubiak. "So, what were you doing there?"

Tommy wasn't the only one in the room waiting for an answer; it was a bar where conversations were shared. Kubiak kept his voice low in case Tommy wanted to keep things personal.

"There's this fellow I knew named Baumgarten. I thought he might have been a friend of your folks, as well."

"I don't get it. You thought he might be living in my parents' house?"

"It was the only address I had. And no, on both counts. He's dead. You never heard your parents mention his name?"

"Baumgarten? No."

"What about this guy, you ever see him?" Kubiak asked, handing him the photograph of Hollinger. Nothing registered on Tommy's face.

"What are you?" Tommy asked. "A cop or something? What makes you think my parents knew either of these guys?"

"I know Baumgarten was familiar with acquaintances of Jack Mackay."

"Oh." The young man's eyes went back to the television screen. "Mackay, sure."

"If this is a bad time to talk about it . . ."

"No, it's okay. It's strange. Right after it happened, I didn't mind talking about it at all. I mean, it's all everybody was talking about. Then, after a couple of weeks, it started to get to me. I didn't want to hear a word. It was like everybody who brought it up to me was getting some kind of thrill by keeping the whole thing alive, and the same talk got old real fast.

"Then, I don't know, just lately it's gotten back to where I don't mind talking about it again. Maybe it's because hardly anybody's bringing it up anymore. Like it's all just gone away and forgotten. The only problem is, every time the subject is brought up, it's that sleazebag Jack Mackay they're interested in, not my parents." He looked at Kubiak, smiled. "Like you, for instance."

"I'm not interested in Mackay," Kubiak said. "I'm interested in Baumgarten."

"Oh, right. Your friend who's dead. Like Mackay, like my mom and dad." He raised his beer bottle in a toast.

"At least you know who shot your parents," Kubiak told him. "I don't know who killed Baumgarten."

"Him, too? Doesn't anybody just have a heart attack anymore?"

"And there are still the questions concerning Mackay's death."

Tommy's smile disappeared. "There's no question about Mackay's death. Jack Mackay shot Jack Mackay."

"Who's telling you otherwise?"

"Nobody in particular. Not that I'd care, anyway. As long as he's dead, I'm fine."

"You don't care to know at all how it went down."

"Not a bit, just so long as it did."

"The only problem with that is you'll never get to ask him why he did it, will you?"

Tommy glared at Kubiak a moment, looked down at the bar, chuckled. He shook a cigarette out of the pack in front of him, chuckled again. "Given the choice, I'm okay with the fact he's not around to answer the question."

"You sure you don't mind talking about this?"

"No, I told you."

"So, what was he doing there in the first place? He was about your age. He's in the house, you're not. He's a sleazebag, you're not. Your folks are decent people. I don't get it."

"Too decent."

Tommy lit the cigarette, looked around the bar. He called the bartender over, asked for two plastic cups. The bartender eyed Kubiak.

"You got to give up your keys," Tommy said. Kubiak noticed Tommy's were resting on the bar next to his phone. He dropped his beside them as Tommy poured their beers into the cups, then followed Tommy out the front door of the dark bar into the blinding light of a Sunday summer afternoon.

Chapter Eight

They walked along a narrow street under telephone and electric lines that sagged into small houses crowded against the curb.

"Legion just wants to make sure you're not taking their booze on the road," Tommy said. "The cops are everywhere. I got a DUI a year ago last January. Day after New Year's, you'd think they'd be sitting fat and happy on their quotas, but no. I'm still paying off the bills."

"Interesting. Mackay had his share of the same."

"What's so interesting? Just look around you . . . what's your name again?"

"Kubiak."

"Look around you, Mister Kubiak. This isn't downtown Chicago. You won't find any cabs here. The only busses are school busses. You watch a football game at point A and your home is point B, you're going to get a DUI sooner or later. When we get back inside, you want me to ask the guys driving on suspended licenses to raise their hands?"

"No, thanks. I take it the neighbors object to glass."

"Yeah, I guess there used to be problems."

"Funny thing about neighbors. That was another thing I wanted to ask you. I hadn't pulled up in front of your parents' house less than two minutes before that Andy Shultz fellow was behind me, asking me what I was doing."

"Like you said, he doesn't miss much."

"Okay, so how is it your parents were shot three times, at seven o'clock in the morning, yet he, and everyone else on the block, left it to your father to make his own call to 911?"

Tommy snorted into his beer, came out of the cup laughing, hardly the reaction Kubiak had expected. "You didn't go anywhere near mentioning that to Andy, did you?"

"I hinted at it."

"Well, you're lucky that's all you did. That whole point burns him. But it wasn't his fault. My dad, he was a carpenter. He was always tearing up the house, moving cabinets, ripping up floors. When he wasn't, he was in the basement building who-knows-what. And he worked in the morning. Early. The neighbors got used to the noise. You try to tell the difference between the sound of a nail gun and a real one when it's waking you up at dawn. Besides, you live in a house next door to the likes of Jack Mackay, you learn to ignore what goes on, whatever the time of day."

"Ignore what kinds of things?"

"The usual. Cars pulling up in the driveway all night, every one of them with a two hundred watt amplifier mounted in its trunk, pounding out nothing but bass. A lawn full of beer cans in the morning."

"Your parents put up with that?"

"It's not like they opened up the house to the party. But

Mackay didn't have a car or a license, so on the nights when he wasn't lifting the keys to my parents' car, his buddies would come to pick him up and dump him off. You know how that goes, there's a lot of lingering involved. Crazy thing is, Jack Mackay just might have been likeable enough if only he didn't have any friends."

"Any of his buddies still live around here?"

"He never had any friends around here. They followed him out of Chicago."

"Know any of their names?"

"How would I? I was never around. I'm just telling you what Andy and the rest of the neighbors have told me."

"That brings us back to the question that got us out here, doesn't it?"

Tommy lost his balance momentarily, recovered nicely.

"I told you, my parents were too decent for their own good. My dad only had two dreams in his whole life: to own his own home, and to own his own business. My mom, I don't even know if she ever wanted anything besides what she already had.

"I don't know, I suppose it had a lot to do with the fact they were pretty old when they had me. I grew up in a house where we waited for my dad to come home, ate dinner, watched a little TV, and went to bed. That was it, and that was all there was ever going to be. When I got a little older, I realized my dad had come up with one more dream, and that was for me to run the lumberyard one day. I didn't want any part of it."

"The lumberyard, or watching TV and going to bed early?"

"The whole package. Move the same stock all day, every day, shuffle pennies into columns every night. I moved out first chance I could, took a job part-time working at a recording studio in Gurnee. Eventually, I put some money down on my own equipment. Now, I do the sound work for most of the bands in the area. Occasionally, I sit in on a set."

"You're a musician."

Tommy shrugged. "I'm familiar with a keyboard."

"So, Mackay stepped into the house when you stepped out."

"Not right away, but yeah."

"You think he was taking advantage of your parents, grooming himself to take over the lumberyard?"

"Oh, it was his to lose, but that was my father's doing."

"How did your mother feel about that?"

"Like I said, she spent her days waiting for my dad to come home."

"And you?"

"I didn't care. That's the truth. I wasn't going to work for my father, counting the days until he died so I could sell the place off. I know it sounds cold, but the way I figured it, my dad was never going to leave the whole place to Mackay. Mackay would be running it, all right, but worst case scenario, he and I would own it straight up, fifty-fifty. I could either take the cash for my half outright, or sit back for the rest of my life splitting the profits, minus his salary."

"So, where did he come from, this Mackay, this stranger who's suddenly sharing your father's lumberyard with you straight up, fifty-fifty?"

They had reached the end of the block. Tommy turned, hesitated a second, then began to walk back.

"How is any of this going to help you find out what happened to your buddy, what's-his-name?"

"Baumgarten. I don't know."

Tommy took a long drink of beer. "My father hired Mackay about a year and a half ago. He had just moved here from Chicago, with his mother and sister. From what I've heard, he was the reason they came out here in the first place. He had gotten himself into a lot of trouble in the city, and they wanted to get him as far away from there as possible.

"But I guess Round Lake Beach turned out to be not far enough. And you can always find trouble anywhere if you look hard enough for it. My father took a liking to him, though, said he was a good worker when he wanted to be. He'd have Mackay over for dinner a couple of nights a week, helped his mom out with a loan or two. At some point, Mackay tried moving out on his own, but that didn't last. So, my folks took him in."

"Why didn't he move back in with his mother?"

"I don't know. I'm sure her house was a lot more peaceful once he was out of it, but you'd have to ask her. As for the year or so that he was staying with my parents, I wasn't aware that things were getting out of control. But I wasn't around much. I asked Andy if he had seen any trouble brewing but he said no more than usual. Of course . . ."

Kubiak gave him time. When nothing more was said, he prodded, "Go ahead."

"I just don't want to sound like I'm making excuses for Mackay. But for all my parents were willing to give him, they would have expected him to take it. All of it. Same as they expected of me. Instead I walked away. Maybe Mackay . . . I don't know."

They reached the Legion Hall's front door. Tommy balanced his beer cup on the rounded top of a trash can, lit another cigarette.

"Look, Mister Kubiak, that lumberyard is mine now, and I don't plan to hang on to it. Between it and the house, I'm going to be coming into a sizeable chunk of money. I told you before, there's nobody really talking anymore about what happened between Mackay and my parents, and the cops never told me anything from the beginning except what they had to. If in your asking around town about your friend, you learn anything you think I should know . . . I don't know what a person would pay for something like that."

"Neither do I."

"I suppose it would depend on what you find out, wouldn't it?"

"I suppose. I'd like to get a look at your parents' car. What happened to it?"

Tommy snorted out another wet laugh. "Hell, that's easy enough for a start." He pointed across the parking lot. "Look all you want. I'm driving it."

Kubiak approached the white Honda while Tommy went inside for the keys. Aside from some rust, the car's exterior was clean. The tires were old. If the police had forced Mackay off the road, they had managed to do it without leaving any traces.

When Tommy returned, Kubiak went through the car's interior. The cloth of the driver's seat, along with a good section of carpet, was stained a faint, dull crimson.

"I couldn't get all the blood stains out," Tommy said, standing beside the car. "But I got them washed down enough so you wouldn't know what they were without asking. To tell you the truth, I don't really mind the stains, seeing as how it was Mackay's blood. You think there's something sick about that?"

"Not especially." Underneath the seat was a scattered sampling of the variety of fast food Tommy preferred while in transit.

"Some people do. Actually, most everybody I know does. But I sold my car after the DUI and was driving a beater I picked up last March that probably wouldn't have gotten me through the winter. You won't find any bullet holes or anything down there, if that's what you're looking for. From what the cops explained to me, the first bullet ran straight down the bone in his thigh and lodged in his kneecap. There is a mark up by the dome light though, made by the one that went out the top of his skull. Found the dent when I was cleaning. What a mess. The blood was everywhere. Everywhere."

Kubiak craned his neck to see a bleach-scrubbed spray of pale stain across the fabric covering the underside of the car's roof. In its center was a tiny indentation which he touched with his index finger.

"You run your hand along the outside," Tommy said, "you can feel the bump."

"That's two. What about the bullet that went into Mackay's cheek?"

"Went right through the flesh and out the window, according to the cops. They say he was trying to kill himself. I think he was taking a shot at them. I think it must have looked like the wild west out there, but nobody's willing to admit it."

"You have any idea of where, exactly, this 'out there' is? Where Mackay wound up?"

"Sure. Up by Loon Lake. In fact, one afternoon, not long after it happened, we all sat around the bar and figured out the route he must have taken."

"Mind drawing me up a map?"

"I could. Tell you what though, let me gather up my stuff and I'll do you one better."

Tommy drove. They rode in the Honda, the football game finishing out over the radio. Tommy seemed unfazed by the fact he was behind the wheel of the same car Mackay had driven, tracing the exact path the man had taken to his death, even while his buttocks warmed the cloth that held the man's bloodstains. Kubiak would have given the irony of it all more consideration if only Tommy's driving under the influence of beer was any better than his walking. The young man had dutifully returned the plastic cups to the Legion's bartender. What was left of their contents, however, was riding in a travel mug secured in the driver's side cup holder.

"Nobody's sure what side streets Mackay took to get him from my parents' house to this point," Tommy said, about ten minutes into the ride. "Probably the same ones we just took, though. The cops first spotted him right about here."

Route 83 was a four-lane road, busier than Kubiak had imagined it would be. Five minutes later, both the road and traffic thinned. The strip malls disappeared and the woods closed in.

"The gun that Mackay used belonged to your father," Kubiak said, turning down the radio.

"That's right. He kept it at the lumberyard. He worked late there sometimes, and he did have a problem with theft. For some reason, people who wouldn't dream of lifting a ten dollar bill out of your pocket seem to think it's okay to steal a dozen or so two-by-four's if they've got a project they're in the middle of. My dad used to say, 'What, they think this stuff grows on trees?' "

"Funny guy."

"That was about as far as his sense of humor went."

"What kind of gun was it?"

"A Smith & Wesson." Tommy thought a moment. "Combat Masterpiece. I only remember the name because I always thought it was kind of strange, like you didn't know whether to take it into battle or frame it and hang it on the wall."

"How did Mackay get hold of it?"

"They kept it locked in a desk in the office. Mackay had keys."

"Anyone else besides him?"

"Just my dad, though he was never too careful with them. He was always lending them out or leaving them laying around, then having to look for them. He was a trusting guy. That's what got him killed. Too decent."

They passed a small lake on their left. Just short of the Antioch town limits, Tommy took a hard right. The road dipped down, curved, came back up. Tall grass grew up along the pavement's edge. An occasional solitary house set back from the road provided distraction. Tommy turned left, then left again, slowed as the road coiled into tighter curves. Kubiak caught a glimpse of water in front of them. Tommy turned away from it, continued on another two tenths of a mile, finally stopped.

"This is it, for what it's worth. I'd take you right into the ditch, but we'd need a tow truck to get back out."

Kubiak got out of the car, walked along the narrow road's edge. Tommy followed. The afternoon felt hotter out here, the air thicker.

"I take it you've made this run before."

"Sure. I was curious."

"How do you know this exact spot?"

Tommy pointed past Kubiak's head. "One of the old

men at the Legion knows a guy who lives here. There's not much traffic on these roads, so when a half dozen cop cars with their lights flashing came running through, he and his neighbors were out here quick."

Kubiak climbed down into the ditch, which proved to be deeper than the tall grass made it appear. Barely able to move through the thick growth, he pulled himself back up on the other side, grunting at the effort. He made a quick scrutiny of the area, which showed no sign of anything having occurred here.

Nothing but a thin strip of road cut through the weeds. Kubiak tried to guess what it was about this place that would make a twenty-four-year-old choose to finally give up the chase, pull off to the side, and take his own life. Maybe it was that glimpse of water ahead, putting forth the idea of a dead end, or the way the road narrowed and twisted back into itself, sending Mackay back in the direction from which he was escaping. Then again, he might simply have lost control of the wheel for a moment and wound up stuck in the ditch.

But he still had to put the barrel of that gun into his mouth and squeeze the trigger, this city kid so cocky and full of himself that he carried his life of trouble out here with him when given a second chance by his mother; this boy able to stumble into a job in a lumberyard and inside of eighteen months, take the place of two men, both old man Wheeler's manager and his son.

Perhaps he still had his head on straight enough to realize that the very reason he was suddenly so hopelessly alone was that he had just murdered the only two people in the world he could rely upon for shelter and comfort.

Kubiak thought he saw a glint of metal through the trees to the left of him. He squinted; it was gone.

"What are you looking to find anyway?" Tommy called out across the ditch.

"I don't know." He saw the flash again, recognized it for what it was.

"You know," Tommy said, "there's a bar on this lake someplace. You up for a quick one before heading back?"

Then he, too, turned in the same direction as Kubiak to view the Lake County Sheriff's cruiser coming around that last curve, followed immediately by a second. A minute later, a third approached from the other direction.

"For a road that doesn't see much traffic . . ." Kubiak began, but Tommy was already being hustled aside by one of the uniforms from the first car. Two more stationed themselves on the other side of the ditch and called Kubiak over. When he took too long fighting his way through the weeds, one of them climbed partway down and yanked him out just zealously enough to keep him from gaining his footing until they were up on the road where a smiling detective in a sweatshirt and gleaming white sneakers was standing beside the Honda waiting for him.

"Just can't keep your butt safe and sound on the other side of County Line Road, can you, Kubiak? Turn him around."

Two more hands gripped Kubiak's other elbow. The scenery spun a hundred and eighty degrees, stopped cold.

"You might want to keep your sidearm holstered, Strom," Kubiak said. "I understand the locals here are known to turn out for a good show."

"All you have to worry about right now is letting me know when these cuffs get too tight."

Kubiak obliged him with a yelp and a curse.

Chapter Nine

"Trespassing?"

Strom had left the room again. Dunning was taking his turn, along with a kid in a uniform who had a sour look on his face and liked to move silently along the room's walls.

"I know it might not seem like much to a guy accustomed to breaking down doors and lying to the police about his involvement in a felony, Kubiak, but it is breaking the law, nonetheless. Add to that the container of open liquor in your vehicle—"

"Lying to you about my involvement in what felony, exactly?"

"Well, if I have to specify, then we have more to discuss than I thought, don't we?"

"That's good, Dunning. You're enjoying this too much."

"I'm not enjoying a bit of it. It's late. It's Sunday. I'd like to go home as soon as possible, and I'd think you would too."

"How late?"

They had taken Kubiak's watch. They had taken his photograph. They had taken his fingerprints.

There was no clock in the room, no windows. Nothing but plastic and tile reflecting bright under buzzing fluorescent lights. Kubiak might have been sitting for six hours or it might only have seemed like six hours. Occasionally, when left alone, he would get up and attempt to walk the ache out of his muscles, but a voice over a speaker would tell him to sit back down again.

Immediately.

"Let's go again. Whose idea was it to drive up to Loon Lake, yours or Tommy Wheeler's?"

"What does that matter?"

"I just want to know what you were doing out there."

"Standing in a ditch. Evidently breaking the law, nonetheless. Where is Tommy?"

"He's home. Probably eating dinner. Imagine that."

"He give you the answers you wanted, or was he just on the proper side of the ditch?"

"Do you hate your own home that much, Kubiak? We treating you too good here? What were you doing out at Loon Lake?"

"I already told you twice. Tommy was looking for a place where we could get a drink."

"You left a bar to go find a drink?"

"We wanted to see some football. All they were broadcasting at the Legion was the local game, so we headed north."

"Sorry, Kubiak. We phoned the Legion. They showed the Packers game."

"Packers? I was talking Vikings. Seeing as the line is open, may I phone my wife now?"

The wall ghost sighed, followed Dunning when he stood and left the room. Kubiak was expecting another long period of being left alone to examine the backs of his hands when the door opened and Strom entered again. He pulled a chair up uncomfortably close to Kubiak, sat, crossed his legs.

"All right," he said. "What is it you want to know about Jack Mackay?"

"Only the details of what happened out on that road on that Tuesday morning last June," Kubiak said.

"Sorry, not possible."

"Why not? The investigation's closed."

"That's precisely why."

"And you want to keep it that way. So much so you yank me down here the minute you catch me snooping around Loon Lake."

"That isn't the reason you're here, and you know it. Go ahead and snoop all you want, there's nothing to find. What, you think we don't clean up our crime scenes?"

"Oh, I'll bet you do."

Strom leaned in so their faces were close. He had been drinking coffee.

"You know what bothers me about you, Kubiak?"

"It seems just about everything."

"We both know that all this hooey being bantered around about Mackay's death being anything but a suicide is just that. Hooey. And not one of the dirtbags responsible for it ever gave a damn about Jack Mackay, including his family. The only reason for any of it is that it's one more excuse to embarrass the department, maybe roll a few heads just because it's fun to watch cops' heads roll.

"Now, I can understand your typical street dirtbag getting his kicks that way, or your local bleeding heart, liberal, defense attorney type, maybe. But you, you used to be one of us. Granted, you worked Latent Prints, so you were never really on the front line like those of us who get called to chase down killers carrying firearms like Mackay, but you were still a cop. So, I question why you'd sign on with those dirtbags."

"Come up with any answers?"

"Yeah. And I like one less than the next."

"Care to share any of them?"

Strom sat back, recrossed his legs, said nothing.

After a moment, Kubiak said, "You were there when that bullet went through Mackay's head, Strom, which means I don't have to trust you any more than you trust me. But you've had the opportunity to go through my pockets. You've found the photo of my son-in-law, and you know I'm not carrying it because I'm that fond of him, so you have to be aware that I know less than you thought. For what it's worth, I'm willing to give it all up to you, but I want some indication you're not going to use it against me. An indication of trust."

"And what would that be?"

"We could start with access to your reports on the Mackay investigation. You can arrange that much. And a fresh set of eyes just might find something you've overlooked that would prove your dirtbags and liberal types wrong."

It struck Kubiak this was the precise conversation Baumgarten had been eager to purchase Friday afternoon in Union Station's food court. Oddly, if either of them had been able so foresee the circumstances under which it would take place, it might have been Kubiak chasing Baumgarten down that escalator.

"What makes you think I'd even consider doing such a thing?"

"If your actions at Loon Lake were on the up and up, you have nothing to lose."

"Not a chance, Kubiak."

"That's too bad. So, what do you suggest as an alternative to get us both out of this room?"

"Simple. Explain to me your relationship with Baumgarten, your son-in-law's end of the business, and what part Mackay played in all of it. Satisfy me you didn't kill Baumgarten, and give me the name of the bastard who did."

"That's all?"

"It's my idea of a start."

There was a knock on the door and Dunning poked his head in. Strom shot him a cold look, but Dunning refused to retreat. Kubiak was left alone again. Time passed. When the door finally opened, there was only Dunning and the sour-faced uniform.

"I hope you've had all the chuckles you can stand," Dunning said, angrier than Kubiak had seen him. "You shot my Sunday all to hell. I won't forget that."

"Is that a threat, Detective?"

"All I'm saying is you could have dropped a name when we picked you up."

"I don't see how."

"I'm supposed to give you this." It was a business card for a Matthew P. Osgood, Member, Illinois State Bar Association, Member, Lake County Bar Association. The address was in Round Lake Beach. Written on the back was a request to be in his office at 8:00 Monday morning.

"This isn't Chicago, Kubiak. Your clout will only carry

you until I can get you back into this room. If you understand that, you can go."

The uniform escorted Kubiak to a grimy pay phone beside which was pasted a weathered card with a list of numbers. The bottom three belonged to taxi companies. Kubiak connected on the second try and was led outside the building to wait for his cab.

Cool had returned with the evening. Downtown Waukegan was dark. Kubiak was staring down the same empty street he had walked along when he was heading to Baumgarten's vacant apartment some thirty hours ago.

After ten minutes, he began pacing out on the sidewalk. After twenty, he was thinking of what Tommy Wheeler had said about the dearth of cabs and busses outside of Chicago. After thirty, his stomach growling, he was considering hiking down to the Metra station and taking his chances on their lean Sunday schedule when a cab pulled slowly around the corner.

The driver wasn't interested in making conversation. Kubiak watched the meter click, watched the dark woods roll by outside. He thought again of the lonely salvage yard in which Baumgarten was murdered. An idea popped into his head, one he quickly dismissed as a waste of his time; after all, even Dunning would have had the sense to check Friday night's trip sheets of every cab company in the area.

The Legion had closed. The Contour stood cold and alone in the unlit lot. Kubiak told the cabbie to wait while he tested the driver's door. It swung open. The set of keys he had left on the bar were tucked in the visor.

Tommy Wheeler's work, or standard operating procedure at the Legion? When the engine turned over, Kubiak felt as close to home as he had all day.

Just before the expressway, he found an open diner where he downed one beer, then sipped another and chatted with the counter girl while he waited for a burger to go. He ate the burger and fries in the car as he drove down the Edens, arriving at the condo at a little after 10:00. Denise was in the front room, reading a magazine. He was both relieved and disappointed to discover that she had not held dinner for him.

"Maybe it's time we give up on suppers all together," he told her. "Concentrate on breakfasts."

"Oh no, Kubiak. I couldn't stand the thought of your having to climb out of bed at four in the morning just to be certain I eat my eggs alone. You could have phoned."

He might as well have baited a hook.

She softened little as he related his adventures up north, meticulous in his descriptions of his discomfort and righteousness.

"I don't understand," she said when he was done. "Have you been charged with a crime or haven't you?"

"I'll find out at eight o'clock tomorrow morning." He handed Denise the card Dunning had handed him. "Looks like we finally have a lawyer."

"Matthew P. Osgood. I would have preferred one with a name that wouldn't get him beat up in the schoolyard." She passed the card back. "I picture him with little, round spectacles and a manicure."

"Poindexter or not, he's connected enough to trump Strom and Dunning."

"How did he find you?"

"I don't know. At first I thought Tommy Wheeler must have phoned him. After all, he was the only one outside of the sheriff's department who knew I was being held. But how would a kid like that have access to the home phone number of the kind of legal eagle who can shake me out of there against the wishes of the two detectives holding me?"

"How do you know it was his home number?"

"Sunday afternoon. Osgood was probably barbequing steaks. I'm sure he didn't bring this card out to Waukegan, himself, or I would have seen his face, but he arranged to have it brought to me."

"Maybe Osgood was Tommy's father's lawyer," Denise offered. "He's handling the sale of the house, the business. Tommy might have his home number."

"No, that type of lawyer doesn't create friction in the Lake County Sheriff's Department. Dunning was so upset he couldn't be bothered to hide his anger from me. Somebody in the department ordered him to cut me loose."

"All because of the clout wielded by a bespectacled, manicured lawyer working out of Round Lake Beach?"

"It's possible. Especially if our two detectives were begging to get reigned in anyway. Strom was involved in the slow speed chase that finished off Mackay. I wonder if his partner was involved as well. I wonder if that's what made them partners."

"You think they might be working alone?"

"No. At least, I don't see how. There must have been a dozen cops chasing Mackay down that road that morning. But the incident might have caused a rift in the sheriff's department which Matthew P. Osgood used tonight to my advantage. If he's enough in the know to manage that, I'm looking forward to talking to him tomorrow."

"Dammit, Kubiak, what are you doing up there in the first place? Why are you so interested in Jack Mackay?"

"Maybe because Baumgarten was chasing me down a flight of stairs shouting out Mackay's name just a matter of hours before turning up dead in our son-in-law's truck?"

"In which case it might not be too bright an idea to follow in his footsteps."

"With two of Lake County's finest so hot on my heels, how much trouble can I get into?"

Denise only glared. The room was quiet. Awfully quiet.

"Where's Maurice?" Kubiak asked.

"He's off again, making his rounds of the building. Why?"

So, her nurse had left her.

"Funny."

"What?"

"You haven't once mentioned Maria's name."

"You haven't given me a chance."

He waited.

"She called. This afternoon. As she promised she would."

"You weren't going to tell me?"

Denise tucked her magazine into the rack by the sofa, rummaged through those behind it. "Of course I was."

"When?"

"When you gave me a chance."

"Did she hint at where she was?"

"Of course not."

"Did you ask?"

Nothing.

"It might have been a good idea."

She rummaged and rummaged. "To do what? Press her until she hung up angry and entirely cut off contact with us? Kubiak, sometimes you can be such an idiot."

"What then, did she say?"

Denise stood. For a moment, Kubiak was afraid she

was going to go to the bookcases and begin rearranging them. Instead, she moved to the front room window.

"She wouldn't tell me anything specific. She sounded fine. Better than yesterday. She said David is all right. He knows he's in a mess, and he's working at getting himself out of it. She swears he didn't do anything wrong."

"Anything covers a lot of territory. What's his idea of a mess?"

"How would I know? I told you, she was deliberately vague."

"You must have asked her why he's not talking to the police."

"She said he wanted to keep his name out of the papers."

"By becoming a fugitive. That's a hell of a way to go about it."

"I told her about the visit from Strom and Dunning she just barely missed."

"Even that didn't shake anything loose?"

"On the contrary, it actually managed to get a laugh out of her. That is, the part about their suspecting you."

He pictured the two of them, his wife and his daughter, giggling over the phone like two schoolgirls.

"Well," he said. "I'm glad I could be of some service."

"It was nervous laughter, Kubiak. She's too much like you. She can't fathom the kind of destruction wrought upon you by one of your own."

Kubiak left Denise at the window, went to the kitchen for a beer. He supposed he couldn't blame her for accepting Maria's vague assurances in order to keep their line of communication open. After all, he had insisted she stay home by the phone, alone in this empty apartment for two days now, alone with her thoughts, catastrophes playing themselves out in her head, alone with that silent phone which he was certain she carried with her from room to room, a phone that, when it did ring, must have startled her like an electric shock.

She was behind him now. She moved past him and took down a glass for his beer. He ignored it, uncapped the bottle, and drank from it.

"By the way," she said, "since when did I become your secretary?"

For a moment he thought she'd been reading his mind. She must have read the surprise on his face, as she didn't wait for a response.

"A very nasty sounding man called for you at about six. He said you told him to leave his number with your secretary. This doesn't have anything to do with Mackay?"

Secretary? Of course. He had been so busy telling Denise about Round Lake Beach and Waukegan, he had forgotten to mention his prowl through Loyola Park and handing out their phone number.

"You've got it?"

"I wouldn't be much of a secretary if I threw it out." She led him back to the front room, handed him the pad from beside the phone. "He wouldn't tell me anything, just said he wanted to talk to the boss. Does this mean I'm getting paid now?"

It was a local number. He dialed. "Actually, if this pans out, the boss may be asking you to front him some cash."

The call was answered on the first ring. A gruff, "What?" came from a cellular phone with a weak connection.

"Hello?" He could hear voices in the background. The sound was muffled, but opened up again.

"What?" the gruff voice asked again. "Who is this?"

"I'm the fellow on the beach today." Nothing. "The one giving away five hundred dollars."

Still nothing. Finally, "I don't know anybody giving away five hundred dollars."

"Sorry," Kubiak said. "My secretary must have gotten the message wrong." And he hung up.

"Who was it?" Denise asked.

"I don't know. But he's either just plain not interested or unusually busy for eleven o'clock at night."

"So you just hung up on him?"

"He has our number. And he may be the type who feels more comfortable initiating—"

The ringing of the phone interrupted him. Though his hand was still only inches from the receiver, he let another ring sound before picking it up, offered the same hello with the same question mark behind it.

"Okay." The voice on the other end was the same, just as gruff, but not as impatient. "Hold on a minute, crazy man."

The receiver was cupped again. So, the name Squarejaw had given Kubiak had stuck.

The voice came back. "I told you, I don't know anybody giving away five hundred dollars. But I might want to know somebody giving away a thousand."

"A thousand? Who said anything about a thousand?"

"I did."

"A thousand dollars is a lot of money. Hell, five hundred is a lot of money. All I'm asking for are directions."

"Well, I got this problem. I got too many friends."

"Some problem."

"You like to take walks on the beach, maybe you've met them. You've opened up your big mouth about how much money you've got to drop, maybe you've already got every one of them excited."

"Fine. I'll take another walk along the beach, look for somebody who's excited, and give them my original offer."

"When? Tomorrow? I was under the impression you were in kind of a hurry."

It was Kubiak's turn to cup the mouthpiece. He asked Denise if it was possible to pull a thousand dollars out of an ATM in one shot. She shrugged.

Into the phone he said, "I expect to be meeting David face to face."

"David who? I think my battery's going. You want to talk?"

Kubiak said yes. The voice gave Kubiak an address. The line went dead.

"A thousand dollar bribe to access your son-in-law," Denise said. "How do you manage it, Kubiak?"

"I know all the right people in this town. Just ask Dunning. In fact, if we all had fewer friends, I'd have gotten Hollinger for half that. And before you even think what you're thinking, I'd rather you be by the phone in case Maria or David does happen to . . ."

But she was already going for her jacket.

Chapter Ten

Sullen, he sat behind the wheel of the Contour, parked illegally on Clark, and watched her as she stood in line for the ATM in the bank's vestibule across the street. Traffic passed between them. The vestibule was lit so showroom bright she might as well have been on display. The line was short, but moving slowly. Directly in front of her was an animated couple, all whispers and giggles, probably reloading their pockets between late-night stops.

He would have preferred she not be there at all, but there was no stopping her at this point. She was a mother determined to cross a very dirty playground in order to grab up her children by the wrists and drag them home, and he could no longer justify his arrogant insistence she sit by the phone while he strolled through that playground, especially when the simple act of movement toward her goal seemed to brighten her spirits.

Nevertheless, he did not plan to introduce her to the voice on the other end of the phone, nor to the odd fellows he had run across in the park, and he was working out a way to keep from doing so when his thoughts were interrupted by the blare of a car's horn. He looked up to see Denise quickly crossing the street against the light, dodging traffic. She entered the car with a wide swing of the passenger's door and a hard landing in the bucket seat.

"Good news and bad, Kubiak," she told him. "The bad news is, our ATM card has a five hundred dollar withdrawal limit. The good news is, with our charge card we can do just about anything short of opening an account in the Cayman Islands. Check it out."

She fanned a stack of hundreds, fifties, and twenties in a manner that caused him to glance over his shoulder, snatch them from her hand, and securely tuck them into the pocket of his jacket.

The address where they were headed was on Ashland, and he took Ashland all the way up, slowing down on the other side of Ridge. While traffic sped past in the left lane, Denise squinted at the addresses of the businesses on their right, until she spotted the number she had written down. Devon was only two blocks beyond; Kubiak drove to it, eased the Contour to the curb just short of the intersection.

"What are you doing?" she protested. "There are plenty of spaces two blocks back."

"I don't mind the walk."

"Well, maybe I do."

Kubiak took the money out of his pocket, counted out half, offered that half to Denise.

"Put this in your purse."

"I don't understand . . . oh, no, Kubiak. I told you, I'm going in with you."

"David isn't in there. Neither is Maria. I'm going to be walking in with five hundred dollars; I'd like some insurance for my walking out. You have the address and you know why I'm going in. If things turn unfriendly, it will be to my advantage to let them know you're around."

"Around?"

"Around the block. Just keep driving in loose circles, passing by here every few minutes. Once I'm back out I'll meet you here—"

She was already shaking her head. "Sorry. I'm not going anywhere where I can't keep my eye on the front door of that building."

"You don't understand. The safer you are, the safer I am. Get it?"

"Oh, I got it. And right back at you. Got that, yet?"

He opened his mouth to run through the argument yet again, but realizing it would do him no good, he sighed. "All right. But don't back up any closer to the building. And keep the engine running, and the doors locked."

"How long should I wait?"

"I don't know. Thirty minutes."

"Thirty minutes is a long time."

"Your presence is the insurance," he told her, getting out of the car. "The half hour is only a last resort."

"Okay," she said, sliding over behind the wheel. "But in precisely thirty-one minutes I will have the police here if I have to use the jack handle in the trunk to break a plate glass window or two."

"Personally, I'd probably just locate a pay phone and dial 911, but if you prefer dramatics there's nothing I can do to stop you. Oh, and if any sailors happen by, try not to catch their eye."

The car door closed on her reply, so she settled for offering a gesture. He glanced back at her when he was a few yards away, at the back of her head through the glass of the windshield as she sat alone, out on the street at midnight on a night that had turned downright cold, and he resolved never again to feel guilty for arguing that she wait for him at home—for either of their sakes!

As busy as the street was, the sidewalks of Ashland were empty, all the businesses closed. By the time Kubiak reached the address, the Contour was barely in sight. The building before him was four stories, narrow, dark, and bordered by two others just as uninviting. The front door opened freely (Kubiak noted the latch had been removed) to a filthy, L-shaped lobby dimly lit by bulbs recessed around the tops of the walls. The glass covering the directory was missing, and only a scattering of tiny, white numbers and letters were left plugged into the black background, with no trace left of a name for the office to which Kubiak was headed. He didn't like the looks of the elevator, but liked the stairwell even less, so he pressed the lobby button, waited while the elevator door slid noisily open, and took the slow, labored ride up to the third floor.

The hallway was narrow. All doors were shut tight but one, from which came light and the sound of voices. Kubiak approached softly, stationing himself in the doorway without being noticed. The office was small, held only a desk angled in the far corner and two wooden chairs facing it. There was a window beside the desk, but it didn't look out on much of anything. Still, one of the four men in the room had his eyes pointed in that direction as he lazily leaned against its frame. He was the same one who had been incessantly looking over his shoulder in Loyola Park. Sitting slumped on one of the wooden chairs was the kid in the baggy pants who had taken off after the fifty dollar bill. Square-jaw was on his feet, leaning down on the back of the other chair, angrily describing to the room why someone of their acquaintance was worthless. He was directing most of his opinion at the man sitting at the desk, the red-haired, stocky fellow Kubiak had seen from a distance.

No one was stationed at the door or the elevator. So far, the meeting was casual enough for Kubiak's liking.

As Square-jaw was the one addressing the group, his eyes happened to scan the doorway first. When he saw Kubiak, he stopped short, straightened.

"Hey, it's the crazy man." He checked his watch. "You're still in some kind of a hurry, huh?"

The room was at attention, but no one was moving. One at a time, each turned to Red. Kubiak hadn't noticed the man's goatee from afar, it was so sparse and light. And what he had mistaken for fat looked to be chiefly the bulk of muscle.

"Come on in," Red said, and Kubiak recognized his voice from the phone. "Shut the door."

Square-jaw offered the chair with a grand gesture. Kubiak crossed to it, but remained standing. He left the door open.

Red's cell phone rang. Keeping his eyes on Kubiak, he flipped open the phone, barked his standard greeting into it, and listened. Kubiak noticed there were no other phones in the room. No pictures on the walls. No papers on the desk. Instead, the desk was littered with open cans of soda. A discarded pizza box lay on the floor in the corner of the room.

Red told the person on the line he would get back to him, stood up, moved halfway around the desk in that stilted gait of his, evidently deciding that was far enough. "So," he said, "I finally get to meet you."

"Seems to me you had that chance yesterday."

"Oh?"

"In the park. Why did you run when you saw me?"

"I didn't run."

"What do you call it then?"

Red moved back behind the desk. "I had some business with my friends. You looked like a businessman to me. I didn't want to step on your toes, figured I'd come back later."

"Step on his toes," Square-jaw snickered, which set the kid in the chair beside Kubiak into a fit of giggles.

Kubiak aimed a thumb at the kid. "Is that what this one was whispering in your ear? That I was a businessman?"

"No," Red said. "He told me you like to take off your shoes and socks and toss fifty dollar bills into the wind. You gave these guys a kick. They think you're a little nutty."

"I had a dog once," Kubiak said, "used to like to roll over on his back. He made a lot of friends that way."

Red's eyes narrowed. "Yeah? So what? I had a dog liked to chase cars, he got run over. Maybe he didn't like people. I don't get it."

He looked around the room to see if anybody else got it. Nobody got it. He sat, again told Kubiak to do the same. This time, Kubiak did. Square-jaw moved to the door, quietly closing it.

"I'm beginning to think you are a crazy man," Red said. "How did you know to approach these guys about your lost friend?"

"You're charging me a thousand dollars to answer my questions. You want me to name my fee?"

"Excuse me, but I don't recall saying anything about answering any questions. I'm charging you for a service.

Some people I know agreed to do some work for you. All I'm doing is distributing the payment to them."

"And keeping a small percentage for your services."

"Well, of course."

"Because we're all businessmen."

Red only smiled.

"Fine, then. Let's get our transaction over with."

The smile disappeared. "I wish it was that easy. If it was, you'd already be out of here."

Square-jaw had moved back behind the chair, so close Kubiak could hear him breathing.

"What's so difficult?" Kubiak asked. "You lead me to David, I drop the thousand in your—"

Red shot up a palm, shook his head in disgust.

Behind Kubiak, Square-jaw snorted, "You see what I mean?" Kubiak half expected a slap to the back of his head. "This guy's going to skip barefoot all the way to Stateville and think he's in a sandlot."

The glare Red gave that comment quieted the room. After meeting everyone's eyes in the manner of an exasperated schoolteacher, he sighed, then settled back into his chair with a creak.

"It might be best, Crazy Man, if you just respond to what I say to you. We all got our liability to worry about. Including yourself."

He waited out what he must have thought was a decent interval before continuing. "You got the finder's fee on your person?"

Kubiak nodded.

"Good. Now, I understand you might be looking for a certain friend of yours who's holed himself up in a safe place for the past couple of days, is that right?"

"That's right."

"Okay. I assure you I know where that place is, and one of my associates is ready to take you there now. But before he does, seeing as how I've been plopped into the middle of all this, I'd like some assurances from you that no trouble will come of it."

"What kinds of assurances?"

"Well for instance, this morning you said there was something these boys ought to be aware of concerning Paul Baumgarten. You want to elucidate on that?"

"You mean the fact that he's dead?"

"That's right."

Kubiak tilted his head back to address Square-jaw. "He's dead."

Red sighed, sat back in his chair with his hands folded over his stomach. He enjoyed playing chairman of the board.

"A hell of a thing," he said. "Tell me, how do you manage to beat somebody to death with a hammer while sitting behind the wheel of a car?"

"Well, you don't, do you? You drag him out behind a storage shed and beat him to death there."

This caused another exchange of glances among the three men on the other side of the desk.

Kubiak checked his watch. Over fifteen minutes had passed since he had left Denise.

"Look," he told Red. "You want to rub it in these boys' noses, I'm headed up that way first thing tomorrow morning. Baumgarten's blood is still all over the shack, they can see it for themselves. I'll even pack the picnic basket. But in the meantime, can we just get this transaction over with?"

More glances. Behind Kubiak, Square-jaw muttered, "Crazy Man, you are one sick piece of work."

The remark seemed out of the blue, until Kubiak realized he had been so wary of his position he had read everything into the men's looks but apprehension. Now, he noticed that he had commanded the full attention of the lazy man at the window, and that the kid in the next chair had squirmed about as far away from Kubiak as he could manage without getting up.

"Oh, hold on one minute, fellow businessmen," Kubiak said, meeting the eyes of every man in the room. "I don't know what your CEO here has been telling you, but you may have been given the wrong impression."

"Impressions don't concern us," Red said. "We were talking about assurances."

"I assure you, I did not kill Paul Baumgarten."

"Baumgarten is water under the bridge. The only problem he might make for us now is if somebody dragged this buddy of yours out of his safe place tonight and took to beating on his head with a hammer. Or just as bad, carry him up to the next county and introduce his body to law enforcement up there, where they might realize the two knew one another and start looking around for friends they shared. Like I told you, I got too many friends."

Kubiak crossed his legs, drummed his fingertips on his knee. Ten minutes left before Denise began hurling tire jacks through plate glass windows. He had timed a three to four minute stretch between this room and the car which meant he now had, at most, seven minutes to shake hands with Red and turn toward the door, and he hadn't even shown him the money yet.

"I promise you, while I plan to introduce the subject of Lake County to my friend, I have no intention of taking him anywhere but south."

"That's fine. The farther south the better. Now, you have to understand, this place where your friend decided to hole up, it doesn't exactly have my name on the lease, but me and my associates have been known to use it in the past. So, I'd prefer you both leave it as clean as he found it."

"I have no doubt he'll agree to leave quietly with me."

Red nodded, scratched his belly, stared up at a spot on the wall while he thought. The seconds ticked away on the clock on the Contour's dashboard. Kubiak had pulled the concept of a half hour out of his hat. He might just as easily have pulled forty-five minutes out of the same hat.

"One last thing," Red finally said. "Your friend, he has a roommate. A cute, little thing. What do you plan on doing with her?"

"Nothing," Kubiak said. "I plan to leave her to her mother."

"You can't just cut her loose."

"So I keep finding out." Kubiak stood. "Don't worry, she'll be taken care of. I was under the impression you preferred I didn't give you any details."

Red aimed more thoughts at points on the wall. "Okay," he said. "Let's finish it." He nodded at the kid in the chair, who jumped to his feet. "He'll take you where you're looking to go."

Kubiak dropped the money onto the desktop. Red counted it, moistening his fingertips with his tongue, had bills clenched in both fists when he came up short.

"What the hell?"

"The kid will get the rest when we get there."

"The agreement was you give the money to me."

"You'll get it. You got that fifty back from him, didn't you?"

It took another half minute, but Red finally gave the kid the nod. Kubiak headed for the doorway, stopped when Red called out, turned to see one of the bills being offered back to him.

"Just a question," Red said. "Who hired you, anyway? It's worth half a hundred to know."

"Would you believe me if I told you Paul Baumgarten?"

Red soured, tucked the fifty back into the pile. "Forget it. You stay away from the beach, Crazy Man. I don't care how much you like to walk through sand, I don't ever want to see you back there."

And with a nod, Kubiak was finally out the door.

They took the stairs, the kid asking all the way down what the hurry was all about.

Chapter Eleven

The kid insisted on riding up front. There was no reason for it, except that he probably didn't like sitting in the back, which was where Kubiak was relegated.

All conversation took place in the front seats. The kid warmed immediately to Denise, and while Kubiak hadn't heard a word from him until they were in the staircase, once he started talking, he never stopped. He pointed here and there along their short journey, going on about relatives and friends who were living or had lived a few blocks this way or that. The talk died down only for a moment, when in response to a comment he made about his mother, Denise asked her age and he said she was all of thirty-something, but still spry enough to work and even go out to the movies once in a while.

They drove a few blocks along Devon. A good number of the Indian restaurants whose neon signs crowded this section were just closing, and traffic was heavier than Kubiak would have expected at this hour. Just past Western, their chattering tour guide led them through a tight zigzag of dark side streets until they stopped in front of a two-flat building that looked bulky standing against a line of bungalows. The windows on the second floor were lit; the first floor's weren't.

"Who lives downstairs?" Kubiak asked the kid.

"Nobody. Nobody supposed to live upstairs, either."

Kubiak asked Denise to park up the street. She found a spot close to legal, killed the lights and engine, and the three of them got out of the car.

Denise was wasting no time and was quickly ten paces ahead of Kubiak, while the kid was holding back, gesturing for Kubiak to wait. Kubiak called out to his wife, who stopped, staring up at the lit windows. He backtracked to the anxious-looking kid.

"Sorry, junior. You don't get the money until I see his face."

The kid aimed his chin at Denise. "You taking her in with you?"

"Seems she's the one taking me in."

"She won't do you no good. I seen this friend of yours. He's a big guy, and young. You need better help than that."

He reached into one of the many pockets of his baggy pants, extracted a knife with a painting of a nude woman on its handle. The blade was long. Even in the street's dim light, the shaft's contours gleamed, as did the teeth in the young owner's mouth as he grinned.

"Three hundred bucks," he said. "I give you more help than you can use."

A car passed on the adjacent block. Kubiak told the kid to put away the knife, and he did.

"Three hundred dollars," Kubiak said. "Is that what they're paying on the street these days to snuff out a man's life?"

The kid's face fell. "Hey, come on. You're handing out all kinds of money to everybody else. This is your best bet yet."

Kubiak told him thanks, but no thanks, that he already had made plans to deal with his friend, and besides, Red had made a point of leaving the two-flat clean. The kid offered to ride with Kubiak and finish Hollinger in the car, even dropped his price to two-fifty. When Kubiak shot down his offer a second time, the kid, evidently insulted, reverted back to the silent, distant young man Kubiak knew before their run together down the stairwell.

When they reached the landing of the two-flat, the kid surprised Kubiak by producing a key to the front door. The foyer was about the size of a freight elevator, with the door to the first floor apartment on the left, a short set of carpeted stairs directly ahead. There wasn't enough room on the second floor landing for all three of them, so the kid remained two steps down. Kubiak had to nudge Denise to the side in order to position his body as the first to be encountered when the door did swing open, which sent one of her heels one step lower, as well.

She raised her fist to rap on the door, stopped short, and whispered, "What if they run out the back?"

Kubiak shook his head. "From what I heard in that office, I'm guessing they've had their share of visitors." What he didn't tell her was that if it weren't for her, he would have been behind the building already.

She addressed the door again, hesitated, and then turned to the kid. "I don't suppose there's a secret knock or anything silly like that."

The kid only looked at her quizzically. As her fist was still poised, Kubiak grabbed her wrist and rapped her knuckles lightly against the door. She shook off his grip, knocked herself, this time only a bit louder. There was a moment of silence, made very uncomfortable due to the cramped quarters, followed by the muffled sound of footsteps approaching on the other side of the door.

The Frankenstein monster. That was how Hollinger's downstairs neighbor had described those footsteps. Funny, Kubiak thought, how a stranger, by simply lying in bed at night and trying to get to sleep, could become so much more intimately familiar with the footsteps of his family member than he was himself. As the footsteps came nearer, Kubiak grabbed the kid by the sleeve and pulled him up beside him so that only Denise's face could be seen through the peephole.

More silence as the body on the other side peeped through the hole. Denise, to her credit, stared up into the tiny, glass button with the countenance of one who would not be dissuaded. The door opened the length of its chain and David's face appeared in the gap. Kubiak would have liked to have seen its look of surprise when it first gazed upon the mother-in-law through the peephole, but his face managed a good enough show when it landed on his father-in-law. After that, it ran through a pitiful morphing of emotions, from embarrassment to guilt to shame to resignation, finally burning in anger when its eyes settled on the kid in Kubiak's grip.

The door shut. The chain slid free. David didn't welcome them in, merely turned away and let the door swing open. He was already in the middle of the room by the time Kubiak, behind Denise, crossed the threshold.

"Hey, Crazy."

The kid didn't want to leave the landing. Kubiak extracted the five hundred from his breast pocket and handed it to him. He stuffed the money into his pants without bothering to count it.

"So, what now?" he asked Kubiak. "You want me to wait in the car?"

"No. I want you to go away."

"What? I don't get a ride back?"

"It's a dozen blocks. I think you've got enough on you to cover the limo."

The kid shrugged, scampered back down the stairs, and disappeared into the night, apparently cheerfully oblivious to just about everything, including the fact that, at that moment, Kubiak would have just as cheerfully traded places with him.

Chapter Twelve

The room was too large for its sad furnishings. Hollinger remained standing in its center, his hands in his pockets. The white shirt and gray slacks he was wearing looked slept in, while the dark circles under his eyes spoke of no sleep at all. Aware of Kubiak's scrutiny of his appearance, he raised a hand to rub the stubble on his cheek, managed a weak smile.

"I'd offer you a drink . . ." He gestured toward the back of the apartment where Denise had disappeared. The fact she hadn't returned meant she must have found Maria.

"Girls in the kitchen," Kubiak said. The floorboards groaned every time he took a step. "Boys in the parlor."

Another timid grin. "Not much of a parlor, I'm afraid."

"No." Kubiak straightened a filthy lampshade, wiped the dust from his fingertips. "Rather humble digs for a professional real estate speculator and his wife. A fixer-upper. What is this place?"

"Just a place a few people know about and most don't. Nobody's sure who owns it; nobody in his right mind would buy it, and I'll lay odds nobody's been paying taxes on it. Electric, phone, cable all hooked up illegal. But it hasn't been boarded up yet because nobody cares enough to bother. How did you find me?"

"That's obvious, isn't it?"

The smile was gone, but the good son-in-law was taking the arrows without spitting them back. "I guess it is. I just never pictured you turning over Trejo's rock, is all."

"Is that the kid's name?"

Hollinger nodded.

"What about the stocky one with the red goatee?"

"Brady? Neil Brady, too. How did you manage it?"

"Your neighbor. She thinks you waste your days playing checkers on the beach."

It took a few seconds to register. When it did, Hollinger muttered a curse.

Kubiak described Square-jaw and the window gazer, and Hollinger assigned them names, as well.

"Padilla's the one to watch out for," he said, referring to Square-jaw. "He's slick."

"Who are they?"

"They're day laborers. Or were. Now they work for Brady. When were you on the beach?"

"This morning."

"Sunday. I'm surprised they were there at all. If it were a weekday you would have run across a couple of dozen men waiting for work."

"Construction?"

"Mostly. Some landscaping. Tearing up and laying carpet. Whatever's contracted on the cheap."

"Why Loyola Park?"

Hollinger shrugged. "This summer it's the park. Last Christmas, it was a doorway across the street from the

Granada. The work's off the books, and twenty to thirty men loitering around at all hours of the day, every day, tend to wear out their welcome pretty fast. The word on the street is if you want to work twelve hours for cash at the end of the day, and you're sober enough to swing a hammer, you can find Brady's boys by the checkerboards in the park. Brady's office is his money clip and his cell phone. And the number on that phone has changed twice just since I've known him."

"How long is that?"

Hollinger sighed, glanced at the empty hallway behind him. "Look, I can only imagine what we've put you and Denise through these past couple of days."

"I hope for your sake it hasn't taken your mind off your own troubles."

"Sit down. Let me get you a drink."

"No, thanks."

"Well, then let me at least get myself a cigarette, will you? A minute to gather my thoughts. You two were the last people I expected . . ."

Kubiak acquiesced, figured that if his son-in-law were to run out the back door at least it would give him an excuse to phone the police and have him safely arrested. Hollinger did return, however, carrying two short glasses holding brown liquor, a cigarette burning between his lips, the perfect, if rumpled, host.

They did sit, Hollinger in a worn armchair, Kubiak on a couch that smelled sour.

"I used to walk past them every day," Hollinger began, balancing an ashtray on the chair's arm. "Last winter, weather permitting. I was taking a lot of long walks back then. Maria and I had done all the moving in we had to do. She was already back at her old accounting job, leaving me home all day with the classifieds. I know the economy isn't what it was a few years ago, but I honestly never expected the maze of dead ends I'd run into coming into Chicago from Wisconsin.

"I must say, it took me longer to gain their trust than you managed. But after a week or two I was picking up an odd job here and there, not so much for the cash as the possibility of making a few connections. Neil Brady might not be the most respected contractor in town, but there isn't a developer who doesn't know his name. By the start of spring, I was pretty thick into their little club."

"How thick?" Kubiak asked.

"I was essentially a supervisor, until I realized I wasn't going to get anywhere working for Brady, not with his reputation. However, I did float the idea of a loose partnership, strictly project by project, again just so the people he knows got a chance to get to know me. Together, we rehab'd a couple of apartments and a small store on Morse."

"You were doing all this, and I never heard a word."

"Well, I didn't plan on being involved with Brady for long. I figured he probably had some kind of a record, so I wasn't anxious to have Maria bring up his name in front of you. Besides, it's not the most . . . scrupulous way of doing business, working these poor stiffs to death off the books for a fraction of union scale."

Hollinger didn't like the look on Kubiak's face.

"You do realize," he added, "that the types of men who line up for day labor do so for a reason. They're unskilled, and half of them aren't legal. But for the most part, they're hard workers, with families. You pull Brady off the street, where do they go?"

He still didn't like the look on Kubiak's face.

"Listen," he said, this last part coming through his teeth. "I'm no friend of Neil Brady. I never respected him, and I don't trust him. But my first business partner was a man I loved, trusted, and respected, and you know what came of that situation. I'll take my chances with the devil I know's a devil, especially in this city of yours."

He stabbed out his cigarette. The ashtray rocked in every direction.

Kubiak sat back, gave him a second, then asked, "What about Baumgarten?"

"What about him?"

"Those long, lonely walks of yours along the beach didn't take you all the way up to Waukegan?"

Hollinger drank, grinned, aimed the index finger of the hand holding the glass at Kubiak in a subtle touché. It was perhaps his son-in-law's one annoying gesture, and Kubiak was grateful for its appearance at the moment.

"No, he found me, all right. Thanks to you."

"Oh, that's right. I forgot I introduced you two."

"In a way, you did. Baumgarten was never around much, which was fine with me. When he was, he spent most of his time drinking with whoever he could pull off the job. He came down from Round Lake Beach with the building supplies, maybe once or twice a week, or whenever Brady called him. The whole operation was so sloppy, every day you'd be in the middle of a project only to find out half of what you needed hadn't shown up."

"Round Lake Beach is a long way to go to shop for nails."

"Not if that's where the nails fell off the back of a truck."

"Jerald and Bernice Wheeler's truck."

Hollinger leaned forward, lowered his voice. "Look, I

only found out about most of this a few days ago. I did know that a good portion of the supplies Brady was getting had to be stolen. It was one of the reasons I was anxious to put him behind me. But just when I was beginning to get fed up with the lot of them and was giving serious thought to simply walking away from the whole mess, Baumgarten disappeared, everything in Round Lake Beach dried up, and the business turned pretty much legit. As legit as Neil Brady can get, anyway. That was why I felt confident enough to float the partnership."

"When was that?"

"Right around the first of June."

"After the death of the Wheelers and Jack Mackay."

"Of course, Baumgarten explained that part to you."

"How did he explain it to you?"

Hollinger finished his drink, leaned back in the chair.

"He showed up, literally on my doorstep, out of the blue. This was . . . about three weeks ago, after I hadn't seen him once all summer.

"You see, there was this incident last spring that Maria and I didn't put much thought to at the time. We were out doing burgers and beers, and Baumgarten just happened to be there with us. Somehow, Maria's maiden name came up. Baumgarten didn't say anything about it, but his demeanor changed, not for the better, not worse, just different. I remember because Maria and I talked about it afterwards, but we didn't put two and two together. After all, we had no clue you two even knew of each other's existence. Well, when he showed up three weeks ago, it was you he wanted to talk to. He said he had a job for you, a little investigation with a big payoff. He wanted me to talk to you first, arrange a time when you two could meet. He even hinted at a small cut for my just doing that much if everything turned out the way he thought it would."

"Did he tell you anything about what he wanted investigated?"

"Not at that time. Of course, I guessed it might have to do with the death of the Wheelers, and I questioned him about that, but he was vague. As for arranging a meeting with you, I stalled him. I didn't want to turn him down outright and have him hunt you down himself, and I certainly wasn't going to approach you about it. Maria and I didn't even want you to know I associated with any of these characters; bringing one of them to your doorstep was out of the question.

"I was hoping Baumgarten would eventually give up, but he only became more and more insistent. When I suggested he find somebody else to do his investigating for him, he told me it was you or nobody. He said you were the only cop he ever trusted."

The only cop he ever talked to he didn't have to. Funny thing, the weight of a compliment, from whatever the source. While Kubiak hadn't been able to shake the hollow ache of guilt he'd felt over his dismissal of Baumgarten in Union Station since news of his death, it wasn't until now he actually missed the man's presence on this earth.

Hollinger continued. "Anyway, as he kept on pressing me to get you involved, he began to feed me bits and pieces of how he believed the death of Jack Mackay went down. I suppose he thought he could bring me into his cause, but it all seemed so ludicrous, the entire Lake County Sheriff's Department involved in the cover-up of a cold-blooded murder."

"How much did he tell you?"

"Not enough to give me much help now that he's gone. He did verify that it was Mackay orchestrating the theft of the lumber, as well as everything else Wheeler was selling. He was the only manager in the yard, so he was able to pull it off pretty easily, and he was paying off the bookkeeper, some girl named Christine Hughes, who Baumgarten led me to understand Mackay was seeing, as well. But you can only get away with so much, especially when everybody down the line is so greedy.

"Old man Wheeler must not have been as soft or blind as Mackay took him to be. He realized how badly he was being ripped off and hired a full-time security force, made up of five or six off-duty sheriff's deputies."

"When was this?"

"Late March, early April."

"But Wheeler was soft and blind enough that he still had no clue it was Jack Mackay facilitating the thefts?"

"According to Baumgarten, yes. But it's at this point I begin to wonder how much he's telling me is true, and how much he believes to be true because it fits the argument he's making."

"How do you mean?"

"Well, at first he said the sheriff's deputies jumped in for a cut of the action, and that was why they shot Mackay, because they were afraid of what he'd confess about their involvement in the thefts if they picked him up for the murder of the Wheelers. I told him it was pretty unlikely that even a small group of cops would fall in together so fast for such a paltry take, much less commit murder to cover it up. Besides, I had heard there was bad blood between Mackay and the Lake County cops, and I knew for a fact that, around that time, Brady started having to pay out more for what he was getting out of the

Wheelers' lumberyard. The next time I saw Baumgarten, his story had changed. Sure enough, the off-duty cops and Mackay were at odds from day one, they were the ones who alerted the Wheelers it was Mackay ripping them off, and when the Wheelers confronted Mackay and he killed them, the cops chased him down, ran him off the road, and shot him dead."

"Because they hated Mackay that much."

Hollinger rattled the ice in his glass. His left hand kept clenching into a fist, then unclenching. "I don't know. I told you, Baumgarten's story kept changing. I do believe one thing, though. He swore to me he had a list of the names of the cops who were moonlighting at Wheeler's lumberyard. Like everything else, the job was off the books. He said he wanted to compare it to the list of the cops involved in chasing down Mackay that morning. That was one of the things he was hoping you'd find out."

"Where did he get this list?"

"How would I know? From Mackay, I guess. He wouldn't even tell me whose name was on it."

"I don't understand," Kubiak said. "Aside from the IRS, I don't know who would be interested in seeing it. Even if some of the names did match, it wouldn't necessarily mean anything."

"Well, dammit, it means something." Hollinger leaned forward in his chair. "Because he's dead, isn't he? It means something because Baumgarten was murdered. You do believe at least that much."

Chapter Thirteen

Kubiak said nothing. After a moment, Hollinger leaned back again, looked up at the ceiling, sighed. The fist clenched, unclenched. When Kubiak spoke again, his voice was low.

"Paul Baumgarten was murdered in your truck."

"Don't think I'm not aware of that."

"Did you ever consider, for a moment, that someone murdered him thinking he was you?"

"What?" Hollinger fished in his shirt pocket, produced a second cigarette which Maria must have given him knowing this session might run long. "No."

"So, if you didn't think the killer was after you, and you didn't kill Baumgarten . . ." Kubiak gave a soft wave of his hand. "What are you doing here?"

Hollinger lit the cigarette, inhaled deep, exhaled. "Last Sunday evening, Baumgarten showed up at our apartment in a panic. He looked a mess, said he had been threatened over the phone, that the caller told him if he didn't stop running around talking about Jack Mackay, he wouldn't live to see the week finish. I told him it was probably a prank, but he was absolutely convinced the threat was genuine. He insisted I take him to see you immediately. Instead, I boozed him up, calmed him down, let him spend the night, and sent him on his way the next morning with some half promises.

"Then, Tuesday night, actually Wednesday morning, around two, the phone woke us up. It was Baumgarten, saying he had been threatened again. He said he was on his way over and wanted you in my apartment by the time he got there. Well, I'd had it, and was half asleep, so I finally set him straight, told him there was no way I would consider hooking him up with you and to leave me alone, and hung up. I barely had time to turn to Maria to tell her what it was all about when the phone rang again. This time the threat was for me."

"It could have just been Baumgarten," Kubiak said. "Trying to reel you back in on a bluff."

"That's what I thought at first, and I told the caller so more than once. But I don't see how it could have been him. The voice was dead calm and flat, and when I hung up on Baumgarten not five seconds before, barely time to dial my number, he was positively raving."

"Would you recognize the voice?"

"Not possible. It was a man's, but he whispered."

"What did he say?"

"He kept it simple. He said Baumgarten was a dead man, and I would be, as well, if I didn't forget everything Baumgarten ever said and forget I ever knew him. It was a short conversation, and I'm sure I missed some of it, what with my constantly yelling into the phone, 'Hey, Baumgarten, who are you trying to kid, it's two in the morning.' "

"Did he mention Maria?"

"No. But he kept referring to me by my full name. It was never just 'you,' always 'David Hollinger, you.' When I hung up, I still thought it had been Baumgarten, just for the reason you said. Then, Baumgarten came by Thursday. My god, was it only four days ago?"

He smoked some more. Kubiak waited.

"He told me he had looked you up on his own and you had agreed to meet with him Friday. I was upset, of course, but at that point there was nothing I could do, and I asked him why he even bothered to stop by and let me know. He said he was doing it as a favor to you, and that was when he let me know why I got that threatening phone call. It seems his conversations with the guy on the other end of the line were a little more extensive than mine. In order to cover his butt, he told him he had an ace in the hole, somebody he had shared all his information with, somebody connected to a retired cop set to step in and shake up things in the Lake County Sheriff's Department. He even hinted that he had given me that list of names."

"He gave up your name?"

"He claimed he hadn't, but he must have let it slip. How else would this guy have gotten my number? Anyway, Baumgarten told me he was going to warn you that Maria and I might be in harm's way. Obviously, he figured that would get you to jump in on this. I told him he had better not try it, that if I found out he even mentioned to you he knew me or Maria, he'd be getting more than threats from my end, and that if you thought for a second he might have done anything to put your daughter in any kind of jeopardy, you'd see him hang. That sobered him up, and all of the sudden he decided he was my guardian angel. He showed me this place, gave me a key, told me he hid out here whenever he didn't want to be found, begged me to just stay until he talked to you. I thought it was a little silly, but I must admit I was starting to get a little nervous.

"That evening, I met Maria downtown when she got off work. We had dinner, went to a couple of clubs on Division. It had been a while since we did that. We talked all night, decided together that it was best I put Neil Brady and the rest of them behind me, take my chances on my own. Amazing thing, but once we settled on that, it was like a weight was lifted off our shoulders. It was like starting all over again, fresh, just the two of us.

"Well, we boozed it up pretty good, had breakfast downtown. Maria called in sick to work. Baumgarten, thinking we'd be spending the night here, had told me he'd be stopping by here late morning. Maria and I thought it was a good chance for us to start severing ties, and I knew we'd never make it if we went home first—after all, it was already morning. He said he had set us up with fresh sheets, so we crashed here. We didn't wake up until mid-afternoon, were still scraping around nursing our heads when he showed up after having talked to you. He was half livid, half in a panic. I thought I'd send him over the edge when I told him I was walking away from him and the rest, but oddly enough, it calmed him. He grew cold, said he understood, but asked for one last favor, and that was to borrow my truck, which was parked outside. You know, he didn't have a car, and he said he was having the devil of a time getting anything done that day relying on train routes and schedules. He said if I would just lend him my truck for a couple of hours, I'd never see him again."

"Funny how he called that one."

"Yeah. The joke was on us both."

"Did he say where he was taking it?"

"No, and I didn't ask. He was happy to have it, and I was glad to be rid of him."

"He was alone when he borrowed your truck?"

"Yes. Of course."

"Somebody else was driving it when he was killed. Any idea who?"

"No. I just handed him the keys and watched him head out the door. I actually believed he'd have it back in time for me and Maria to make it over to your place for her birthday, and when he didn't I suggested Maria go by herself. She didn't want to, said you'd know right off the bat something was wrong and wouldn't let up until you had it out of her. We decided it was best neither of us went, and I phoned you with the same excuse she'd given her office. We picked up some Chinese food and waited for Baumgarten to come back."

"What time did you go out for the Chinese?"

"Around ten, maybe ten-thirty."

"You just might have an alibi there."

"If the counter guy even recognized my face. The place was jammed. This neighborhood, it's unbelievable if you're hungry."

"Go anyplace else?"

"No. We came back here and ate, didn't want to miss Baumgarten if he showed. Eventually, we drifted off. Sometime in the middle of the night, the phone rang. It was Brady. He was surprised to hear my voice. I figured he was looking for Baumgarten, and I told him the jerk still had my truck. He asked me if I'd tuned in to CLTV lately, and hung up. Well, obviously by the time I turned it on, whatever news item he wanted me to see was over. I called him back, but he wasn't answering his phone, so I waited until the next half hour broadcast, and sure enough, there was my truck. I could only make out the last three numbers on the back plate in the flashes from the squad cars' lights, but there was no doubt, not with that Packers decal I screwed up trying to paste in the back window. All the reporter standing in front of it knew was that whoever was in it was beaten to death."

"Why didn't you call the police?"

"Only because I had a handfull of good reasons not to. I hadn't been home for two nights, and was squatting in an apartment Baumgarten had the keys to. I, supposedly, am holding a list of crooked cops, and had been threatened to keep my mouth shut about it. And the only two people who knew I wanted out of this whole mess were my wife and the dead man in my truck. Besides, I wanted to get Maria clear before I did anything. It wasn't until some time the next morning she agreed to go to your place. I couldn't think of where else to send her."

"Why did you call her back here?"

"I didn't. I promised her I'd phone her, and when I did she said she had rested, felt stronger, and was coming back whether I liked it or not. I asked her to stay with you for just forty-eight hours, to give me a chance to do what I had to do. I begged her, I swear I did, but she refused. You know how she is. She makes her own decisions."

Kubiak sipped his drink. It was the first he had touched it, and he felt bad for not having thought to offer it to Hollinger when his glass had been emptied so quickly so many words ago. The whiskey was cheap, probably came with the apartment.

"A chance to do what?" he asked.

Hollinger leaned in close again. "Baumgarten was killed Friday night. Too late for the Saturday papers. Sure, it was on CLTV, and I caught a couple of minutes on WGN and FOX Chicago, but nothing on the radio. The Sunday papers this morning? Forget it. Nothing."

"You picked up the *Sun Times* and the *Tribune*. It happened in Lake County; the *Herald* would have run something on it."

"I'm sure they printed something, but how much?"

How much? Kubiak could still see the sad, desperate look on Baumgarten's face as Kubiak told him, referring to Mackay, that it was so much more than most men are given.

"Anyway, whether because the Lake County cops would like to keep this all quiet or because nobody really cares if Baumgarten is dead or not, my name hasn't yet been mentioned once in the media. Before it is, I'd like to do something to clear it. I've been trying to get hold of this Christine Hughes. I find it strange that someone so close to Mackay fell off the map so fast after he died. I've also contacted a lawyer who Baumgarten claimed he was working with up in Round Lake Beach, a fellow named Osgood. I'm supposed to phone him tomorrow, see if we can set up a time to meet." Hollinger searched his pockets. "Hold on, I've even got his card here, somewhere."

"Here." Kubiak extracted Matthew P. Osgood's card from his wallet, held it out before him. "You can borrow mine."

Hollinger stared at the card like the victim of a parlor trick. Kubiak continued. "You're not afraid that by weaving yourself in tighter with these people you might not be giving the police a stronger case against you?"

"No," Hollinger said, blinking. "I think it's more likely

that if the cops get hold of me, what little investigating they're doing into the case will end. I never—"

He stopped there, as his eyes followed Kubiak's to the two women who had entered the room and were standing at the edge of the hallway. Maria's eyes were wet and puffy, her shoulders hunched. Denise's arm was wrapped around her daughter's waist.

"We're going home," she stated. "Are you two joining us?"

Hollinger looked to Kubiak, back to his wife, back to Kubiak. "You go ahead," he said. "It's better if I stay here."

"Sorry," Kubiak told him, getting to his feet. "But you're tagging along. I don't want you here if Neil Brady happens to call again tonight. After all, I just paid the man a thousand dollars for the privilege of coming over here and killing you. You surprise him all over again by answering the phone this time, he just might come over and do the job himself."

Chapter Fourteen

If there was anything Kubiak was grateful for as he nursed a beer in as deep a corner of his living room as he could find, it was that at least the party decorations had been taken down. His tiny family shuffled about like boarding house tenants as they prepared themselves for bed. Comments were responded to with nods, nods ignored, passings in the hallway tolerated. When David and Maria were finally, solidly shut into the guest bedroom, he turned out the lights and joined Denise in theirs. The clock on the nightstand read 3:00 A.M.

"What time are you meeting Osgood?" Denise asked, already under the bedcovers.

"Eight."

"You want me to set the alarm?"

"No. I'll wake up."

She waited until he was lying beside her before she asked, "What should I do about the police if they come by while you're gone?"

"If they show you paper, let them do whatever they

please. If they don't, keep the door chained, tell them I'll be back sometime in the afternoon."

"What about David?"

"I'll be upstate asking the questions he wants answered. He should wait around for me to get back. If not. . . . Hell, I don't care. Send him out for Chinese. Take him to the beach. No, whatever you do, don't take him to the beach. Take him to the zoo. In fact . . ."

Denise turned out the lamp on her side of the bed, leaned over him, and turned out the one on his side. In the dark, he felt her hair brush his face, then her lips on his cheek.

"Kubiak," she said, "sometimes you do have an idea or two."

He was asleep immediately, awake again in three hours that passed like minutes. He crept about the apartment to keep from waking anyone else, showered, and was in the kitchen with his second cup of coffee, the news station playing softly on the radio (without mention of Baumgarten or Hollinger), when Maria appeared. She was barefoot, wearing a thick robe that ran to her ankles, and she looked more refreshed than he felt. She scrutinized the sink, the dish rack.

"Aren't you going to eat anything?"

He told her he would pick up something on the road. She told him not to be ridiculous, and went to work toasting bread and cutting fruit.

"You've got time," she said, joining him at the tiny table in the corner of kitchen. They ate in silence for a few minutes before she spoke again.

"Poor David's out cold. This is the first real sleep he's had in days."

"Fine. I want him to have a clear head when I get back."

"What did you say to him last night?"

"Not much. He did most of the talking."

"You told him you paid Neil Brady a thousand dollars for the opportunity of killing him. Why would you say a thing like that?"

"Because I thought it best he know."

"But you didn't." She was trying to peel the membrane off an orange slice and was making a mess of it. "I mean, even the way you twist things, sometimes. You wouldn't make a deal like that."

"The point is, Brady thought I did."

"I don't understand. Why would he want David killed?"

"I don't know. Maybe he has his reasons. Maybe he just couldn't pass up a quick grand. You tell me which is worse, or which is more likely."

Maria stared down at her plate, perhaps contemplating the gravity of an acquaintance's willingness to trade her husband's life for an envelope stuffed with hundred dollar bills. Kubiak saw no reason to mention that her name was brought up, as well.

"David's problem is that he's too pure-hearted," she said, softly. "He trusts too easily." A pause, then, "You wouldn't understand that."

Kubiak couldn't blame her for throwing that jab at the end, not after all the ones her husband had taken from him last night.

"What I don't understand," he told her, "is why the two of you never came to me, with the resources of the Chicago P.D. at my disposal—especially if you thought you were running for your lives from the Lake County Sheriff's Department. Even Baumgarten knew enough to ask for my help."

She rubbed the back of her neck, regarded her father through narrowed eyes. For all her demands for candor, she never knew what to make of it when it came from him. "I thought David explained all this to you."

"He told me he wanted to keep his name out of the papers."

"Well, yes. Of course he did. Not just for himself, but for all of us." She stood abruptly, carried her plate to the sink. "He knew what the media would do with a story about the son-in-law of an ex-Chicago cop involved in a homicide of his own, especially one tied to a shooting by Lake County Sheriff's deputies. He wasn't about to let that happen to you, or to mother. David, if anything, is sensible. He realized what that would do to our family."

"Funny, he left me with the impression it had more to do with his business prospects."

"Well, he would, wouldn't he? I mean, that's his way, to take responsibility rather than throw it back at you, or me. And it's all so bundled up together, after all. Don't forget, it wasn't his idea to settle here. I was the one who wanted to come home. If it weren't for me, he could have just . . ."

She leaned back against the counter, searched a moment for her words. "I was so worried about him when we first moved here. I knew how much he'd miss the north woods, and he seemed so lost wandering around the city. Oh, I don't know why I don't give him more credit than I do.

"We'd been here only about a week or two before he started carting me along with him on his walks through the neighborhood, and I realized that while he had looked to me to be wandering lost, he was actually walking around in awe of everything, even East Rogers Park, a neighborhood I, like everybody else I know, always considered nothing more than a stopover for students or transients, someplace you can rent on the cheap while looking for a real place to live. But David started pointing out to me the differences in architectural points between all the buildings, telling me the decades in which they were built, showing me the cut of their stones, their archways, the courtyards in front of their deep entrances. Do you remember what you always called them when I was a kid?"

Kubiak said nothing, and she smiled.

"Stormed castles," she said. "I told David that, and he said it was more sad than funny. He said he'd never known any neighborhood like it, that with all its languages and different faces, it was a tiny, cosmopolitan city within a city. He said it held more potential than any place he'd ever seen, and that we were lucky to have landed there when we did. I told him he was crazy, that he was ignoring the gangs and the shuttered businesses. He wasn't, of course. He wasn't missing a thing. It's just that, he can see things the rest of us take for granted. I've known that neighborhood all my life, but it wasn't until he walked me through it that I really perceived it. Those castles that were stormed and abandoned before I was ever born suddenly showed themselves to be as grand and proud as they must have been a century ago when they were first built. And I won't be the last one to see it, not if David has his way. Downtown bounced back from its squalor years ago. East Rogers Park is past due. How can it not be? Like David says, it's a mile and a half of fully developed lakefront property sitting smack between Highland Park and the Loop. That's why he couldn't let this horrible mess between Neil Brady, Baumgarten, and Jack Mackay ruin his plans. But he's not like them. He's not here to make a killing in some real estate market. What he wants is something grander than that, to be a part of restoring that poor, sad neighborhood to its former greatness, make it a place where people want to live, another gold coast even, but one where people can afford to raise a family, an exciting, ethnically diverse neighborhood where ordinary people can live in castles and walk the streets at night. And he's already begun. Why, just by rehabing that store on Morse, he's managed to move the gang activity on that block back over to the west side of the El station. He says that when . . ."

She stopped short, and her eyes narrowed again. She was reading his face; he couldn't imagine what she was seeing.

"You haven't heard a word I've said."

"That's not true."

"But you don't believe it."

"I never doubted David's intentions. However he wound up involved in Brady's—"

"No, that's not what I'm saying at all. Oh, I wish you could hear David tell it, then you'd see." A sigh, another rub of the neck. "But no, I don't suppose you would."

She turned back to the sink, washed her plate, glanced up at the wall clock.

"You'd better get going."

"Osgood can wait fifteen minutes."

"No, you're already running late. Traffic will be impossible."

And with that, she left him alone to wonder what he had said, or could have said, or didn't say, not even giving him credit for refraining from comment after her description of Hollinger as a sensible visionary or her remark about his never intending to make a killing in the real estate market. He would have liked to have said as much, would have liked to see her laugh, laugh like mad, the way the two of them used to, not so many years ago. Had the chasm between them grown that great, or was it only that each of them was afraid to make the leap across it for fear of not being caught by the other?

But his coffee was cold, and he was indeed running late, and some things were better pondered over a drink at Jimmy Dee's. So, he took the back elevator down to the garage, concentrating instead on the questions he had for Matthew P. Osgood, and fired up the Ford for another run to Round Lake Beach.

The drive north proved both him and Maria right: traffic was impossible, and Osgood could wait an extra fifteen minutes, because he did. The lawyer's office was tucked into the corner of an L-shaped strip mall. Its reception area was furnished for a finer location, its blinds shut tight against the view of the parking lot, the room's light coming from two heavily-shaded lamps on tables of dark wood with leather trim. Osgoood's secretary was dressed for downtown, as well. She had Kubiak sit just long enough to cross his legs before she ushered him into a back office, more brightly lit, with a window that looked out onto the woods behind the building.

Osgood was half-sitting on the front corner of his desk, looking as casual as a man in a tailored, wool suit can. Six foot plus, with a model's face and an athlete's frame, he was the exact opposite of what Kubiak had expected. He flashed a grin, came off the desk to shake Kubiak's hand and to introduce him to the room's other two occupants. Kubiak had seen them before, but only in the newspapers. Robin and Kimberly Mackay, Jack Mackay's mother and sister, were suited up quite nicely themselves. The dark circles under their eyes that had stood out so starkly in that black and white photo in the *Herald* were gone. Robin had shortened her hair considerably, which softened her face, and her daughter Kimberly might have passed for pretty had she not looked so uncomfortable in her neatly starched pantsuit. Seated in two high-backed chairs pushed together so their elbows were nearly touching, they each nodded primly as Osgood introduced them in turn.

Kubiak took a seat, angled his chair so he could take in any of the three without turning his head. Osgood settled himself behind his desk. He spoke first.

"Before we begin, Mister Kubiak, I suppose you'd like a couple of points cleared up about last night. You are aware you were arrested for trespassing. As it turns out, the owner of the property is not interested in pressing charges."

"What changed his mind?"

"Nothing, really. From what I understand, he didn't even know you were there until the sheriff's deputies knocked on his door and told him so. There are some in the department who think it's their duty to persuade a man in his position that it's expected he take such a matter to court. Thankfully, there are others, more sensible, who would rather not clog the system with that kind of frivolous charge. After all, there is question as to whether you were even on private property in the first place."

"Strom and Dunning were having too good a time playing hardball to give me up without somebody ordering them to do so last night. Who did you contact in the department?"

"Why? What does it matter?"

"Just a point I'd like cleared up."

Osgood picked up a pen and played with it. "Who I phoned isn't important. The point is, the minute I told them you were working for me in an investigative capacity concerning the possibility of a civil suit in the Mackay matter, they cut you loose. They had to. If they'd kept you in there knowing that, they'd have been doing my job for me, wouldn't they?"

"I suppose. Somebody was doing your job for you, though."

"Oh?"

"Whoever phoned you to let you know I was being held."

More playing with the pen. Not a bad trick, if that was what it was, as it provided a distraction for anyone's gaze, including Osgood's own.

"I've been working in the Waukegan courts for nearly a decade," he said flatly. "I have a great many friends there. Seeing as you're a former police officer, you understand why I'd be reluctant to discuss any contacts I might have in the sheriff's department, or elsewhere. Besides, none of what I might have said or done concerns you. All you have to worry about is that, as of now, you're off the hook as far as any charges go. If that should change, or if those two detectives decide to drag you back up here to play hardball again, I can refer you to a colleague of mine who can offer you excellent representation."

"Colleague?"

"Yes. Another lawyer."

"I know what a colleague is," Kubiak said. "I thought you were my lawyer."

"Oh, no. I'm sorry, I couldn't possibly."

"Why not?"

"Well, first off, there's the potential conflict of interest."

"What conflict of interest?"

"I didn't say there was a conflict of interest. I said there was a potential for one."

"What potential conflict of interest?"

Osgood bellowed a laugh. "Mister Kubiak, as much as I'd like to, I can't represent everyone."

"Then, what am I doing here?"

"You tell me. You're the one who drove all the way up from Chicago." Osgood looked over at the women. The ladies' befuddled stares offered him no fuel. Still, he continued, all traces of humor gone, but the smile hanging. "You can leave any time you wish."

Chapter Fifteen

Kubiak did not reply. Osgood let the offer stand just long enough to make everyone uncomfortable before resuming.

"All right, then. Now, you know why the Mackays are here. I hope Mister Baumgarten, in his recruiting you, made you aware of the pain they've been going through. While no amount of money will bring Jack Mackay back to them, it can help make certain this sort of thing never happens again. Right now, these two strong ladies are standing alone against a town opinion that puts law and order over civil rights, and a sheriff's department that's locked itself up tighter than a . . ." Another glance at the ladies. "Well . . ."

"Where does the Round Lake P.D. come down on this?" Kubiak asked.

"They're trying to stay as far away from it as possible, of course."

"Wasn't Jack's first run-in with them? Something about a drug sale next to a schoolyard."

Robin Mackay sat up straight. "That wasn't what that was."

Osgood showed her his palm, along with a smile that must have already reassured her more than once, as she closed her lips and let her shoulders fall.

"That incident," he said, "was the only encounter the local police had with Jack, and it was some time ago. You have to understand, most of what you'd consider Round Lake and Round Lake Beach, isn't. Outside the town proper, the county has jurisdiction, and most of Jack's subsequent infractions occurred there. Any animosities built up over the past year or so were between Jack and the county sheriff's department."

"And you're saying these animosities resulted in the sheriff's deputies murdering Jack Mackay."

"No, that's not what I'm saying."

"Then, what's this civil suit all about?"

Osgood sighed, went back to his pen. "I'm not about to claim that Jack was a model citizen, but basically, he was no different from any young man with too much energy and too little respect for authority. Most of the boys here in Round Lake are allowed to grow out of that phase of their lives. Jack wasn't given that option, and that is what this civil suit is about. A set of circumstances rose up around him and closed back in on top of him, resulting in his death. A number of men are responsible for that. Some are the thugs who followed him here from Chicago. Others are the men up here who left Jack Mackay in the middle when they decided to, as you would say, play hardball with those thugs. I don't want to disparage anyone in law enforcement, but they should have known better than to leave a young man in such a position, especially one still trying to find his way in this community. Jack Mackay was a victim of their incompetence and indifference."

"You're leaving a thing or two out of your opening arguments, aren't you?"

"What's that?"

"Jerald and Bernice Wheeler."

Both ladies shifted their weight, both looked to their lawyer. Osgood offered them a soulful expression, then turned pensive.

"I understand your point, of course," he told Kubiak. "It's one I've been fighting, both in the court of public opinion and in my own mind, since I agreed to take this case. You see, I grew up in this community, and I certainly don't want to disparage the Wheelers. But I have to wonder what old Jerald was thinking. First, he hires Jack, knowing of his past, in fact, because of the hard knocks the kid's had. Then, he gives him a position of authority, basically hands him the keys to the business. At that point, Jack's well-being became Jerry Wheeler's responsibility. When certain . . . troubles became apparent at the lumberyard, instead of pulling poor Jack out of the position he's put him in, which in my opinion was his duty as self-appointed surrogate father, he hires the very select group of sheriff's deputies most antagonistic to the poor boy to work on a day-to-day business with him, or should I say, against him. As I said, the lot of these adults should have known better. If you consider Jack Mackay's death a suicide, don't you think the same could be said for Jerald Wheeler's?"

Before Kubiak could form a response, Osgood was on his feet. "But it doesn't matter what you think, does it?"

he continued, moving behind the Mackays and resting his hands on their shoulders. "I'm the one whose job it is to make the case for Jack. Your job is simply to find out as much as you can and carry that information back to me, and me alone."

Osgood had to have felt Kimberly freeze up under his touch, as Kubiak noticed it from where he sat. Her glare, however, was not aimed at her lawyer, but at Kubiak. She muttered something about vultures. Her mother clutched her hand; Osgood bent down and whispered into her ear. Neither act changed her expression.

"Go ahead," Kubiak said. "I'd actually appreciate hearing it, whatever it is."

She sent two sharp breaths through her nose while she gathered up the courage to repeat it.

"I said you're just another vulture, is all."

Robin tightened the grip on her daughter's hand, leaned into her. "He's just doing his job, Kimmy. He's working for us."

"No, he's not. There isn't anybody in this room who isn't working only for themselves. Even you."

"You know that's not true."

"But it is. Don't you hear what people are saying about us? People who used to be our friends?"

"What they're saying doesn't matter. It's like Mister. Osgood tells us, we have to stand strong."

"Stand strong for what? For a bushel full of money so we can buy a smelly, old shack in a town where everyone hates us for using poor Jack's death to pay for it? And how much money? A thousand dollars? Ten thousand dollars? A hundred thousand dollars? Has this man even given you a hard figure yet? Well, have you, Mister Osgood?"

Osgood touched her shoulder again. It was the first wrong move he'd made. Kimberly shook off his and her mother's grips, stood, and turned on them.

"No. I don't want to hear it again. Jack is gone, and none of this is going to bring him back, and no amount of money is going to replace him. And if letting it all go is going to give the cops an excuse to do it all over again to somebody else, then let them, because I just don't care anymore. I don't want any part of it."

A sudden flow of tears choked off whatever she was going to say next. Then, she was out of the room, slamming the door shut behind her. Robin Mackay and Osgood exchanged glances; his concerned, hers anxious. The door opened again and the secretary's nervous face peered in. Osgood nodded at Robin, who took off after her daughter. He told his secretary to make sure both women stayed put, and she disappeared as well, leaving Kubiak alone with the lawyer.

"Sorry about that," Osgood said as he returned to his desk and fell into his chair.

"That's all right. She couldn't have made me feel more at home."

"The kid can afford to sound as noble as she wants. She knows she'll still get her fair share of any money we collect."

"The tears seemed real enough."

"I suppose. She's going through a tough period. So is her mother. I'd like to help them put all this behind them, which means getting this case moving and settling it quick."

"Too bad you can't get it settled quick enough for Paul Baumgarten."

"I don't understand what you mean."

"You know he was murdered three nights ago."

"Yes, of course. It's tragic, but I don't know what I could have done about it."

"You hired him to snoop around, and he did. He was threatened that he'd wind up dead if he kept it up, and he did. I'm not saying you could have prevented it. You just don't seem as concerned as I thought you'd be."

"I'm concerned about any man's death, Mister Kubiak."

"I was thinking more of your own safety. In your shoes, I might be looking over my shoulder, or at least drawing the curtains over the window behind my back."

"Or frisking strangers coming into my office on a Monday morning?"

Osgood laughed at his own joke. When Kubiak didn't, he folded his hands in his lap and swiveled about in his chair, looking pensive even as he stole a glance through the window behind him.

"You've been the victim of some misinformation. I did not hire Paul Baumgarten."

"Who did?"

"As far as I know, no one. I'm tempted to say he worked alone, but that would give him too much credence. The man, God rest his soul, was more a nuisance than a maverick. He was a busybody who knew the Mackays and the Wheelers, as well as most of Jack's acquaintances from Chicago. When he heard rumors of a potential lawsuit, he wanted a piece of it. I might have once discussed with him the possibility of some future payment for information he could give me that might prove useful, but that was all I had to do with him."

"When was the last time you saw him?"

"Some weeks ago. He phoned me a few times, but I stopped taking his calls. My secretary had orders to turn him away at the door. If he had knowledge of anything pertinent I would have been glad to speak to him, but his idea of investigating was talking unrelentingly about every aspect of Jack Mackay's life to anyone who knew Jack. And Jack knew some unsavory characters capable of . . . well, I'll just say that when I heard Mister Baumgarten was dead, I was surprised, but not too surprised."

"You think Neil Brady would be willing to chance a murder charge just to cover up the theft of some lumber?"

"I didn't mention any names, and I don't intend to. But I will say the thefts were ongoing, and involved more than just 'some lumber.' Do I believe there are men who would think nothing of killing another man in order to sustain what they consider their livelihood? Yes."

"Did you ever receive any threats?"

"No. But, then, I wouldn't have, would I? My issue is with the Lake County Sheriff's Department. I don't have to tell you that's hardly their method of intimidation. There were, however, two phone calls made to the Mackays, both occurring some time earlier this month. Neither of the ladies was personally threatened. In each instance, the caller mentioned Baumgarten by name."

"What did he say?"

"Nothing precise, or too menacing. From what the ladies told me, the conversation was short. 'Tell Baumgarten to let the matter rest or he'll be sorry.' I told them the calls might have come from anyone in this town who was tired of hearing the troubles brought up. Saturday morning they contacted me, understandably hysterical after hearing of Baumgarten's death. I tried to reassure them the murder was not directly caused by our litigation, and that as long as we pursued the matter in court, and not by word of mouth, they had nothing to worry about."

"That couldn't have been an easy job."

"On the contrary, all I had to do was explain that we were suing no one person in particular, but an institution. The idea of the entire sheriff's department systematically killing every person involved in a case simply to prevent its being brought to court is preposterous. The Mackays understood."

"Before or after you reminded them what a shame it would be to everyone involved if the lawsuit were dropped?"

Osgood hardened. "I can see why Baumgarten sought you out. You two have the same narrow vision of people's motivations."

"If we're so much alike, why am I your vulture when he wasn't given the privilege?"

"You're not." Osgood rose. "I'm not offering you anything more than I did him. We'll probably never know what really happened up at Loon Lake, and Jack Mackay's past makes it impossible for us to use any media to our advantage. All we can do is make the other side nervous or exasperated enough to settle. Nobody's going to get rich here, Mister Kubiak. You, me, or the Mackays."

The attorney waited for Kubiak to get to his feet, escorted him to the door.

"There is one thing, though," he added, his hand on the door's knob. "Your friend kept mentioning something about a list of the sheriff's deputies on Jerald Wheeler's payroll. They worked off the books, so I can't get hold of any other record of their employment. I don't suppose he gave it to you?"

"What do you plan to do with it?"

"Nothing. It's enough that I have it. That list could speed matters up considerably. A fellow interested in some quick cash might want to think about that."

Osgood opened the door. Kubiak stopped just on the other side of it.

"I understand Jack had a girlfriend who worked at the lumberyard," he said. "Christine Hughes. Have you asked her about the list?"

"Ms. Hughes has her own bone of contention," Osgood answered brusquely, Kubiak already having been dismissed. "She's wasted enough of my time already, so don't bother wasting yours. And stay away from the Mackays. Any information you want from them you can get through me. They don't need another Baumgarten in their lives right now." He turned his attention to his secretary. "Janet, where the hell are Robin and Kimberly?"

Janet, on the phone, pressed the receiver to her bosom. "In the parking lot. Having it out."

"Well, get them in here."

Osgood retreated to his office. Janet brought the receiver back to her ear, started to speak into it, was interrupted by whoever was on the other end of the line. Kubiak moved to the window, parted a section of the blinds with his index and middle fingers, and peered through the slit. Kimberly had pulled a dulled silver subcompact into the center of the parking lot and was sitting in it, one hand on the wheel, the other on the gearshift. Robin was outside of the vehicle, animatedly arguing through the driver's window. Twice Kimberly popped the clutch, then had to back up in order to counter whatever her mother screamed at her as she had begun to drive away.

Kubiak couldn't hear a thing, the office was sealed up that tight. He turned back to Janet, smiled, tilted his chin at the front door.

"Mind if I . . . ?"

She smiled back, cupped the mouthpiece. "Be my guest."

Robin and Kimberly toned down their argument considerably as Kubiak approached, but it took him under a minute to catch up on what he'd missed. Kimberly had been ready to drive off since the moment she had stormed out of the room, and was still there only because her mother refused to climb into the car. Robin, trying to remain rational but doing a poor job of it, was complaining of her daughter's lack of cooperation, claiming she was too exhausted at this point to continue the good fight all by herself.

Kubiak waited for an opening, then apologized for his timing. He told Kimberly he was on the right side of her mother's good fight, but had had only so much explained to him by Paul Baumgarten and needed to discuss some details before he went any further. The ladies argued some more, until Kubiak, now addressing Robin, added he didn't need both members of the family present, and he could drop her at home when the two of them were finished if Kimberly insisted on leaving. Kimberly glared at him through the open car window, not wishing to cooperate but anxious to take advantage of his offer. When her mother stood too long in indecision, she made up her mind, jammed the rattling, little car into first gear, and roared off.

Robin stared after her, looking more lost than sad. Kubiak touched her elbow.

"You know, I have one of my own at home," he told her. "About the same age."

"She's not always like this."

"You're lucky. Mine is."

The line brought a tiny smile which didn't diminish the dark pockets that had returned under Robin's eyes. Perhaps they had never left, but were more noticeable in the sunlight and the camera's flash. He hadn't let go of her arm.

"Have you had breakfast?"

She said she had.

"Well, then. I know it's early . . ."

She waited.

"I don't know about you, but I think I could use a drink."

She expressed no shock or disdain.

"There's a place in Antioch. Paul told me Jack used to drink there sometimes."

"The Village Inn? It's awfully far."

"I don't suppose it's even open this early."

"Oh, it's open."

She hesitated only once, and that was as he was starting up the Ford and she was about to buckle her seatbelt.

"Didn't Mister Osgood want to see me again?" she asked.

"Oh, he will," Kubiak assured her. "I told him to keep one eye out his window. You might want to give him a wave."

And she laughed out loud for the first time, suddenly a rebel child playing hooky, an outlaw, dressed for Sunday church but taking to the road on a whim, and looking ten years younger for it.

Kubiak only hoped poor Janet, the secretary, didn't catch hell for this.

Chapter Sixteen

"What are you thinking?"

She had left him alone while she used the bathroom, asked the question on her return to their table by the tavern's plate glass window. The Village Inn was empty but for their server and two old men at the bar. It was kept dark, and the old, polished wood tables and chairs kept it darker. Kubiak had been staring out the window at Antioch's well-preserved business district, two intersecting blocks of clean, three-story buildings, many of red brick with shops occupying their first floor, some with second-story bay windows that hung out over the sidewalk.

There were a handful of towns very much like this one along or near the Wisconsin/Illinois border, their two blocks of history jutting up like carved stones in a weedy field, surrounded by a scattering of fine, century-old homes either dilapidated or restored to pink and pale yellow, depending on the size of the village treasury. It had been some time since Kubiak had passed through one of these towns, and he had forgotten they existed.

"Feels almost like home," Robin said, settling back into her chair. "Doesn't it?"

Indeed, except for the district's being dandied up a bit much for the boutique crowd, he and Robin might have been sitting at a restaurant table in any one of Chicago's neighborhoods.

"Is that why Jack drank here?"

"I suppose. He never really said. He didn't come up here that much, didn't have any real friends here, just people he'd meet in the bars. I think he liked that he didn't know them or them him except for what they'd talk about over drinks. Like home again but not home again. Another fresh start. Fresh start! My baby was twenty-four."

Kubiak had brought up the assault charge he had read about in the newspaper involving Jack and the tavern's bartender. Robin had dismissed its significance, as had the waitress, who joined in their conversation now and then, leaning against the back of one of the table's empty chairs. The argument precipitating it, which had taken place late one night the previous summer, had been over nothing anyone could remember. Jack had thrown the first punch, someone had phoned the police, and Jack was arrested. A week later, Jack waltzed back into The Village Inn, paid his tab, muttered his apologies to the bartender, stayed for a few more drinks, and the incident was forgotten, as incidents that happen inside of bars are. The bartender had since moved to Colorado Springs, the waitress thought; Glenwood Springs, one of the old men at the bar claimed. The assault charge, however, had never been officially dropped.

"Those lousy cops were the ones who stopped him from coming up here anymore, too," Robin had said, as the waitress nodded in agreement. "They'd lie in wait for him off Route 83, caught him on two DUI's and a suspended license. He started drinking within walking distance after that."

"You think this might have been where he was heading that morning?" Kubiak asked her. "Home but not home again? Another fresh start?"

"I don't know. Maybe he was trying to get across the border to Wisconsin, thinking that might help somehow. Then again, there aren't that many roads running out of Round Lake Beach. He had to take one of them."

"I get the impression none of the three of you were that happy relocating here out of Chicago."

She at first looked at him as if she didn't understand what he'd said, blinked, shook her head. "Oh, no. No. If that were so, Kimmy and I would have moved back home after Jack's passing." After more thought, she smiled, sat back in her chair. "You haven't spent any time up here at all yet, have you?"

"A day and a night."

"Well, you'll get used to it if you let yourself. Just when you think you can't stand driving past another strip mail, you'll stop at a red light and look out your window and see nothing but blue sky and green fields, everywhere you look. You can sleep with your windows open in the summer, and sometimes you'll wake up in the middle of the night to the sound of cicadas so loud you can hardly stand them, though they'll put you right back to sleep. And in the winter, the snow stays white for days, even weeks, and you'll stand outside your front door in the evening and smell the burning wood from your neighbors' chimneys. It does make it feel like home, even if it's not."

Kubiak nodded a bit of empathy, all he could manage at her description of the rather squalid plot of land where fate had dropped her as if it were some magic kingdom. That damned Hollinger was affecting everyone he came across. He glanced over at the waitress to make certain she was busy with her bar patrons, leaned forward, his elbows on the table.

"Robin, why did Jack kill Jerald and Bernice Wheeler?"

"I don't know, Mister Kubiak."

"But you've thought about it, agonized over it. You must have come up with something."

She took her time. "Jack was a free spirit, the only real free spirit I've ever known aside from his father. That's why everybody loved him, and everybody did love my son."

"What happened to his father?"

She snorted. "Free spirit. He left before Kimberly was born. I'm surprised Jack stayed with us as long as he did. Nearly his whole life, it turned out, didn't it? Jack disappeared often enough, though. Just when you'd give up on him and begin to bear a grudge, there he'd be on your doorstep again. You'd make him breakfast, and he'd make you laugh, tell you about all his adventures, or most of them, anyway. Then, he'd take you along wherever he had to go just then, and you'd go, and be grateful for the time you got to spend with him until he was gone again."

She stared out the window, her memories bringing only a pained, grim look to her face.

"How did he wind up with Jerry Wheeler?" Kubiak asked.

"Two years or so ago, I talked him into taking a couple of courses at Loyola. Kimberly had just started college and was doing all right. In fact, she's doing wonderfully now over at the county college in Grayslake. She has a 4.0 in her dental hygiene courses."

Robin waited for acknowledgement of this news, and Kubiak nodded. The sadness in her eyes lifted for just an instant as she comforted herself with the achievement of her surviving child.

"Jack, though," she continued, "he wasn't much for sitting in a classroom, but he did like the action in the neighborhood around the Loyola campus. He met Neil Brady there, and started doing odd jobs for him. Brady pays cash at the end of each day, that's how he recruits people. Through him, Jack met Jerry.

"Jerry had a son, Tommy. I understand you met him yesterday."

"That's right."

Robin nodded. "He's a sweet kid. He just didn't want to go the way of his father. But for that, and a number of other reasons, I guess, Jerry was disappointed in how he turned out. Jerry considered Jack everything Tommy isn't. Jack always was a good worker, and he was smart. So, he sort of took Tommy's place. Jerry and Bernice used to take me out to dinner, and the talk was always about Jack. Jerry was the one who convinced me to come up here. It sounded like a good idea, get Jack out of the city, away from the gangs from high school he still hung with.

"For a while, everything was so fine. A real fresh start for all of us. Tommy had just moved out of Jerry's house and was glad to be on his own. He even dated Kimmy for a while, so she got to know some people in town and settle in. We saw more of Jack than ever, and the Wheelers and I had dinner together every Saturday night.

"Then, Jack's old friends started coming around here.

The police blamed Jack, and they started harassing us, like we were the ones bringing drugs and gang members into their community. They made it pretty plain they wouldn't mind if we moved back to Chicago. One Saturday night, Jerry suggested Jack move in with him and Bernice. They had so much room in their house, what with Tommy gone, and we were pretty cramped in our apartment. And Jerry was stricter with Jack. I thought that was a good thing. Looking back, I suppose I couldn't have been more wrong."

"How so?"

"Well, the only time you ever had any real trouble with Jack was when you put boundaries on him. That's why I lost control of him back home in Chicago. I'd given up laying down the law, it was just too impossible to do with him. Now, I wish I'd never handed him over to the Wheelers. Sure, I'd probably be visiting my baby in jail right now, but at least—Mister Osgood told me about a poet or somebody who said it wasn't natural for a parent to have to bury her child. The only thing I remember about Jack's funeral is the feel of people's hands on my arms, aiming me this way or that, sitting me down or standing me up. I suppose that's just as well."

Kubiak nodded, though he was thinking of Tommy Wheeler's words. For all his parents were willing to give Jack, they would have expected him to take it. All of it.

"It's just not right," Robin said.

Kubiak's thoughts had been elsewhere. "What's not right?"

"That they have to grow up so fast today. Just the things they're subjected to."

"I'm sorry. What things?" he asked.

"Well, you have to admit, the world is a more dangerous place than when we were their age."

"Is it?"

"Of course it is. Don't you watch the news, read the papers?"

Funny, he felt as if he had just run a long, exhausting circle and was beginning this endless weekend all over again.

"My wife," he said. "She reads me the comics over soft-boiled—"

"Things just aren't as simple as when we were growing up," she said, finishing her thought without hearing him.

"I don't care how old they are, you don't dare leave them alone for a minute. Damn, I wonder if Kimmy ever made it home." She fished a cellular phone from her purse, punched some numbers, listened.

"Simpler times," Kubiak said.

She held up her index finger to shush him, then flipped the phone shut. "Nobody there. I've got to let out the dog." She craned her neck, searching for their waitress. "We left in such a hurry this morning."

He signaled for the check.

Robin was quieter on the ride back down Route 83. Kubiak asked her how she had come to hire Osgood as her attorney. She told him that had been Baumgarten's doing.

"And Baumgarten?"

"What about him?" she asked, suddenly guarded.

"How did you know him?"

"He worked for Neil Brady," she said, staring out the window. "We knew him through Jack."

She guided him to the southernmost part of Round Lake Beach, an old area where commercial spaces mixed with residential, and the streets ran alongside the Milwaukee North railroad line. Her apartment was on the ground floor of a squat, square two-story structure that held maybe a dozen units. She didn't formally invite him inside, but she got out of the car without a good-bye and didn't object when he followed.

The dog, a full poodle, was less concerned with its bladder than it was with greeting every square inch of Kubiak's body, despite its mistress' commands to heel. Eventually, Robin managed to locate its leash and get it clipped to its collar. She tugged "Pootie" outside, leaving Kubiak alone in the apartment, standing, as far as he could tell, in the same spot the newspaper photographer must have stood when he took the photograph of Robin and Kimberly on their couch.

The front room was cut narrow in order to leave space behind it for a good-sized kitchen and a dining area just big enough to hold a table, four chairs, and a breakfront. Small, framed photographs hung on every wall, chronicling the Mackays through the past three decades. He watched Jack and Kimberly grow up from infancy, Robin move out of her twenties, through her thirties, and into her forties. These were the first clear photos of Jack Mackay Kubiak had seen. A handsome young man, with a natural grin that appeared in every snapshot, Jack did indeed look like the free spirit his mother had described, his casual demeanor hinting of a suppressed wink, as though he had just dropped into the frame for a moment at the request of the family.

The pictures continued down a short hallway where two doors stood shut. Kubiak tried the first, found it locked, moved on to the one farther down. It opened to what must have been the master bedroom, Robin's, which looked as though she had, as she'd said, left it in a hurry this morning. The bed was unmade; clothes were strewn over and about a wicker hamper; a jewelry case on top of the dresser sat open, its contents about as organized as those in a cartoon pirate's treasure chest.

He moved to the window, keeping to one side. On the fringes of the building's parking lot, Robin was still admonishing Pootie while the dog busied itself doing everything but its business. Behind them, traffic on the four-lane road had backed up, as a train was pulling into the Metra station and the gates on the adjacent streets had come down.

Kubiak stared at the blinking lights over the railroad gates, then did a quick search of the dresser drawers and nightstand. He found no list of off-duty cops on Gerald Wheeler's cash payroll, but did rummage through two neat piles of men's boxers and black dress socks. The closet held more male clothing, including shoes. They might have belonged to Jack, but were a less contemporary style than Kubiak had seen him wearing in the photographs, and the items were interspersed with Robin's, hardly the way a mother would keep her dead son's personal affects.

A small bathroom lay off the bedroom. Kubiak entered it, leaving the light off so as not to activate the ceiling fan. What light came in from the bedroom showed a sink crowded with lotions and cosmetics. The cabinet held two razors. There were two toothbrushes, as well, one still damp, the other bone dry. He held the dry one, wondered how long it had been since it had last been used, was still holding it when he heard the apartment's front door slam shut.

Back at the bedroom door, he watched Robin pass through the front room and disappear into the kitchen. She called out his name. He closed the door gently, crept back down the hallway, entered the kitchen to find her pulling down two glasses from a cabinet. More glasses. His head was already thick, and it was barely mid-afternoon.

"Where were you?" she asked, tottering a bit as she came down off her toes.

"I was looking at the photographs of Jack."

"I didn't see you."

"How long did you know Paul Baumgarten?" he asked her.

"Not so long. Like I said, I knew him through Jack."

"It must be difficult, not being able to talk about how much you miss him."

She busied herself at the refrigerator. "I don't know what you mean."

"I've been to Baumgarten's apartment. He hasn't lived there in some time."

She said nothing.

"I met him downtown on Friday. As you know, he didn't have a car, so we agreed to meet at the Metra station. He told me his train got into Union around two. The train out of Waukegan doesn't empty into Union Station. But the Milwaukee North line does. That's it right across the street. I'm willing to bet it just happens to land downtown right around the time he told me to be there."

Robin crossed to the sink. Kubiak followed her.

"I'll also bet," he said, "that if I were to look around here, I'd find a thing or two that belonged to him."

"I'll bet you already have."

"You should have thrown them out. The fact you didn't . . . Did you tell Osgood that Baumgarten was living with you?"

"No."

"Why the secret?"

"No secret. Only Paul thought it best that he kept himself what he called a silent partner. He said he was the one doing Osgood's thinking for him, and he'd have liked to have stepped out front and get things done faster, but that with his prison record, his having a stake in things, or being in a relationship with me. . . . Well, none of it would help in any court negotiations. We'd all get less money, he said."

"So, who knew?"

"That's the funny part. Only everybody who knew Paul. He used this kitchen as his office, gave my number out to everybody."

"What about the police?"

"Oh, no. No."

"After what happened to Baumgarten, you didn't think it best to let them in on it?"

"I don't see why, not with all the trouble we've had with them already because of Jack."

"That might be nothing compared with the hornet's nest your lawsuit could stir up."

"Mister Osgood assured me that wouldn't be a problem."

"There's a lot Mister Osgood might not know, aside from what you're not telling him. He can assure you of anything, but he can step away from all this in a second. You can't."

"Well, I have to trust somebody, don't I? With Paul gone . . ." She took in a long breath, let it out. "I'm sorry. But I haven't been able to think straight since Jack died. Every day is like passing through a fog, and all the advice everybody is throwing at me just rings in my ears. It's why I counted on Paul for so much. Oh, I don't know. Maybe Kimmy's right. Maybe we ought to just leave Round Lake Beach and put all of this behind us. Go home again."

"How did it happen?" Kubiak asked after a moment. "Baumgarten's coming into the picture, I mean."

She shrugged, smiled. It was the first memory that brought a smile. "How does it always happen? He stayed with me a few nights, got comfortable here. It was more convenient, with all his business between Chicago and Round Lake Beach. After a few weeks, his stuff just moved in with him." Her eyes tried to read Kubiak's, causing her smile to go lopsided. "I know this sounds funny, the way things turned out, but with Jack gone, I felt safer having Paul here. He'd sit on the phone at the kitchen table all day. Networking, he'd call it. 'I still got a finger in every pie,' he'd say. 'Just waiting for one to cook up right.' He only ate what I cooked for him, and only drank what I bought. But he had a trusting heart. And it was nice to be with somebody who still had dreams, even ones as crazy and hopeless as his might have been. It's just nice to have somebody at all, don't you think?"

She was approaching Kubiak, holding his glass. However, instead of handing it to him, she moved in close, raised herself up again on her toes. Though not expecting the move, he managed to place both hands on her waist and keep her from coming any closer. Her face only inches away from his, she didn't fight his grip, but didn't step back, either. Instead she stood, her eyes locked on his, waiting for him to either relent or push her away. And he knew that even though she had no need to grieve for the loss of Baumgarten, she had been unable to discard those few items he had left behind, as they were holding the space for the next man to take his place.

A voice from the kitchen doorway startled them both. "You two lovebirds don't mind me," it chirped.

Chapter Seventeen

Kimberly uncrossed her arms, pushed herself off the doorjamb. The look on her face announced she had enjoyed every bit of the show.

Robin pulled away from Kubiak. "You were home. Why didn't you answer the phone?"

Her daughter shrugged, crossed to the refrigerator, found a can of soda, popped it open, and sat down at the kitchen table.

"He tried to get in my bedroom," she said, coolly. "While you were out with Pootie."

Kubiak could feel Robin's eyes on him. He knew he looked as guilty as an errant schoolboy, but couldn't think of a word of protest that would make him seem less so. Kimberly saved him by continuing.

"I don't care, really. It's not like Paul didn't go in there to sniff around a time or two himself."

"That's not true."

"No? You don't remember why I put the lock on the door in the first place?"

"Oh, good lord, Kimberly."

Kimberly made a face at Kubiak. Her demeanor had changed entirely from Osgood's office and he doubted it was only because she had exchanged the pantsuit for a pair of blue jean shorts and a T-shirt.

"It's not what you're thinking," she told him. "He was stealing my cigarettes." As if she had just reminded herself she had a pack of them in the pocket of her shorts, she fished one out and lit it, then was up to pull an ashtray off the dishrack and back at the table in one fluid motion.

"I told you," Robin said. "You want to smoke, you do it outside."

"You'll want to get all of me you can now, Mom. I'm leaving tomorrow morning."

"You're not going anywhere."

"I am. I've already started packing. You want to see?" She gestured to her bedroom, turned to Kubiak. "How about you? I should have left my door unlocked, you could tell her."

The argument had the feel of being old and worn. Kubiak remained mute, uncomfortably conspicuous, waiting for the line he knew was coming. Robin was the one who uttered it.

"Do we have to do this in front of Mister Kubiak?"

"Hey, I'm not the one who brought him home," Kimberly replied. When her mother simply shook her head and turned away, she addressed Kubiak.

"Actually, I'm glad I did see you again. I wanted to apologize. I'm sorry for calling you a vulture."

"Thank you. That alone makes the trip here worthwhile."

"No. Mom was doing that." She puffed quickly, not holding the smoke in her lungs long. "I don't know if you are one or not, but I don't want to leave you thinking I usually act the way I did this morning." She ignored a snort from Robin. "It's just that I'm so sick of Osgood and his . . ." She stabbed out the cigarette. "He doesn't believe I don't want anything to do with his stupid lawsuit. He thinks it's all an act. Well, I'm proving it right now. I'm leaving, and I'm not coming back."

"Where are you going?"

"Back to Chicago. So, you can keep the car, Mom. I won't be needing it."

"You're darned right I'm keeping the car. I paid for that car."

Kubiak said, "That stupid lawsuit will be dealing with the details of your brother's death. Even if you're not interested in the money, aren't you curious enough to stick around and see what it turns up?"

Kimberly stared at her soda can, turned it this way and that. "I'll always be curious. But I'll never know, will I? After all, whatever comes of the court case has nothing to do with the truth. It's just one side winning and the other losing, and you can't believe a thing either one says. No, as far as I'm concerned, it's over. We came here for Jack. Now he's dead, and we have no reason to stay. Mom can if she wants, but there's nothing for me in Round Lake Beach. I have one semester of school left, and I can finish that in the city. Then I'll have a degree that I can use anywhere. I plan to take advantage of that."

She looked up. When neither Kubiak nor Robin argued with her, she blinked. The corners of her mouth came down. "You think I'm a total, selfish brat, don't you?"

"Not at all," Kubiak said, and he could feel Robin's eyes boring into him again. "In fact, if I were in your shoes I might be doing the same thing."

"You would?" She looked surprised. "Well, thanks. It's

a nice change to have somebody on my side besides Pootie."

"But I was under the impression you were starting to feel at home in Round Lake Beach."

"Oh? And what on earth would make you think that?"

"You've made some friends here. Dated one of the local boys."

"Oh, god." Kimberly laughed, a sharp laugh that caused her mother's eyes to narrow. "So, Mom told you that, huh. She likes to talk too much, especially about things she knows nothing about, especially with horny guys who will let her as long as they think there's a chance to—"

"Kimmy." This time Robin raised her voice. "That's enough."

The jab having landed, Kimberly, with a slight smile, addressed Kubiak matter-of-factly.

"I dated Tommy for a couple of months. Every once in a while, if he's playing in a band, I'll go see him. That's because I like music. Tommy's a nice guy, but that's about all there is to it."

"You don't like nice guys, or they don't like you?"

"Very cute. Tommy and I got along fine. We're just from two different worlds. And it didn't help that his father wasn't very pleased with our getting together. I was the tramp from the city."

"That's not true, Kimmy," Robin protested. "And you know it."

"You're blind, Mom. We're not Round Lake. It makes a difference."

Kubiak interjected. "It didn't bother Jerry Wheeler in the case of Jack."

"Oh, and that turned out just rosy, didn't it? Jack was

nothing more than another one of Jerry's projects, one that didn't pan out."

This jab landed too hard, and Kimberly saw it in her mother's face. She exhaled smoke through her nose, shook her head. "I'm sorry, Mom, but you'll have to admit our coming up here didn't work out so well for any of us. I'm going home. You two can talk about me all you want when I'm gone."

"Seeing as how you're not leaving until tomorrow morning," Kubiak said, "can I at least count on you to help me until then?"

"Help you do what? Seduce my mom, then wind up dead like Paul?"

"I'll warn you one more time, young lady," Robin said, firmly. "That's enough."

"It'll be enough when you decide it's enough. Besides, I'm just doing him a favor by cutting to the chase. He's only got my help until tomorrow morning."

Robin addressed Kubiak. "She's still scared, Mister Kubiak. You'll have to forgive her."

"What?" Kimberly was even more surprised than she had been when Kubiak had agreed with her about her leaving. "Like hell."

"Then, why didn't you answer the phone?"

She tried a laugh. It was about as convincing as her shrug earlier. "I was busy packing." The soda can spun and spun. "You think I was afraid it was him calling again? I wasn't scared of him when he called the first time, why would I be now?"

"Oh," Robin said, her arms crossed now. "You were scared, all right, just as scared as I was. You remember, you slept on the couch that night, with every light in the house on. And I slept in the chair right next to you just in case you woke up before morning. You're still scared. That's why you're running away."

The spinning can stopped dead in her grip. "I'm not running away. I'm leaving. There's a difference. If you don't understand that, I don't know why I'm bothering trying to explain it to you."

Then, she was up in that fluid motion of hers, out of the kitchen and down the hall. The door to her room slammed shut. Robin stayed by the sink, hugging herself. Kubiak thought of what she had said, about it making no difference how old they are. Without a word, he turned and followed Kimberly, knowing her mother wouldn't stop him.

She didn't respond to his soft knock, and again the doorknob wouldn't turn, so he crouched down to have a look at it. The keyed entry lock was about as cheap as they came. He straightened, opened the door with his Visa card, entered, shut the door behind him, and knocked softly again.

Kimberly was in front of her closet, holding a white blouse. She stood frozen for a moment, glaring at him, then resumed her packing.

"I could have you arrested for doing that," she said.

"Didn't Osgood tell you? The police can't hold me in this county."

"I don't trust anything Osgood says."

A large, square-cornered suitcase stood looking heavy beside the bed. She was currently stuffing a smaller canvas bag. Its sides were bulging.

"We keep finding common ground, Kimberly," Kubiak said. "Does that bother you as much as it does me?"

"What bothers me is a guy old enough to be my dad trying to be cool around me. Especially in my bedroom. Are you a creep, Mister Kubiak?"

He didn't bother answering, lifted the square-cornered suitcase, let it drop.

"What are you taking, the family silver?"

She let out a chortle. "If we had any."

"Was Paul a creep, Kimmy?"

She stopped packing, pulled out another cigarette. "Oh, I get it. It's Kimmy now. Look, in spite of what my mom thinks, I'm not a child. I'm twenty-two years old, and perfectly capable of kicking a man where it hurts if he touches me when I don't want him to. And no, Paul wasn't a creep. I told you, all he ever wanted from me was these."

She held up the cigarette, and lit it, taking another one of her short puffs. She looked so damned silly doing it, he wanted to slap it out of her mouth. No, that wasn't it. What he wanted to do, and God help him if he ever brought this up in front of Denise or Maria, was to slap little Kimberly's face until she began to cry, and then to hold her until she stopped. He wanted to kiss her once lightly on the forehead, the way he kissed his own daughter, then load those heavy bags into her mother's car for her, along with the title and every penny he had squandered on Neil Brady, wish that if she did find herself some handsome Wisconsin northwoods real estate speculator that he be bright enough to keep out of trouble with the police, and then wave good-bye, counting himself maybe one for two, maybe better, only time would tell.

"Where in the city are you going?" he asked.

"I've got friends who will put me up until I find a place."

He nodded.

Kimberly's face had softened. She might have been reading his.

"I'm not afraid," she said. "Really."

"Then why are you leaving, really?"

"You haven't figured it out yet? I just don't want to someday wind up . . . where my mom is. It's that simple. I suppose you think that's a cruel thing to say."

"Only if you say it to her."

Another chortle. She resumed packing, stopped again. "You know, Paul really wasn't such a bad guy, as far as the line that marches through here goes. I wouldn't have minded if he cracked a smile every now and then, though. It might have cheered things up a little around the house. He told us all about you."

"Oh?"

"That you're an ex-cop. That you were supposed to be working for him. I don't get it. How come you don't seem to be? Working for him, I mean."

"Maybe because he's dead."

"You know what I mean. You're supposed to be going on about how the cops killed Jack."

"The cops weren't the ones who called here and made those threats. Even Osgood believes that."

"So, who was it, then?"

"I'm not sure. But there's something in Jack's life that someone wants to keep covered so badly they're willing to kill Baumgarten to keep it covered. When I find out what that is, I'll know who was on the other end of the phone."

"And you think I can help you. I don't know how."

"I'm looking for secrets. You're his sister."

She was holding a straw beach hat with a brim too wide to fit in the canvas bag. She contemplated the hat, sat down on the bed with it in her lap, contemplated it some more.

"That doesn't mean everything you think," she said.

"We didn't see much of Jack after he moved out of here. He only came around every so often to give my mom money."

"How often was that?"

Kimberly smirked. "The end of every month. You probably noticed my mom has a little problem with . . . well, with what you've been feeding her all day. She hasn't held down a job for more than a few weeks since we came up here."

"Maybe I got it wrong, but I understood Jerry Wheeler supplied her with a loan or two to keep her on her feet."

"Yeah, you got it wrong. Those weren't loans. They were gifts."

"Even nicer. What's your mom doing right that everyone shows up at her door every month to give her money?"

"That's funny. Because, in Jerry's eyes it was everything but what she was doing right. Jerry and Bernice were determined to make a new life for Jack. I suppose when Jerry found out Jack was running over here every time the rent was due, he got a little nervous he might decide to stay, if only to make sure Mom wasn't opening up Pootie's cans to make her own dinner. It all came from the salary Jerry was paying Jack anyway, so he just cut out the middleman. Here's some money, Mrs. Mackay, mind if I pretend your son is mine for another thirty days? It was a sick arrangement any way you look at it."

"But Jack still came around every month."

"Yeah. I don't know if it was because he missed us so much or if he felt guilty for leaving. And my mom always took his money. I don't blame her for a minute though, if that's what you're thinking."

"I wasn't. I was thinking that, sick arrangement or no,

Jerry Wheeler was paying everybody's bills. I still can't figure out why your brother put two bullets into him."

She played with the hat some more, then stood and tossed it back into the closet.

"The only reason you're in this is to take somebody else's money to pay your bills," she said. "Just like the rest of the world, including that vulture, Osgood. I can't stand him, and you haven't yet given me one good reason why I should help you."

"It's like you told your mother," Kubiak said. "If you don't understand, there's no use my explaining it to you."

She glared, reached back for another cigarette, thought better of it, tucked her hands into her pockets. She pondered a full minute before speaking again.

"My brother wasn't much for worrying about how much he spent or where he spent it. Money went through his hands pretty quick, and he was always looking for more. Jack might have managed the lumberyard for Jerry Wheeler, but he still worked for Neil Brady. He always did."

"Was arranging for the free transfer of the Wheelers' merchandise to Brady's business really lucrative enough for Jack to throw away the second chance Jerry Wheeler was offering him?"

"It wasn't just what Jack could get away with at the lumberyard. It was everything Brady and his little group of thugs were promising him, a future as a rich punk. Jack never pushed drugs to anybody before he fell in with Neil Brady and Manny Padilla. Oh, he used, everybody knew that, and maybe he sold a little to his friends to pay for it, but he wasn't pushing for profit. That was Padilla's idea, to make a little money on the side. They followed him up here and found themselves a nice, lucrative market. Can you blame Jack, really? After all, everybody he ran into his whole life, including Jerry Wheeler, was doing all they could to change him from a happy, footloose guy into a first class businessman."

"What kinds of drugs?"

"Are you kidding? Whatever you can get hold of in Chicago and drive up to the dead heads in Round Lake Beach. A regular country buffet, everything but the corn relish."

"And as his trusting sister, Jack let you in on all of this?"

"Only some. But I live in this town, too. I mean, come on, he was busted for it once. Osgood has to know, as well, but he hasn't brought it up once with me or my mom. That's only one reason why I don't trust him."

"What are the others?"

"You're working under him. You figure it out."

"There's a lot I'm trying to figure out. I can get why Jack might consider everything Jerry Wheeler was offering him as nothing more than keys to the candy store, but I still can't fathom what Jerry Wheeler was thinking."

"You're asking the wrong person."

"Well, I can't ask Jerry."

"I told you, it was a sick relationship. All the yokels up here who would jump at the chance to clip on a tie and shuffle away their lives managing that lumberyard, look at the two the man insisted on foisting it on."

"A couple of free spirits."

"Exactly."

This time when she reached back she came up with another cigarette.

"Jack was busted for dealing marijuana," Kubiak said. "He had to stash his supply somewhere. He didn't keep it here?"

"Of course not."

"The Wheelers? How would he manage that?"

"I don't know. I didn't deal in my brother's business." She glanced at the large suitcase Kubiak had picked up and dropped, then back at Kubiak. "What, you don't think . . ."

"That isn't what I meant."

"Go ahead. Open it. I'm serious, you have my permission. You've been through everything else in the house." When Kubiak didn't move, she lit the cigarette, held it up before her. "This is the only drug I do, Mister Kubiak. I've seen what they did to Jack, and what they've done to my mom."

"I was thinking of a space larger than a suitcase. Your mother said Jack disappeared for periods of time. Any idea where he might have been?"

"He was with the Wheelers. My mother might like to think otherwise, but he lived with them."

"Sure, but he wasn't dealing out of their home. What about his girlfriend?"

"What girlfriend?"

"The bookkeeper at the lumberyard. Christine Hughes."

"Girlfriend? Christine?" She tilted her head back in a laugh. "I guess you could call her that. I guess she'd call herself that, wouldn't she? Everyone else knew better. I don't know who you've been talking to, Mister Kubiak, but if that's the kind of information you're getting, you've got your work cut out for you. The only reason Jack even spoke to that pig was because he needed her to cook the books. He'd do her once every pay period and she'd scramble up whatever numbers he needed scrambled so bad Jerry Wheeler couldn't make heads or tails of them."

Kimberly zipped the bag shut, swung it off the bed and

onto the floor. Hands on her hips, she gave the room a quick survey, nodding to herself at a job well done.

"Poor Jack," she said. "I hope Neil Brady appreciated the things he did for him."

Chapter Eighteen

Wheeler Lumber and Hardware was located about ten miles outside of Round Lake Beach, due east toward Waukegan. Robin and Kimberly each offered Kubiak directions, then argued over which route was quickest until Robin changed the subject by bringing up Kimberly's smoking habits again. When he left them in the kitchen, the debate had moved on to whose suitcase was whose. Kimberly waved a dismissive good-bye; Robin asked if she would see him again, seemed satisfied with a probably; Pootie didn't even bother following him to the door.

The drive didn't take long. Just as Kubiak was repeatedly surprised by the amount of traffic up here in what he considered far country, he had yet to grow accustomed to the distance one could cover on a two-lane road in a short period of time when street lights were spaced apart by miles rather than by city blocks. He missed the lumberyard among the clutter of businesses lining this section of state Highway 120, spotted it a quarter-mile on the backside of his U-turn. He pulled into its parking lot, left the

Contour in a space away from the front building, and took a stroll around the company's perimeter.

The property ran deep, about the length of a football field. Only the front lot was paved. Four long, open, corrugated steel sheds covered rows of twenty-foot high stacks of bundled units of lumber. He spotted no security cameras. With only a free-standing gate at the lot's entrance to ensure Jerry Wheeler's lumber stayed in his yard at night, Kubiak was surprised the owner hadn't hired his off-duty cops for security duty sooner than he had.

And with all this space available to the lumberyard's manager between dusk and dawn, Kubiak had to wonder if Jack might have been running his and Neil Brady's other lucrative business out of this address, as well. It would be audacious, but audacity fit into the profile Kubiak had so far of Jack Mackay, and unless he was shuttling himself somewhere besides here, the Wheelers' home, and his mother's apartment, he was doing it directly under someone's nose. If that were the case, Kubiak wondered further what might have happened when the off-duty cops who were on that list Baumgarten claimed to hold discovered what Jack was dealing behind their backs while they stood sentry at the detached gate.

He stared out past the long sheds, at the expanse of sky and green fields Robin had talked about. No, he had already dismissed that possibility. Too little take with too many palms to take it, too many honest cops, too many mouths that talk. Add to that however many employees worked at the lumberyard who might overhear or stumble across something, it was miraculous Jack was even able to spirit away any lumber.

Was this how Baumgarten had come up with his crazy theories, staring at that country sky, getting sucked up into its vast emptiness as one character after the next spun their version of Jack Mackay's life until a vision of conspiracy formed before his eyes? For the first time since coming up here Kubiak felt a touch of apprehension for his own safety. After all, might not Baumgarten have stood in this exact spot just a few days ago, staring out past that same shed, with the same thoughts running through his head? And hadn't Kubiak been warned by just about everyone he had come across in the past forty-eight hours, including his own wife, against walking forward in Baumgarten's footprints?

One of Wheeler's employees was approaching him now, a teenager in a polo shirt and khaki pants, wearing a sales floor smile. He asked if he could help him, and Kubiak said he was looking for Christine Hughes. The kid told him he wouldn't find her out here, guided him back around to the parking lot and into the front building.

Kubiak followed him through the hardware department, past the bathroom fixture displays to a counter in the back with windows that looked into a row of small offices. The kid knocked on the door of the last, opened it without waiting for a response from the other side, an act which got them both a frown from the young woman at her desk whose work they had interrupted. The kid backed out, leaving Kubiak to the frown.

With Kimberly's reference to Christine as a pig still in his head, Kubiak was expecting something very different from what sat before him, though the pinched face she aimed up at him kept her from qualifying for anything pleasant. She asked him what he wanted in a tone that said she didn't care to know.

Hers was the only chair in the tiny room, so Kubiak stayed on his feet. He began by introducing himself, which didn't change her expression at all. When he dropped Baumgarten's name, her face pinched even tighter. When Jack Mackay's landed, her eyes went back to her computer screen, her fingers to the keyboard.

"I'm sorry, Jack Mackay no longer works here."

"It would be quite a feat if he did."

Thankfully, her glare was directed at her computer. "If you have any questions, you'll have to talk to George."

"Is that company policy or personal?"

Christine tapped at her keys.

"So, George took over when Jack killed himself?"

"George is the office manager, so yes."

"Well, Tommy Wheeler now owns this place, and when I talked with him yesterday, he basically gave me carte blanche to find out everything I can about the circumstances of his parents' death as long as I got back to him."

"Tommy is very busy today. He and George both."

"I didn't say I wanted to talk with Tommy. I said I talked with Tommy."

Christine tapped. Tapped and tapped.

"Yesterday." He was facing the back of her computer. The power line ran to a surge protector which ran to a wall outlet only two paces in front of him. He took the two paces, bent, and pulled the plug from the outlet. The sound of tapping stopped.

"Oh my god."

He straightened. "I don't own a computer," he said, holding up the plug. "But I understand this sort of thing isn't good."

"Oh my god. Do you have any idea of what you've just done?"

"Not really. But if you'd like, you can call in either of your bosses, I'll plug this thing back in, and we can open up their books and show them how you managed to cover up all the merchandise you and Jack stole from them."

She blinked, blinked again. "I don't know what you're talking about."

"You don't have to bother denying anything to me. If I had any intention of sharing my information, somebody else would have pulled that plug before me. And if I don't get any from you, I'll see to it somebody will."

The door to the office was still open. Christine gave the doorway a glance. The kid in the khakis was back in it, curious. Kubiak shut the door. The kid's anxious face moved to the window. Kubiak glared at it until it disappeared, then turned back to Christine. Her expression had changed. Her eyes had narrowed. She looked capable of about anything.

"What do you want?" she asked.

"I want to know what happened between Jack and Jerry Wheeler that morning last June, that's all. I want to know why both of them are dead. I want to know why Bernice Wheeler was cooking bacon and eggs one minute, and lying in a pool of her own blood beside her kitchen sink the next. And the only thing I can come up with, is that the Wheelers finally found out it was Mackay robbing them blind. Jack is dead. You're still here behind your desk. It makes me wonder if the Wheelers were aware of your involvement, or if Jack killed them before they could do anything about it."

Kubiak watched her think.

"Who are you?" she asked.

"I told you, your boss wants some answers about that morning. Lucky for you, I was approached to find out those answers by someone else in Chicago last Friday.

I'm under no obligation to tell Tommy anything, and I would prefer to get back to Chicago as soon as possible."

"How do I know I can trust you?"

"You can't. All you can do is convince me not to talk to Tommy."

He watched her think some more.

"I never took a penny of the Wheelers' money for myself," she said, finally. "I only did what I could to keep them from finding out about Jack."

"But they did."

"They had to have, sooner or later. I told Jack as much. It was out of control. I did everything I could to stop him, you have to believe that."

"How did they find out?"

"I don't know. Honestly. I got a call from Jack that night."

"What night?"

"The night before he died. Monday. Jerry hadn't shown up to work that day. Jack said he was waiting for him when he went home after work, that he told him he knew, and to get out of his house and his life."

"Did Jerry say he was going to call the police?"

"No."

"This was the night before, you say."

"That's right."

"Did Jack call you from the Wheelers?"

"No. Jerry told him to get out, and he did."

"Where was he, then?"

"I don't know."

"He didn't say?"

"No."

"You must have some idea."

"No, I don't. You have to understand, Jack would just go away sometimes. It was just better not to ask. But he wanted to warn me, even though Jerry didn't mention my name, about what might be coming down the next morning. That was the kind of guy Jack was."

"And what did you do?"

"There was nothing I could do. Of course, I was scared to death, but I came in as usual, hoping for the best. When neither of them showed . . . Then, later, George took us all into Jerry's office. . . ."

It was Kubiak's turn to think. "What time did he call you?"

"Around eight."

Eleven hours before all three were dead.

"Was the gun still here that Monday, or had Jack already taken it out of the office?"

"What gun? Jerry's gun?"

"The Combat Masterpiece."

"Jerry's gun. He took it home himself."

"You said he wasn't here that day."

"He took it out of here a good five, six months ago." She read his look. "Ask anybody around here. Jerry didn't make a secret of it. In fact, I typed up the memo we posted for the security guys that it wasn't there anymore. They wanted to know if there were any firearms on the premises."

"Why did he take it?"

"Because he didn't like Jack's friends from Chicago coming around his house. He thought he'd scare them off."

"Neil Brady's gang?"

She nodded.

"Did he?"

"What?"

"Scare them off."

"Well, it doesn't matter, does it? What matters is that the old man got used to waving a gun around to make his point. And that's what got him killed."

"And Jack Mackay just happened to be there."

She leaned forward in her chair. She was no longer guarded, but still angry. "It was Jerry's gun. It was Jerry's house. I don't know why Jack went back there the next morning. Maybe he just wanted to pick up a thing or two he left there. Maybe he wanted to make things right. And nobody was there but the three of them, so who's to say what happened?"

"It's pretty obvious how it turned out."

"Jerry's no more dead than Jack. But nobody's going to take Jack's side over his, are they? Nobody in Round Lake Beach. Nobody in this lumberyard. Not even you. But how do you think Jack got those wounds in his leg and face? Are you going to believe the cops? That he shot himself? Like I said, it was Jerry's gun. It was Jerry's house."

"You think Jerry Wheeler shot him."

"Of course he did. He waved that gun at Jack, and this time it went off. It went off when Jack was trying to take it from him. It went off into his leg, and into his face. But Jack still managed to get hold of it, and when he shot Jerry he didn't miss. And then he shot Bernice, too, and I don't blame him a bit for that, either, and if either one of them had been the one to make it out of that house alive, they'd have been called heroes. But it was Jack who came out, so the police chased him down like some kind of animal, and made up that crazy story about him shooting himself just to keep Jerry and Bernice's names clean."

"If Jack had been wounded in that house, there would have been evidence of it."

"Evidence covered up."

How had Osgood put it? Her own bone of contention.

"I'd guess you didn't mention this theory to the police?" he asked.

"How could I? I told Jack's mother, and she took me in to talk to their lawyer, but he didn't seem interested. I hoped that when that Baumgarten came around he might . . ." Her eyes darted to the window behind Kubiak. "I don't suppose . . ."

The office door opened abruptly. Kubiak hadn't noticed the small crowd gathered on the other side of it. A man in a white oxford shirt and a tie set one foot into the room and asked Christine if she was all right. Surprised and trying to figure which way to play the situation, she didn't answer him quickly enough, so he turned his concerned face on Kubiak, was about to open up his mouth when the familiar figure of Tommy Wheeler pushed his way past him.

"What the hell, George? Hey, it's Mister Kubiak."

Tommy stood, gawking, his hands on his hips. Like George, he was in a shirt and tie, but he was also wearing a corduroy sportcoat that had seen its share of use. He shook his head, smiled, and the tension in the room dissipated, as did the crowd outside the door. Christine muttered something about her computer, her eyes still on Kubiak. Kubiak pointed at the wall where it should have been plugged in. While George tended to the task, Tommy gently escorted Kubiak out of the office. They were followed by a heavyset man in a dark suit carrying a soft leather briefcase.

"You should have called and told me you were coming in today," Tommy said as they moved back past the bathroom fixture displays. "I could have arranged to introduce you to everybody, save you from having to break the ice, or whatever that was you were doing in there with Christine."

"I didn't think you'd be here."

"Well, you're right, I'm usually not. It's just luck we happened to be doing another walk-through this afternoon."

"We?"

"Oh, sorry." He and Kubiak stopped so the heavyset man could catch up. "Dan Allen. He's an old friend of my parents, even sold them this property back when they moved the business out here."

Kubiak recognized the name from the realty sign on the front lawn of the Wheelers' house. Allen transferred his briefcase to his left hand, extended his right.

"He's taking over the power of attorney for this place, and the house, so I don't have to walk through any more walk-through's. The three C's, right, Dan? Care, control . . . and whatever that third C is."

"Custody." Allen's smile was strained.

"Right." Tommy touched Kubiak's arm, got the three of them moving again. "Sorry, it's been a long afternoon."

Kubiak nodded. He could smell the bar tab on Tommy's breath.

"Mister Kubiak and I go way back, ourselves," Tommy said over his shoulder to Allen. "All of twenty-four hours." He let out another of his wet snorts. "We got arrested together yesterday."

Allen plastered the smile on again, this time wound up looking more like a red-faced lunatic. All buttoned down for business with a briefcase full of freshly signed forms, this wasn't the sort of small talk Kubiak imagined he liked to hear from his clients.

"Brothers," Tommy said, squeezing Kubiak's shoulder. "Breakin' the law."

"How did you make out?" Kubiak asked him.

"Yesterday? Not too bad. I got a long lecture. They threatened me about that beer I left in the cup holder, but they were happy to let it go when I answered their questions about you. I only told them that you were interested in seeing where Jack Mackay died because that was pretty obvious. I didn't say anything about Baumgarten. I figured that was how you'd want it."

"Thanks. You talk to your lawyer?"

"No. You think I should?"

"What's his name?"

"He's a her. Amy Martin. She handled my DUI. Why?"

"You talk to anybody else once they let you go?"

"No. They had my car towed, and I had to get it out. By the time I got home it was pretty late. Detective Strom gave me his number, told me to stay away from you, that if you tried to contact me again I should give him a call."

"He say why?"

"No."

"You plan to?"

"No. Maybe he knew you were coming by here today?"

"I don't see how. I didn't. You got the number on you?"

"Sure." Tommy fished a card out of his wallet, passed it to Kubiak, who copied the number. When they reached the front door, Tommy held it open for both Kubiak and Allen, paused to light a cigarette, then came back up beside Kubiak.

"I haven't forgotten about our deal," he said. "You run across any information about my parents' death I ought to know about?"

Kubiak thought of the conversation he had just finished with Christine Hughes, couldn't imagine the contortions

Allen's face might go through were he to relate it back to Tommy verbatim.

"Like you said," he told Tommy. "It's only been twenty-four hours."

"Yeah, seems longer, though." Tommy took a deep drag on his cigarette, blew the smoke up at the sky. "Boy, it's good to be out of there. This place makes me nervous. It's been years since I put any time in the yard. Except for George and Christine, I don't know the name of a single employee, but everybody seems to know me. Dan, am I done with this thing or what?"

"Pretty near. A couple more points."

Tommy once more steered Kubiak by his shoulder, pressed him another few feet ahead of Allen. "By the way, you figure out yet how we got busted yesterday?"

"I'm still working on it."

"Well, it might have been my fault. You remember, after I agreed to run you up to Loon Lake I went back into the Legion again to pick up my stuff? Charlie, the bartender, asked where we were headed. My big mouth, I told him. Charlie's an ex Round Lake cop, and the place is full of off-duty cops, anyway, and every geezer who isn't is some old soldier who's signed up for one of those citizens' police academy things and has 911 programmed into his phone. I'm sure one of them called the chief of the Round Lake Beach P.D. just because they thought he ought to know. What I don't get, though, is how we wound up getting busted by the county sheriff, and why they sent three cars for just the two of us. You think you're more wanted than you realize?"

"I think it's more likely that the Round Lake P.D. didn't want to come near either of us, and didn't have to as long as we were heading out of their jurisdiction. As for the number of cars, I'd imagine Strom felt more comfortable with witnesses if he was going to be busting anybody up at Loon Lake."

"Yeah. I guess that makes sense."

"Was Strom the one who contacted you about the death of your parents?"

"No. It was a couple of Round Lake cops. Why?"

"Where were you when they notified you?"

Tommy's face darkened. "I haven't been asked a question like that since it happened."

"I'm dredging things up. You'll be asked more like it."

"I was in Wisconsin that morning. Madison, doing sound for a band I do a lot of work with. They played a college bar with a four o'clock license. We finished breaking down about four-thirty, decided to have breakfast. The band dropped me back home late that morning. There was a message from the cops on my machine. I called them, the two cops knocked on my door with the news five minutes later." Tommy inhaled deeply on the cigarette, stared back at the lumberyard. "I look back on that breakfast, we never laughed so hard. I don't remember at what. Maybe we had all just been up too long. The way we figure it, though, it was right at that time that Mackay and my folks . . ."

Tommy flicked away his cigarette. "You go ahead and do your dredging, Mister Kubiak. Remember, you find out anything, let me know. If I'm not around, you can always call Dan. Dan's always around."

Allen produced a card from his palm quick as a magician, then he and Tommy turned and disappeared back inside the building, leaving Kubiak standing beside his car, just where Tommy had deposited him.

Chapter Nineteen

"This is Crawford."

"Crawford, don't hang up."

There was a pause, then the line clicked and a dial tone sounded. Kubiak pumped more coins into the phone, punched the same numbers again. The pay phone, attached to the wall of a convenience store, was too close to the noise of the street traffic, the cord from the box to the receiver so short he had to press himself against the metal enclosure in order to stand up straight.

He counted nine rings before Crawford picked up the phone again.

"You know, the kid at the White Hen could only spare me so many quarters."

"Listen to me, Kubiak. I'm going to say this once. When this mess is over, you and I will have a nice, long conversation over the phone. Probably with a sheet of lexan between us."

"That's funny."

"Until then, I can't afford to be involved in whatever it is you've gotten yourself into."

"But you already are involved. You were the one who brought those two jokers, Strom and Dunning, into my living room."

"I was doing you a favor. You chose not to take advantage of it, and that's why you're out on your own right now."

"Okay, have it your way. Grant me this favor, and I promise to take advantage of it."

"Sorry. Good-bye, old buddy."

"Hold on, Crawford. Listen to me. Three days ago I was right where you are now, only I was holding a pretzel and a beer, and across the table from me, Paul Baumgarten was asking for my help. I didn't listen to him. I turned around and walked away."

"And now he's dead. Kubiak, are you actually intimating that if I refuse to do your bidding I might personally be responsible for your demise?"

"You don't have to sound so thrilled at the prospect."

The line clicked, and a woman's clipped voice interrupted, demanding twenty-five cents for the next minute. Kubiak dropped another quarter into the phone.

"All right, Crawford, I'm just about out of change."

"Thank goodness for that."

"You can either help me or leave me hanging, but I don't have time to argue which. I want you to get hold of the Lake County Sheriff's Department and find out if they've got a list of their boys working security for Wheeler Lumber and Hardware. I'm not certain how it works up here, but I'm pretty sure any freelancing has to be approved by the sheriff himself. I don't need the list, I just want to know if there is one and if they're willing to share it with somebody out of Cook County."

"You want them to share the list, but you don't want to see it."

"No, the fact is I don't care to see it. And while you're talking to them, see if you can get the dispatch records for the Tuesday morning Mackay died. I want to know the time the 911 call from Jerry Wheeler came in, the time the description of Mackay's car went out, when they spotted it and where, and if possible, when they ran Mackay into the ditch."

The voice demanding money interrupted again. Kubiak dumped his last two quarters into the slot.

"Crawford, you there?" He pressed his finger into his free ear to muffle the noise from the traffic, heard a sharp, angry sigh on the other end of the line. "Okay, you got a pen? I'm going to give you three names and spell them out. Neil Brady, Christine Hughes, and . . . George."

"Is that George with an e?"

"You know, you get funnier as time passes. This George took Mackay's place as manager at Wheeler Lumber and Hardware. I only want to know something about him because I don't know anything about him. Find out whatever you can from the investigation on the Wheeler homicide. The same goes for Christine Hughes, but I also want her home address, and if you can manage, whether she lives alone or with a roommate or her parents. And I want you to verify that Tommy Wheeler was where he says he was that morning, having breakfast in Wisconsin.

"Neil Brady's out of Chicago, but the information I need about him you'll have to get from up here, as well. He's a contractor, but also buys and sells fixer-uppers."

"Another real estate speculator."

"That's right. I'm curious as to whether he owns any

property up here in Round Lake Beach. It's after five, and the village offices are closed. Somebody will have to get hold of the assessor and drag him or her back to their desk."

"How on earth do you expect me to do that from down here?"

"I don't. I expect Strom to do it for you. Like I said, Brady works out of Chicago, but he doesn't have an office. As of last night, he was using a vacant room on the third floor of a building on Ashland." Kubiak gave him the address. "Check it out, he might still be there. I'll guarantee he's got a record. Throw it in front of Strom, along with the fact I'm back up here and these questions came from me, and he'll get moving quick enough, if only to cover his butt. In fact, let me give you his direct number, and you can tell him that came from me, as well."

"I've already got a direct line to Strom," Crawford stated flatly. "In fact, he even gave me the number of his personal cell phone."

"And you wonder why I call on you. You have access to everyone and everything."

"He contacted me this afternoon. He wants your son-in-law, and he's got a warrant. Where's Hollinger, Kubiak?"

"I don't know."

"They've been to your apartment. Nobody's there. Where are Denise and Maria?"

"I don't know."

"What do you mean you don't know? Stop screwing with these guys. Give up your son-in-law to them and worry about sorting things out later. They're serious, and they don't like us, and if they decide to go after you there's very little I or anybody here can do to stop them."

There was another click, and the voice asking for money came on the line again. This time Kubiak was relieved to hear it. He began an apology for being out of change, then depressed the cradle in the middle of his sentence, putting the blame for the disconnection, as far as Crawford was concerned, solely on SBC Ameritech.

Chapter Twenty

The sun was setting behind the house. Silhouetted, its face in shadow, the wood-sided ranch looked older, more weathered than it had yesterday under the flat light of midday. Kubiak had been staring at it for some time, parked at the curb again, as he finished the coffee he had purchased at the convenience store. Now, he dropped the empty styrofoam cup onto the passenger's seat and climbed out of the car, opened the trunk, tucked the windshield ice scraper into his back pocket, and headed up toward the Wheelers' home.

This time he didn't approach along the driveway, but walked across the lawn, past the FOR SALE sign advertising Dan Allen's name in fat, block letters, and around the side of the house opposite the garage. The backyard was small, the trees old, tall, and full. The neighbor directly behind the Wheelers had put up a privacy fence, which made the area behind the house feel even more condensed and dark. There was no back door, only three shoulder-high windows looking into the raised first floor and two deep window wells leading to the basement. With a glance over his shoulder and a grunt, Kubiak climbed down into the closest well, squatted out of sight in its filthy bottom, and addressed the window's frame.

The wood was old, rotted. The ice scraper slid in easily. Funny, he thought, tapping with the heel of his hand on the base of the scraper, that of the dozen or so entrances he had jimmied in his lifetime the last three break-in's had taken place in as many days. His method must have been improving as well, as opening the swollen window wide enough for him to squeeze through proved to take more effort than had freeing the lock. When he guessed there was enough space for his body to pass, he slid into the basement, limbo-style, and shut the window behind him.

His eyes still adjusting to the light, he began to move across the cement floor, brushing against a pull-cord dangling from above. He tugged on it, and fluorescent bulbs flickered on to coldly illuminate Jerry Wheeler's workshop. Jerry had kept it neat, except for a clutter of works in progress stacked in one of the basement's corners: a bench without legs; a hard-edged, unvarnished set of shelves; a chunk of carved wood leaning against that, pieces of a whole Kubiak couldn't put together. Unfinished projects that never would see completion, bits of work meticulously measured and cut, now lucky to be sold for garage sale pennies.

The basement staircase was wider than average and led up to a set of double doors, evidently more of Jerry Wheeler's handiwork. Kubiak could imagine him finishing his first masterpiece in his new workshop, only to realize he couldn't fit it into the house through the existing basement door. So, another project, another pounding of the nail gun at 7 A.M. Kubiak wondered if one of the finishing touches might have been to put a bolt on that double door, but he found it unlocked. Tommy had said his father was a trusting man.

The doors opened at the end of a hallway, with the kitchen directly to Kubiak's right. He entered it first, crossed to the outside door with the small window through which he had peered into the kitchen yesterday, looked out across the short walkway at the garage's side door, then turned and took in the room where Bernice had died. It had been cleaned up thoroughly. But then, it would have to have been before the FOR SALE sign went up. There were services that did that sort of thing, though Kubiak assumed that Tommy had managed it himself, probably with the help of neighbor Andy Shultz. Even the grout in the kitchen tile had been scrubbed spotless. Kubiak couldn't guess where Bernice's body had lain.

He went back into the hallway. There was a pungent odor, familiar, chemical, that he couldn't place, maybe cleaning solvents. The sun's slanted rays coming in through the windows played crazy shafts of light and shadows throughout the house. The front room, with its single, wide window facing east, was dark. Except for a large screen television set, the furniture was old, but clean. There was an upright piano against one wall, and Kubiak thought of Tommy practicing as a child, his mother and father listening, perhaps sitting together on the couch, perhaps busy in another room but listening all the same, tracking his progress, never imagining that one day he would defiantly declare that he was stepping away from the family business in order to attempt to make an impossible bohemian living as a musician.

Kubiak continued on, found the source of the odor in the master bedroom. New carpet. It nearly matched that in the rest of the house. He went around to the other side of the double bed where Jerry Wheeler had lain after he had been shot twice while phoning the police. At least one of the bullets had gone through his body, as the wall had to be spackled near the base and repainted. Aside from that, the fresh carpet laid down in only one room, and the tile grout scrubbed too white, prospective buyer Kubiak might have thought the home's previous owners had simply retired to Tampa.

But the scene Christine Hughes had painted for him had not taken place here. There had been no bloody footprints, no errant shots, or he would have seen some evidence of the clean-up afterward. Besides, just the one bullet she accused Jerry Wheeler of sending through Jack's cheek in a struggle for the gun would have provided a finished canvas on any wall or ceiling for the crime scene crew, resulting in a police report that would have squelched any chance of Osgood's bringing a case into court against the department and sent Baumgarten shuffling, stoop-shouldered and penniless, back to Waukegan.

He made a cursory inspection of the rest of the rooms, was heading back toward the kitchen when he had the feeling something in the house had changed. He thought it might have been only the light, then realized it was the air in the hallway; the stagnant mustiness of the house had been displaced, if only for a moment, by a wash of fresher air, as if someone had opened a window or door. He stopped, heard nothing, felt a ghostly chill between his shoulder blades, continued into the kitchen and was nearly to the outside door when he heard the sole of a shoe scrape against the tile floor behind him.

He half turned. Andy Shultz had taken two steps into the

room and had stopped. He was holding a steel blue, semi-automatic pistol aimed at Kubiak's torso. He held it low.

"Be careful, Kubiak."

Kubiak didn't move.

"What's that in your back pocket?"

For an instant Kubiak couldn't guess what he was referring to, then he realized it must have been the ice scraper and told him so.

"Like hell. Let's see it."

"I'll be glad to show it to you, Andy, but be warned, if you shoot me while I'm taking it out of my pocket you'll feel even sillier than if you don't."

Kubiak extracted the scraper slowly, gently set it on the kitchen table. Shultz glared at the piece of plastic, then at Kubiak, then back at the scraper.

"I thought I might run into you here," Kubiak said. "I didn't expect the gun, though. Where did you get it?"

"It's mine. Why?"

"Ever use it?"

"Haven't had to yet."

"Well, let's keep it that way. You people in Round Lake ought to consider putting in alarm systems rather than keeping pistols in drawers. You all might live longer."

"You broke in here. I have every legal right to shoot you dead."

"Do you, Andy? Even if it's not your house?"

"I have a key. I'm caretaker and custodian."

"You're a neighbor, and you have a phone and could have dialed 911 in the time it took you to get that gun. The only difference between you and me is that I came in the window and you used the door. We're both trespassing, and I found out yesterday how Lake County deals with trespassers. I was only walking around in a field of weeds and they kept me in Waukegan half the day. Imagine if you blew my brains out in the Wheelers' kitchen. You'd have to put a hold on your mail."

Shultz said nothing. Kubiak could hear the deep, heavy breaths passing through the man's nose. The room had grown dimmer in just the short time since Kubiak had examined the floor tile, the sun's horizontal rays turned a darker gold.

"So," Kubiak said, "what do we do now?"

"You tell me."

"Well, I count three options. You can shoot me, or you can call the police, or you can shoo me out of here. I'd prefer you don't shoot me, and you've already called the police on me once and it only brought us back around to this point."

"I don't know what you're talking about."

"No? Then, why did Tommy go out of his way this afternoon to set me straight on that phone call? He wanted to make excuses, claimed that when he mentioned at the Legion yesterday that we were running up to Loon Lake one of the old veterans in there picked up the phone to let the Round Lake P.D. in on that bit of gossip. I don't think that happened. When he left me outside, his cell phone was still sitting on the bar. You had just called to inform him I was on my way to see him. I think he called you back to let you know I found him, and he told you where we were headed. I don't know why you phoned the police, and I doubt he was too happy about it. I imagine you got an earful last night when he finally got home."

"You talked to Tommy today?"

"Just a couple of hours ago. He was with his realtor at the lumberyard."

Shultz thought that out a moment before he spoke. "I

didn't know who you were. Neither did he. After what happened to that Baumgarten fellow the other night, he was a fool to get in a car with you and go up to Loon Lake."

"You didn't simply dial 911 and ask the dispatcher to send a few cars to meet us up there just in case I had a claw hammer in the pocket of my jacket. Who did you talk to, Strom or Dunning?"

"What does it matter? Let me tell you something about those two detectives, Kubiak. Of all the cops who came down on this house that morning and in the days after, those two were the only ones who ever gave me the impression they cared about what happened to Bernie and Jerry. The rest, I'd watch them go about their business and then gather around together and have a smoke and a laugh. But Strom and Dunning never joined that group. They treated what happened here as the grievous matter it was, and I'll always appreciate that."

"Maybe it was as personal to them as it was to you."

"You can believe what you want, but you don't have the right to come around here and throw it in everyone's face. What happened happened, and I don't see where it's any of your business."

"It became my business when Paul Baumgarten tossed my daughter's name at me six hours before he got himself bludgeoned to death in my son-in-law's truck. You've got your dead acquaintances, Andy, and I've got mine."

"It's been gone over, Kubiak. Over and over."

"Has it? Then, what are you protecting right now besides the Wheelers' good china? What secrets are worth placing yourself one squeeze of that trigger short of murder?"

Shultz's face grew darker; the breaths through his nose came slower, deeper. "Jerry Wheeler gave more to this town than it ever gave back to him."

"Yeah, so I hear. I don't care what he did or didn't do, I'm only concerned with how and why he died the way he did."

The two men glared at one another.

"Okay," Shultz said. "Okay. So, I answer a couple of your questions and then send you out of here. What guarantee do I have you won't be back?"

"You still don't get it. Nothing is going to stop Osgood from bringing his civil suit to court. Whatever you don't tell me in this room you're going to be subpoenaed to tell at a hearing, anyway. At this point, you can't do anything to stop it."

Shultz breathed some more. Leaning against the kitchen table, he looked around the kitchen as if he had just entered it after a long absence, or was about to leave it for some time. Then, he sank into one of the table's chairs, sat back until his face was in shadow. The pistol still glinted in the last of the sun's light.

"There aren't any secrets, Kubiak," he said, "but if you think you can understand why Jerry died without concern for what he did in his life, then you might as well walk out of here right now. You say you got a daughter?"

"That's right."

"She happy? Healthy?"

"More of the latter."

"That's enough. You count your blessings every day?" Then, before Kubiak could answer, "Well, who does?" Shultz shifted his weight. The pistol's aim didn't waver. "Anne, my wife, she passed away four years ago. She never worked a day in her life. It wasn't that she didn't want to, it's just that she never planned to. She was going to raise our family. So instead, she made our home what it was, spent her time with her friends, watched them, one after the next, become mothers twice, maybe three times over. Those first five, ten, hell, fifteen years, we were ready to join them any day. Expecting to be expecting. You're younger than me, Kubiak, but not so young you don't remember a time before they were freeze-drying sperm and shuffling eggs from one womb to the next. You remember when all that started. When was that, the seventies, right? One day it's science fiction, then it's a newspaper headline, the world's first test tube baby. Before you know it, there are a dozen clinics in downtown Chicago advertising fertility in the yellow pages. When was it that all changed?"

"I don't know. It could have been the late seventies. Maybe the eighties."

"No. I'm telling you, it was the seventies."

"Okay, Andy. You're the one holding the gun. It was the seventies."

"I remember, I'd clip out every newspaper and magazine article I'd run across, and show them to her. I saved them, too, kept them all in a manila envelope. One morning, I was in the kitchen having my breakfast, saw another piece in the paper about what all those scientists were up to. Anne was always a late sleeper. I cut it out, left it on the table for her, went out to clear the snow out of the drive. It had snowed that night. I remember, it was the first snow of the season. I got about half done, and came inside to warm up, and there she was at the table, holding that article and crying like a child. It took all morning for me to get out of her what had set her off. She said she couldn't stand it anymore, that she felt like she was lying in a hospital bed dying of cancer and reading about a cure for the disease coming down the line so close for everyone else, but too late for her. She asked me to stop bringing up the subject, that it was nothing but torture every word I said about it, and we never brought it up again. That afternoon, I took that manila envelope out and dumped it in the trash, one article at a time. It was nothing but a stack of old, yellow paper, but I never had more trouble letting anything go.

"The funny part is, Anne came from a family of seven kids, her three sisters all fertile as cats, which only made it worse. All that was ever expected of her in life was that she be a mother. Eventually, we tried to adopt, but with our age and situation there was no way we were ever moving up the list. Tried foster care, and got a couple of kids for a period of time, but they were older, came with their own sets of problems. It didn't work out. Strangely enough though, I think that might have been what put the spark in Jerry and Bernie's head to take in Mackay."

"Kimberly called their taking Jack in just another one of Jerry's projects," Kubiak said. "Was that what it was?"

"No. It was simpler than that. Just an empty nest that was aching to be filled back up. I'm sure Jerry thought he could make a better go at that sort of thing than we had, or than he had the first time through with Tommy. And at first, I, like everybody else, thought he would. The families came together well. Jack was a charmer from the get-go. Robin was grateful for the help. Bernice certainly had the time, and both she and Jerry had the will. That was back when there seemed enough time and spirit to make everything turn out right as rain. Of course, that didn't last long. That part never does."

Andy leaned forward, and Kubiak could see the outline of his face. "You know," he said, "how there's that point in people's lives where, when you look back, you can recognize it as that fork where they make their choice that determines everything? You move one way, and everybody's life just keeps humming along the way it has. Turn just a bit in the other direction, though, and even though the path doesn't look any different, it leads straight down into a world of darkness. That was the path they took, and not a one of them had a clue they'd taken it.

"Of course, the whole idea behind Jack's moving in with Jerry and Bernie was to give the boy a cleaner environment, but that was the start of the trouble. Jack refused to let go of his friends, and vice versa. For a number of months, this house was a magnet for every lowlife Jack had ever known. Jerry finally drove them off; he had to threaten to use a gun more than once. I don't think a home alarm would have done the trick."

Shultz waved the barrel of his own pistol to punctuate the sarcasm.

"The problem was," he continued, "that it drove off Jack, too. He'd take Bernie's Civic and disappear for days at a time, he wouldn't say where. Jerry did know that he sometimes stayed with his mother, so he thought it might be best to distance the boy from her, as well. I don't suppose Robin factored that part in when she handed her son over to him."

"So, he started paying her a cash stipend to stay in her good graces."

"What choice did he have? He couldn't sit by and watch her get thrown out on the street. And if she turned Jack against him, they'd all be right back where they started, which wouldn't have been such a bad thing as it turned out, though, like I said, nobody could have known that at the time."

"Somebody could have. You paint people into corners, they have to come through you to get out of them."

"Jerry only meant the best for Jack. They were both strong willed, but Jerry had spent his life bending people in the direction he thought they should go, which was usually the right direction, and the right direction for Jack Mackay was to bury him in work at the lumberyard. Jerry gave him responsibility, a twelve hour day of honest work, and a future. I don't have to tell you how Mackay returned that favor."

"Evidently, Mackay didn't consider it a favor."

"No. He considered it an opportunity, one he could take advantage of. I'm not saying Jerry didn't sometimes come down too hard on people. He pushed, and sometimes he pushed too hard. He pushed his own son out of this house, and pulled Robin Mackay in close where he could keep her under his thumb. He broke up Tommy and Kim Mackay's relationship when he thought it wouldn't do either of them any good, and was in the process of doing the same with Jack and Christine Hughes because he would have rather believed it was her stealing his money than Jack. And when he figured he couldn't trust the local P.D. to find out who was taking his lumber, what did he do? He put them on his payroll. There wasn't anyone painted into a corner, Kubiak. Jerry had no power over anybody who didn't mind giving up the taking of his money."

Suddenly Shultz shoved his chair away from the table. The sound of its feet scraping along the floor seemed incredibly loud. He moved, casually, back to the doorway through which he had come, flipped on the switch to the overhead light. Both men squinted as the room became an island of bright tile and shiny walls painted semigloss white.

"Take a look around you. You've been through the

house. You've seen the car Bernie drove. Jerry didn't even have his own car, he used one of the lumberyard's vans. They never had any money, the business was always just making it. Those thefts hurt. Jerry didn't know how bad they were hurting him until the end. He never wanted to believe it was Mackay, either. That's why he let things go on so long. But the cops he'd hired finally convinced him otherwise.

"I saw him the morning of the day before he died. I came over to return a video I'd borrowed. It was around ten o'clock, and Jerry still hadn't gone in to work, which was unusual. Bernie was making up a late breakfast and insisted I stay and join them. Right here." Shultz bent and rapped his knuckles on the top of the kitchen table. "Where I last saw them. They both looked an unhealthy kind of tired, and when Bernie was out of the room Jerry told me he'd made up his mind. He'd given up on Mackay. He had packed Jack's things and they were in the garage. He wasn't going in to work because he didn't want to confront Mackay in the yard, so he was going to wait until the end of the day, then let him know he was not only fired but was no longer welcome on either of his properties. He told me he'd made a mistake giving away his son's bedroom to a stranger, and that he was going to go back into the yard the next morning and take back the reins of the business he'd built, then get hold of Tommy and get on his knees if he had to, but bring that boy back into the family. He'd tried to substitute his son with a son of his own making, and by refusing to admit he'd failed to manage the task he'd brought them all nothing but grief."

"I don't get it," Kubiak said. "You were aware of all this, why is Tommy still offering me money to find out why Mackay killed his parents?"

"Because he doesn't know."

"You haven't told him."

"Nobody knows, Kubiak, except me, the police from the pieces I bothered explaining to them, and now you. Imagine Tommy inheriting everything his parents owned and then being told they died only because they wanted him to have it. He'd walk away from it all over again. I can't let him do that."

"But his father. Didn't Jerry try to get hold of Tommy before dealing with Mackay?"

"No. He wanted to stop the bleeding first, then take the time to make amends. Of course, he never had the chance to do either."

"Why you, Andy?" Kubiak asked after a moment. He asked the question with his eyes set squarely on the pistol's barrel now carelessly aimed at the floor. It didn't turn upward.

"Why me? Because I'm all the boy has right now. I never really knew Tommy but through Jerry and Bernie when they were alive. I never knew how decent a kid he was until they were gone and there was no one left to keep their memory alive but him and me. Besides, I owe at least that much to Bernie and Jerry for that morning."

He looked around the room again, and when his eyes lingered on a spot on the floor next to a low set of cabinets, Kubiak at last knew just where Bernice Wheeler's body had lain.

"I slept through it all," he said. "Didn't know anything had happened until the cop pounding on my front door finally dragged me out of bed. After Anne died, I discovered a surefire way to put myself to sleep every night. Start drinking around three, four in the afternoon, and just keep at it. It works like a charm, believe me, and I didn't have anything to do, anyway no one to see. By midnight every night, I managed to be stone, cold out. I don't know that I could have done anything to help if I had woke up at the sound of those gunshots that morning, but I haven't touched a drop since. So, now instead, I watch this house when I probably don't have to, waiting for it to sell so it isn't my responsibility any more, keep an eye on Tommy until . . . Until what, Kubiak? What do you do when they're all gone and there's nothing left?"

"I don't know," Kubiak said. "Something tells me I'm not going to live long enough to have to worry about it."

"That's what I thought. But look at me now." Shultz smiled then. The only smile Kubiak would ever see on his face, it held more melancholy than his vacant stare. He was alone with himself for a half a minute, then rediscovered Kubiak sharing the kitchen with him. "What?" The sad smile turned bitter. "Get out of here, Kubiak. Go home to your wife and daughter and leave these families to what's left of their lives." Shultz brought the gun's barrel back to horizontal. "I mean it. Get out."

Kubiak didn't argue nor hesitate. He did, however, pull the Contour around to the block behind the Wheelers' home and park where he could see their kitchen window. A good half hour passed before the light in it went out and Andy Shultz's figure passed slowly between the houses.

Chapter Twenty-one

"This is Crawford."

Kubiak liked this tone less than the one he had hung up on earlier. "What's the matter?" he asked. "What have you found out?"

Silence. Then, in a voice even colder, "Only what you wanted me to. You know, if you want to take the fall for your son-in-law, there are easier ways to do it. Just walk into the nearest police facility and confess. At least that will leave me out of the mix."

"Sorry, Crawford, I don't get it. Tell me what I'm missing."

"That's the problem, Kubiak. You don't miss a trick. Listen. Tell me where you are, I'll send a car up there to bring you back to Cook County. We can hold you here for forty-eight hours as a suspect in the Brady assault. That's two days Strom can't get to you but through us. After that, you're on your own. It isn't much, but it's the deal you set up."

The deal he had set up.

The Brady assault.

The tavern's pay phone was in the vestibule by the front door. Out of the corner of Kubiak's eye he caught his waitress far down the line of booths waving to him, holding high his plate of food. He waved back and she set it down.

"Would that be," he asked, "the Neil Brady assault?"

"I think if I were you I might have phoned it in anonymously, then burned some time and asked me about him after I'd gotten the news. But you had to jump the gun, same as you did with the Baumgarten homicide. I sent Griffith up to that address you gave me on Ashland. You remember Griffith?"

"No. I don't remember Griffith."

"He has little nails that scratch. He's interested in what he found up there, and I made the mistake of calling Strom concerning your errands before Griffith got back to me. Right now, I'm in as tight a spot as you could have put me."

"What happened to Brady?"

"The word is he's dead."

"Whose word? What word? Griffith was there; either Brady's dead or he's not."

"When did you find out about it?"

"I haven't, yet. I'm still trying, but you're only giving it to me in bits and pieces."

"You told me Brady was using that office space as of last night. You were personally aware of that?"

"Yes. I was with him there."

"Too bad, because that's when they figure it probably happened."

"When I left Brady he was not only alive and well, but was graciously offering me fifty dollars to stay and chat.

Come on, Crawford, if you're going to cut me loose at least give me the details."

More silence. A sigh. "Somebody was cut up in that office, and badly enough that he should be dead. He's a horse if he managed to walk out of there on his own; more likely he was carried. Griffith's still out on the street. He's hearing it was Brady."

"He hearing why?"

"Only that Brady had it coming for some time. A risky business, that real estate speculation."

"That's why we chose law enforcement. What about the information you got out of Lake County?"

"Forget it. Deal's off."

"Strom didn't get back to you?"

"He did, but you'll never hear it, and that's for both our sakes. I'll give you this offer one more time. Tell me where you are, I'll send up a car, you greet it with your hands over your head. That's it. You have fifteen seconds before I hang up."

The waitress was holding up Kubiak's plate again, gesturing down at the table, then back in the direction of the kitchen's heat lamps. He nodded at her, bent in close to the phone not knowing where the plate would wind up. Ten seconds had passed.

"New deal, Crawford."

"I think not."

"When I left Brady last night there were two men in the room with him. A third followed me out to meet my son-in-law, and he flashed a blade thinking I might want him to use it. I sent him away, and I'm sure he was headed back to that office. I can give you his name and the name of the only one of the three who could have decided to turn on Brady. You can use them to either trump Griffith or placate him. All I want in return is the information I asked you to get."

"What's the part you're not telling me?"

"This is straight up. No jokes, no tricks, no obfuscation."

Crawford told Kubiak to wait a moment, put him on hold. Kubiak pumped three quarters into the phone. Crawford came back on.

"Okay, what are the names?"

"The one with the knife is Felix Trejo. The other is Manny Padilla. The third name I got last night, but I don't remember it, and don't ask me to spell the first two. They all work for Brady, or did, recruiting day laborers out of Loyola Park. They also were the ones stealing lumber out of Jerry Wheeler's lot, and on the return trip running drugs out to Jack Mackay to sell in Round Lake Beach. By the way, if you get your hands on them and there happens to be a thousand dollars in one of their pockets, it's mine."

"You feeding a habit or remodeling a kitchen?"

"Neither. I told you, Brady led me to my son-in-law. That's what the directions cost me."

"So, where is Hollinger?"

"I don't know."

"Dammit, Kubiak—"

"We took him home last night, but I set the family adrift this morning just so I wouldn't have to answer that question. Now, how about your answering mine?"

"Sorry. I wish I could tell you everything you wanted to know, but those boys didn't want to share much."

"Funny you didn't mention that before I gave you your names."

"I'm glad you didn't want to see that list of off-duty cops working for Jerry Wheeler, because you're not going to. They wouldn't put me through to the sheriff, but the information officer kept assuring me that if there were sworn officers working freelance for Wheeler it was only because there was nothing wrong with it. He was so interested in why I was interested I couldn't get anything out of him. He did give me the exact time Wheeler's 911 call came into dispatch. Seven-oh-seven."

"That's all?"

"It's more than I would have given him. Strom was a little more cooperative. That George fellow you asked about does have a last name. You want to get a pencil and write it down?"

"Not especially. Is there a reason I should?"

"Is there a reason . . . ? I don't get you, Kubiak. You send me to fetch a list you don't want to see, ask me to inquire about a man whose name you don't even want to know and, of all the questions you choose to channel through me to Strom concerning the Mackay homicide, whether Mackay's old girlfriend lives with her mother or a roommate finds its way into the top ten. I'm beginning to understand why you spent your career in Latent Prints."

"Well?"

"Well, what?"

"Does Christine Hughes live with her mother or a roommate?"

"She lives with her parents in their house in McHenry. Mind telling me why it matters?"

"I'm curious as to where Jack Mackay spent his nights when he wasn't with the Wheelers. The odds of it being her place would have been better if she lived alone."

"Well, he wasn't with her the night before he killed the Wheelers. When Strom became aware that she and Mackay had a relationship, he put a little extra care into determining where she was and when. That Monday night, she went straight home from work, ate dinner with her parents, and the three of them watched TV until they went to bed. She was at the lumberyard the next morning when the Wheelers were shot. That fact was verified by just about everybody, including George Millings, who was right there with her. That's your George's last name, by the way. He's worked for the Wheelers for three years, has a wife and two kids, decent, quiet guy from what Strom has heard. As for Tommy Wheeler, he was up in Wisconsin, all right. Everything checked and double checked . . ."

"What about Brady? Did Strom get hold of the assessor?"

"Yes. Brady does own a house up in Round Lake, or, did."

"Careful, you're not sure he's dead yet."

"I was referring to the house. It burned recently."

"How recently?"

"Just a couple of weeks ago."

"Arson?"

"Strom doesn't know. The Round Lake P.D. told him the place had stood vacant for a couple of years and was a magnet for kids and squatters. They say it just as easily might have been a match discarded by some derelict, that their only regret is it didn't burn to the ground."

"How much of it is still standing?"

"I suppose you'll tell me. You got a map?"

"It's all I've been staring at the last couple of hours." Kubiak pulled the map from his jacket pocket.

"1820 North Willow. Strom says it's on the far northeast end of Round Lake."

"Got it."

"Got what? So, it might have been where Mackay spent

his nights when he wanted to light up and be left alone. If you suspect it burned for a reason, answer me why was it left standing for over two months after he died?"

"The question might as well be why it was torched two weeks before Baumgarten was killed. After all, what's a little arson when the next item on your agenda is murder?"

"Okay, but the question is still why?"

"Take a look at the map, old buddy. The house just happens to sit smack halfway between the Wheelers' home and where Jack Mackay's car was spotted that morning on Route 83. I owe you, Crawford."

"Wait a minute."

The receiver was on its way to the phone's cradle when Kubiak heard the three words come faint and tinny. He nearly ignored them, thought better of it, brought the receiver back to his ear.

"What?"

"I promised Strom I'd call him when I hung up from talking to you. All he's got to track you down is that address. He's probably staking out the property already, but he's guaranteed to meet you there once he knows I've given it to you."

"You don't have to tell him I called you back."

"Yes, I do. If you don't understand that . . ."

"You don't have to tell him when."

"Thirty minutes," Crawford finally said, his tone again as cold as it had been when he had picked up the phone. "It's a couple of minutes past ten now. At ten-thirty, I'll call Strom, give him our conversation verbatim, and I'm finished with this."

The receiver was in its cradle before the word 'verbatim' could get to Kubiak's ear. A dozen long, quick strides took him back to his booth. He was hoping to find a bit of food there he could stuff into his mouth on the fly, but the waitress had done him the favor of taking his plate back to the kitchen to keep it warm. He dropped a twenty on the table and strode out of the tavern, turning the minute hand of his watch back to synchronize it with Crawford's clock.

Chapter Twenty-two

Willow was a narrow residential street without curbs or streetlights, its squat, ramshackle homes buried behind the thick growth of untended lawns. Yellow lights burned here and there through tiny windows. Kubiak drove up the street slowly, reading what few addresses were posted under lit bulbs. He was counting through the sixteen hundreds when the street apparently ended at Rollins Road, a four-lane thoroughfare.

He turned right on Rollins, made a U-turn as soon as traffic allowed it, came back slowly in the right lane, ignoring the horns and flashing headlights of the cars passing around him. He passed Willow again to his left, but couldn't find it opening up to the north, pulled right off Rollins at the first opportunity, a drive that led to the paved lot of a long, one-story office center. He angled into a parking space, killed his headlights, switched on the dome light, and studied his map again.

As far as the map was concerned, Willow might have continued as a short squiggle somewhere on the other side of Rollins, might just as well not. He wondered if Crawford had taken the address down wrong, though if that were the case he would have driven past a burned-out house or vacant lot. Then again, he hadn't run the entire length of Willow from its south end. He was staring vacantly straight ahead through the Contour's windshield, debating whether or not he had the time to do just that, when a Crown Victoria with Lake County Sheriff's markings rolled slowly out from behind the office center.

Kubiak hastily killed the dome light, and sank down low. A few office windows were still lit, and a good half dozen cars were scattered around his in the lot. The squad car continued its roll toward Rollins, stopped at the end of the drive, waited past too many openings in traffic, finally slid out in a left-hand turn, and disappeared.

Maybe nothing more than a routine patrol of the parking lot. However, the rounds of this lot most likely would have belonged to the Round Lake P.D., and the office center ran fewer than a hundred yards; in the time Kubiak had been parked here, he would have seen the front end of the swing-through.

He reached down to put the Contour into gear, then changed his mind. Instead, he switched off the engine, rummaged through the glovebox for his penlight, tested it, found the batteries weak but passable, and climbed out of the car. The evening was beginning to cool. Alone but for the traffic passing on Rollins, Kubiak walked across the lot and around to the other side of the building. The back alley was narrow, with a high fence running opposite the backs of the offices. He started down it on foot.

From the front lot, he hadn't noticed that the building, through a series of wide angles, curved around in a slight U. Here, in this dark passage, he was making a blind turn to his left every fifty feet. The occasional incandescent bulb over a rear door only seemed to make the shadows on the other side of it deeper and blacker, and if another squad car were to come rolling at him he would have to back up flat against the brick wall to keep from being run down, in which case he would very well have to greet it just as Crawford had recommended, with his hands over his head.

Finally, the alley ended, with a set of Dumpsters and a gravel road that continued on and down, twisting around old, broken, hollow trees and gnarled brush. The north end of Willow, its entrance displaced at some point in its sad existence by the building of the office park, lay before him. Ironically, he had Strom's diligence and mistrust to thank for it.

The houses here were spaced farther apart, each nearly invisible from the road, marked only by a mailbox. Somewhere off to the right a dog was barking itself hoarse. The ground below the gravel felt soft beneath the soles of Kubiak's shoes. Those cicadas Robin Mackay had mentioned, the ones that, incredibly enough, sang her to sleep at night, were screeching all about loudly enough to swallow the sounds of Kubiak's footsteps as he made his way down the uneven path.

He didn't need an address to spot 1820 North. The charred face of the two-story structure loomed up so dark at the end of a long curve it seemed to lighten the night sky behind it. Patched with squares of raw particle board over the gaping holes of its punched-out windows, it was set a good two acres away from its nearest neighbor. Kubiak stopped, listened. Convinced he was alone but for the chattering cicadas, he walked up the weedy drive and made a quick inspection around the outside of the house.

Someone had been there since the place had been boarded up, as the wood patching one of the back windows had been torn loose. Kubiak switched on his penlight and leaned inside, dimly illuminating a dingy bedroom empty of furniture save for a bare mattress in one corner. He climbed through the opening, examined the room's four walls and ceiling, then flipped the mattress over and inspected it as well as the floor beneath it. After a cursory check of the empty closet, he moved out into the hallway, playing the light in slow, wide circles before him.

Closed off from air or sunlight, the house's interior was still soaked from the hundreds of gallons of water the fire department had pumped into it. The smell of mildew mingled with that of smoke, and the blackened walls gleamed with a thin coating of mold and damp. The ground floor's thin carpet spongy under his feet, Kubiak could only imagine what the basement looked like, hoped he didn't have to find out.

He came upon the kitchen. Evidently, this was where the fire had been started. Everything burnt to black, appliances unrecognizable, the debris rose up two stories, as the floor above had come down. He shone the penlight's weak beam upward, only to have it swallowed in the charred void. Behind the walls, water dripped into water. He aimed the penlight at the face of his watch. Crawford would be making his phone call to Strom in a little under fifteen minutes.

It took Kubiak half that time to go through the house's front room. The furniture was typical squatter's fare, a hodgepodge of broken, overstuffed pieces lifted from curbs and Dumpsters, each now so waterlogged Kubiak didn't attempt to budge them from their places. The room gave up nothing, or had nothing to give.

An empty foyer led him to the staircase. Little of the railing was left, and each step sagged deep under his weight as he ascended. He kept close to the wall, and at the top found himself standing precariously over that black chasm that had once been the kitchen. What was left of the second floor hallway led in only one direction, to a room at its end.

This bedroom was made up for more comfort. A cheap futon, still extended for sleep, rested against one wall. Opposite it was a small television set perched on a plastic end table. Discarded clothing lay everywhere, as did empty beer and soda cans. Kubiak's eye was drawn to a pile of blankets shoved against the corner of room. He started for it, stopped just short, knelt, ran the penlight's beam across the floor. This section of carpet had been scrubbed, but the bloodstains remained. He went to the blankets which, in spite of the smoke, still smelled of bleach. A good area of the wall above them had been scrubbed, as well, but nowhere near as thoroughly as had been the Wheelers' kitchen tiles, and the scrubbing had occurred before the fire, as the thin layer of soot was relatively even from floor to ceiling.

He ran the light along it, spotted the tiny hole about seven feet up. Behind the wall was a shallow closet, and he stepped back to where he could see inside of it, played the beam up at the hole, watched the point of light dance along the closet's opposite wall where the bullet had lodged. He lifted his left foot to step into the closet, heard a distinct report sound from downstairs, and froze.

Nothing. He wondered if maybe the shifting of his

weight had caused a stress in what was left of the house's structure, or if he had only imagined the noise. Perhaps his mind had exaggerated its loudness, or that the water dripping behind the walls . . .

Then it sounded again, and again, and series of poundings echoing sharply throughout the house. He switched off the penlight and crept out into the hallway in time to hear the screaming of nails being torn from their foundation, the splintering of wood, a curse, followed by the heavy thud of footsteps directly below but out of sight. Then, a second set of shuffling feet. Another curse, a grunt, and, finally, the sound of a voice he recognized.

"What about you, little prince? What, you gonna stand sentry out there all night?"

The reply was muffled, but the questions clearly came from Padilla.

"Don't be lonely," he continued. "Come join the big dogs." His tone grew menacing. "I mean it. I trust you out there by yourself about this much. You, help him inside."

"Help him inside yourself."

Kubiak recognized the second voice, as well: the kid with the knife, Trejo.

Padilla spoke again. "What, I can't ask you for a simple favor any more? You're useless, you know that?"

"I'm good for something."

"Put that thing away before you slice off your own . . . give me a hand, here."

More grunts, then a clatter and more curses.

"What's the matter with you?" Padilla shouted. "You're going to kill me and Trejo both, you can't climb through a hole by yourself?"

The voice of the third man, now inside the house, came drifting up all too sharp and clean. "Maybe I'm not as accustomed to climbing into holes as you two are," Kubiak's son-in-law said. "As for the rest of it, don't give me any ideas."

"Oh, that's funny! That's funny."

"Why don't you shout it again a little louder, just in case there's some half-deaf geezer in this neighborhood still asleep?"

"Neighborhood? To you this is a neighborhood? Oh, I forget, you live in East Rogers Park." A long howl came up out of Padilla so sonorous, Kubiak, fearing its vibration might shake him loose and down into that black kitchen, had to resist backing against the wall. The cry petered, and Padilla continued, without missing a beat. "See, there's nobody around here. Why do you think Mackay operated out of this place?"

"All right, fine. Let's just get around to finding what we're here for so we can get out."

Padilla muttered something. The beam of a flashlight much more powerful than Kubiak's played erratically through the kitchen, then disappeared as all three sets of footsteps moved away in the direction of the front room.

Kubiak gingerly placed his foot on the top stair. The resulting loud creak caused him to step back again. He switched on his penlight, aimed it at his watch's face, switched it back off. Strom was probably on his way here already, and if he were to discover the four of them in this house, he'd toss them all in jail, with Hollinger the least likely to ever come out again. Kubiak couldn't have arranged a worse predicament if he had done so deliberately. He considered whether he should back into the bedroom and chance the three finding whatever they came for and leaving before Strom got here. However, if they were turning things upside down in a search, that closet in the bedroom was the last place he wanted them, and he had a better shot at keeping them downstairs if he were to go down there himself, and announce his presence, even if that would hardly speed their exit. He was still weighing his options when the flashlight's beam was back and he heard the voices of Padilla and Trejo approach.

"Man, what a stink," Padilla was saying. "I didn't think this place could smell any worse than it did before the fire."

"Who do you think torched it?" Trejo asked.

"Brady, of course."

"What, his own house?"

"The house is worth jack. It's the property, stupid. Watch out on those stairs."

"They're strong enough. Check it out."

Kubiak heard the sound of bouncing up and down on one of the stairs, then its splintering, and Trejo's scream.

"My ankle!"

"I warned you."

"I think it's broken."

"Serves you right."

"No, it's okay. See?"

Hollinger's voice sounded from the bottom of the staircase. "Look, you two clowns, why can't you just give me the list, and I'll let you get on with your business? You know where I live; you know I'm good for the money."

"You give us the cash, you get the list. That's how things work."

"This is crazy. You said yourself, Mackay never kept more than a few hundred bucks worth of anything stashed here. You'd be spending your time better helping me look for my father-in-law."

"A few hundred bucks is a few hundred bucks. Besides, it's my car out front. How do you plan to get home?"

"I have a thumb. But you might as well leave with me. If it's true that every punk in the area knew about this house, the chances are whatever was worth taking is already . . . oh, my god."

An instant before Kubiak stepped into the beam of the flashlight, he caught a frozen glimpse of the three of them, Trejo halfway up the staircase, Padilla four steps behind him, and David at its base, staring up with the same look on his face he must have had when he peered through the peep hole at his mother- and father-in-law last night. Kubiak finally got to see it; then, Trejo aimed the light directly into Kubiak's eyes, and they were only voices again.

"Well, well," Padilla said. "Look who's here. Come on down, Crazy Man. You can hide, but you can't run."

"How long have you been up there?" Hollinger asked.

"Long enough, little prince," Kubiak told him.

The pounding of feet came up the creaking stairs. Kubiak guessed they were Hollinger's. Trejo yelped out at him to be careful of the wood, and Kubiak, once again, couldn't help but feel affection for the kid who didn't think twice about cutting people's flesh for a day's bonus pay.

Hollinger gripped Kubiak's arm, maybe just to save himself from falling into that abyss on the other side of the top step. Trejo pulled back the light so he could take them both in, and Kubiak could see Hollinger's face again.

"Are you all right?" Hollinger asked.

"So far."

Hollinger ran his hand through his hair, squinted down at the two men standing on the stairs, then turned back to Kubiak. "I know this looks bad."

"At least you know that much. Aren't you supposed to be at the zoo or something?"

"What? No, I've been running all over this town searching for you."

"I don't get it," Padilla interjected. "Yesterday, you're looking for him. Today, he's looking for you. Why don't you two just travel together, save yourselves all that time and money?"

"Brady is dead," Hollinger told Kubiak. "I went to see him at that office he uses on Ashland. There was blood everywhere. I called Padilla to find out what went down. He's got that list I told you about, the names of the cops on Jerry Wheeler's payroll working security. Brady had it all the time. Mackay had given it to him months ago, when the cops were first hired, along with the times they were posted at the lumberyard."

Kubiak stared down at Trejo. The kid was wearing that ear-to-ear grin again.

"Was that what turned you against Brady, what you thought that list might be worth? I didn't think it was just my thousand bucks. I suppose the two, together, put enough blood in the water."

"Nobody meant to hurt Brady," Padilla said. "But he was too greedy. A man keeps making promises and then breaking them, he's going to eventually pay a price."

"I'm not arguing your cutting him up. I just think it might have been better for you if you had killed him."

"What are you talking about? He's dead, all right."

"You leave him there after you were done?"

"What, I'm going to take him home, mount his head on my wall?"

"You should have checked his pulse. I just got done talking to a lieutenant in the Chicago P.D. Brady walked out of that office."

"Bull."

Kubiak turned to Hollinger. "You said you went there. Did you see a body?"

Hollinger blinked. "No, but I sure as hell didn't go searching for one. One glance at that room was enough."

"You had to have seen him," Padilla said. "He was lying right in the middle of the floor."

Hollinger didn't need to say anything. Padilla only had to read his face.

Trejo read it, as well. "I told you, you couldn't finish him with that lamp," he told Padilla. "Not with his hard head."

"Shut up. If you knew how to use a blade for its purpose and not your pleasure—"

Kubiak interrupted. "Did you let Brady know you planned to come up here and clean out this place?"

"Of course not," Padilla said. "Why should I have had to let him know that?"

"You didn't mention this house at all before you started slicing him up, or what was in it? You didn't argue about how much money he pocketed from your little side operation here, or maybe how much he didn't?"

Padilla was doing his best to maintain his cocky air, but Trejo couldn't control his nerves. He glanced back at Padilla, received a nasty glare in return.

"That's too bad," Kubiak said. "I understand Brady knows a lot of people, and this address is on the short list of places you're likely to be found. Where we're all to be found. The fact is, there's at least one car on its way here right now."

"Oh, yeah? And how could you know that?"

"What do you think I'm doing here? I wasn't waiting for you three to show."

There was a moment of silence, interrupted by Hollinger.

"I appreciate your concern for the welfare of these

two," he told Kubiak, "but the point here is that list Padilla is holding. All we have to do is match up any of the names on it to those of the cops who ran Jack Mackay off the road, and bingo."

"Bingo, eh? Is that the game you're playing?"

"It's no game. Baumgarten is dead because of that list, and if I can't produce it in my defense I might as well be too."

"How much does he want for it?"

"Two thousand."

"Twenty-five hundred," Padilla announced.

"You told me two thousand."

"I said twenty-five hundred."

"I have . . ." Kubiak said, taking his wallet from his pocket and thumbing through it. "Thirteen dollars."

"Crazy Man," Padilla said. "You're getting too crazy for your own good. What happened to that wallet you had on the beach yesterday?"

"You happened to it. I have found out since, though, just how much cash one can get out of an ATM after banking hours."

"So," Trejo said anxiously, "it's time we take our business there."

"I'm staying," Kubiak told him. "I told you, I'm expecting visitors. My business with them takes precedence."

"If Brady is alive," Padilla said, "he won't let you leave here that way."

"You forget, I'm not the one who tried to kill him."

Trejo had moved down five steps and was standing just below Padilla. The two leaned close and conducted a brief, whispered business meeting. In the time it took Padilla to straighten and face Kubiak, Trejo had scampered to the bottom of the staircase.

"So, when will you have the twenty-five hundred?"

"How long could it take? Tell me where I can find you."

"I'm not that stupid. I'll meet you." He pointed at Hollinger. "What about him?"

"He stays here. Like you said, it's time he and I stopped chasing after each other."

"Okay." He addressed Hollinger. "You call me from that place where we met. But don't take forever. I'm sure there are people who will pay just as much, if not more, to keep this list buried."

Then he joined Trejo, and the light disappeared as the two of them shoved and cursed their way back out through the entrance they had forced open. Kubiak started down the stairs even before they were outside.

"What's wrong with you?" Hollinger complained, following close behind. "Why aren't we going with them?"

"Because they're not going far. Where are my wife and daughter?"

"They're fine. They're safe. You couldn't possibly believe that I would—"

"You were supposed to stay with them."

"Yes, as per your orders, touring that stinking museum beside the mothers and schoolchildren, gawking at mummies and stuffed animals all day. How long did you think any one of the three of us could put up with that?"

"Actually, my suggestion was the zoo. Was it Denise's idea to see Brady?"

"No," Hollinger said, though the half second's hesitation told Kubiak it had been. "I couldn't take it any more, so I brought up the idea," he lied. "She and Maria went along with it."

Kubiak could picture his wife bored and fidgety at the museum, staring vacantly at the displays, while the conversation among the three of them centered solely on Baumgarten and Neil Brady. Plots would be hatched; David's ideas of how he might clear his name would begin to make sense.

"Did they see the gore in that office?"

"Of course not. They waited in the car. I didn't even tell them what I found, but after I called Padilla and he told me he had that list, we decided it was important we come up here and track you down."

Kubiak led Hollinger down the first floor hallway and into the back bedroom through which he had entered the house.

"Well, you managed that much. At what point did you switch traveling companions?"

"I didn't want Padilla anywhere near Maria or Denise, so I agreed to meet him up here at eight at this pizza joint he had told me about where he used to hang with Mackay. I thought that would give the three of us enough time to find you first. But we were hours behind you all day, couldn't even get in to see Osgood until nearly five. Eight o'clock rolled around fast. I had to cut Maria and Denise loose because I was afraid if they knew where I was meeting Padilla they might come after me the way we came after you. So, I talked them into dropping me off a few blocks short of the pizza place and waiting for me at a Denny's we'd passed well outside of town. I figured I'd talk Padilla out of the list and be back to them within an hour, but Padilla kept arguing price, and then insisted on running up here, as long as he was in the neighborhood, to collect whatever drugs and cash Mackay might have left laying around. I wanted to keep him in my sights, so I tagged along."

"You think they're still at the Denny's?"

"They promised to wait as long as it took."

Kubiak bent, peered out through the bedroom window. The blue and red flashes of police takedown lights on the other side of the house were already illuminating the tops of the surrounding trees. He straightened, handed Hollinger the keys to the Contour, along with the penlight.

"I thought you said I was staying."

"You did. Now, you're leaving."

He described where he had parked the Contour, told Hollinger to plunge deep into the woods and stay as far away from the road as possible as he made his way back to the car.

"Drive it directly back to that Denny's, and then wait there. Alone. Tell Maria and Denise to go to the police facility here in Round Lake Beach and to tell whoever's in charge there that they will gladly give up your whereabouts the minute I give the okay, but not until then. Emphasize that they are not to cooperate in any way with the police until I see them, face to face, and to make certain the police are aware of that."

"Let me get this straight. While all of you are doing this, I'm supposed to wait, sipping coffee in a Denny's, until the cops show and put me in handcuffs."

"That's right. You'd prefer it happen here?"

Hollinger glowered, glanced back into that dark hallway, sighed. He lifted one foot onto the window sill, but when Kubiak reached forward to help steady him, he stopped.

"I'm aware this is my mess," he said. "But I'll have you know I was fully prepared to claw my way out of it by myself. I never asked you for your help, and only let you come up here today because, one, I knew I couldn't stop you, and, two, Maria wouldn't have it any other way. I've come to realize, God help me, that your daughter has more faith in your judgement than she does in mine. I know that's my fault. And if everything does go sour, I could live with her hating me because of it. Or you. But I couldn't stand to think of her blaming herself. So, I hope you know what you're doing, if only for her sake."

He didn't wait for a reply, but leapt through the window and landed running. The woods swallowed him up in an instant. Kubiak stared after him, left alone in a silence that pressed against his eardrums, until the sound of the cicadas came up again, followed by the distant cacophony the police were making at the front of the house. He made his way back through the hallway to the home's foyer, stood in its center, with his legs spread apart and the palms of his hands resting on the top of his head, and braced himself for their arrival.

Chapter Twenty-three

He had to empathize with the staff of the Round Lake P.D., even if they did show him nothing but contempt. In cooperating with the County Sheriff's Department, they had virtually handed over their entire facility. Not only was every aspect of their agenda put on hold, but each officer was, in effect, reduced to the role of assistant. Complicating the matter was that it was taking place during the shift change from afternoon to midnight, meaning everything that could be explained had to be explained twice, to everyone from shift commander down to dispatcher.

The most difficult chore was keeping all the guests separated. Kubiak spent most of his time either in a holding cell or parked at a corner desk in the patrolmen's room. From what he overheard, his wife and daughter were tucked in the chief's room, for which he was grateful, while Robin and Kimberly Mackay rested in the investigations room where the detectives put up their feet while on duty. Tommy Wheeler had kept asking if he could go out to the station's garage to smoke, so they stuck him there permanently, while Andy Shultz was shuttled around to whatever room was unoccupied at the moment. Christine Hughes was parked somewhere, Kubiak could only guess.

Padilla and Trejo were the ones keeping the interrogation room busy. Kubiak caught some of the show before one of the sergeants thought to disconnect the video monitor. Just after one in the morning, a patrolman brought in a drunk driver, and his addition to the mix sent everyone scrambling. Some sort of altercation started up in the holding cells, and Kubiak heard Brady's name discussed immediately afterward.

Nothing happened over the next forty-five minutes. Kubiak was alone in the patrolmen's room, staring at the spins and twirls of a computer's screen saver and thinking about food, when Crawford entered and shut the door behind him. This was his third visit with Kubiak since his arrival at around midnight. He wouldn't say whether he had been pressed into service or had come up to Round Lake on his own, but he was presently being used as mediator between Kubiak and every sworn officer in the building. He rolled a chair up close, sat, and waited for Kubiak to speak first.

"Brady's here?"

Crawford nodded.

"Where did he turn up?"

"He stumbled into Stroger's E.R. right around this time yesterday, claimed he was homeless and had been cut up by some street punks on the west side. Even the nurse doing triage caught the manicure and forty dollar haircut. It only took Griffith a couple of hours to track him down. The guy is made of rock. The hospital was going to release him later this morning, but he was raising such a ruckus all night they were glad to be rid of him."

"How did you manage to shuttle him up here?"

"It has nothing to do with the scheme you're trying to arrange. In Cook County, he's just another lowlife knifed by his friends. Lake County wants to use this spat to get these three to indict one another. They can be awfully serious about their drug infractions here, and could put the lot of them away longer than we would bother to on assault charges."

"The scheme I'm trying to arrange is an indictment on the charge of murder."

Crawford leaned back, crossed his arms like an impatient judge. "So you've said. But so far you haven't given up a name or specifics. Hell, I'm not even sure anymore whose murder you're talking about." He uncrossed his arms, leaned closer. "Listen, Kubiak, if that bullet you found tonight turns out to be what you claim it is, of course it changes everything about what we thought went down the morning of the Wheeler murders. But your not giving up Hollinger only makes things look worse for him. Tell us where he is, let Strom book him on suspicion, and let the investigation take its course."

Kubiak looked at the clock, wondered if Hollinger was doing the same as he sipped his coffee at Denny's.

"I can't trust Strom not to use any information I give him as a further indictment of my son-in-law," he said. "And I have no doubt the minute I hand over Hollinger to him, he'll dismiss everyone here, except for Brady, Trejo, and Padilla, with a polite thank you and a pat on the back. Just how did he manage to talk them all into coming down here, anyway? He won't tell me."

"Simple enough. He sent a Round Lake officer to each of their residences, asked them if they'd please come down and answer a few more questions on the Baumgarten homicide. They were all willing to cooperate. Of course, he didn't say the questions were to come from you."

"Or at least they wanted to appear willing."

"Kubiak, I've seen you work a room and produce your rabbits often enough in the past, but you have to understand Strom's point of view."

"Sorry, Crawford, I do understand his taking one last shot at my giving up Hollinger without any fuss, but he wouldn't have gone to the trouble of getting these people down here if he wasn't willing to give me what I want. And I suggest we get started while they're all still here."

Crawford sat for a moment, silent, then stood and left. A few minutes later, Strom entered the room. He didn't sit.

"How long is this going to take?"

"I don't know," Kubiak said. "That depends not so much on me as on everyone else."

"Whether it goes your way or not, we get Hollinger."

"That's the deal."

"And I pull the plug when I decide we've all had enough. I don't plan to be here all night."

Kubiak nodded.

"Osgood is here. He's just about convinced the Mackays to go home. I don't suppose you'd want to do this without them. It might be easier without a lawyer present."

"No."

"Okay, have it your way."

Strom ushered Kubiak out of the room and through the station's maze of hallways, staying close beside and one half step behind as if he were expecting an escape attempt at any second. He led him to a much larger room that held three long, rectangular tables. At its head was a desk, behind which a chalkboard ran the length of the wall. Dunning was standing beside the desk, chatting with Crawford and one of the station's shift commanders. The conversation ended when Kubiak entered.

Aside from the sheriff's deputies, all of whom were on their feet, the room's occupants were scattered about the three tables in plastic chairs, looking like anxious students on their first day of class. Closest to the desk were Denise and Maria. Both looked exhausted, probably from the grilling Strom must have given them trying to get Hollinger's location. As Kubiak entered, Denise offered him a discreet wave from just above her lap, the type a mother might give a child taking the stage in a school play. It gave him no solace. At the opposite end of their table, Neil Brady sat alone. He moved stiffly and wore bandages on his neck and his forehead, but he looked angry enough to warrant the two officers flanking him. His chair was angled sideways so he could take in his business partners who were seated in the chairs farthest away from him, at the back table. Padilla and Trejo, with one empty chair between them, were concentrating on ignoring his glare. Also in the back, but spaced well away from those two, Tommy Wheeler sat beside Andy Shultz, with Christine Hughes close by, though outside of whispering range. The middle table was occupied solely by the Mackays and their lawyer, Robin planted smack dab in the center chair, her daughter on her left, Osgood on her right.

Aside from Denise and Maria, who had to twist their bodies in order to see Padilla and Trejo directly behind them, everyone in the room could view any other person with a smooth quarter turn of the head. All eyes turned to Strom as he addressed the group.

"I've told each of you this already, but it's important enough I mention it again." He pointed a finger at Kubiak. "This man holds no authority here. You don't have to tell him anything, and you're under no obligation or expectation to stay and listen to a word he says. The officers present in this room are here solely for your safety, but they are sworn officers. They cannot, and will not, disregard anything you say if it implicates you in a crime. Again, I want to thank you all for agreeing to come down here, and to tell you you're free to go any time you wish. Just come up to the front of the room, and I'll have a car drop you back home."

Kubiak thanked Strom for his heartening introduction, and received a shrug in return. The light rustling that comes from a group of people shifting their weight and glancing at those around them when confronted with a decision rose up. Trejo stood and took a step toward the door. A set of heavy palms belonging to the officer behind him cupped his skinny shoulders, and pressed him right back down again.

"Not you," the owner of the palms stated.

Trejo showed his own palms, asked the officer if he hadn't understood that his boss had just set him free. Padilla took the cue and addressed the room's occupants, looking each one in the eye and asking if they weren't, in reality, all prisoners. The act was too much for Brady. He let out a curse and called Padilla a thief and Trejo a murderer. One of the officers behind him placed his hand on his shoulder, but must have squeezed a sensitive stitch, because Brady let out a howl that silenced the room. Kubiak took advantage of the moment to begin.

"First of all," he said, "I don't want to be here any more than any of you. But through an unfortunate set of circumstances, my son-in-law is about to be charged with the murder of Paul Baumgarten. You all knew Baumgarten. Some better than others, but you all knew him."

Robin Mackay didn't flinch.

"For weeks," Kubiak said, "he was running around here asking questions and making accusations concerning the death of Jack Mackay. And he was murdered because of it. Each of you having had contact with him, I'd imagine the killing caused you to lose some sleep this weekend, whether you admit it or not. Am I right?"

No one said anything. Osgood shifted his weight, but when Kubiak stared at him, the lawyer only stared back in his condescending manner.

"I'm sure," Kubiak continued, "that's part of the reason most of you agreed to come down here. However, allowing my son-in-law to be put away for a crime he didn't commit will only make the wrong people sleep better tonight."

"I didn't arrange this," Strom growled, "in order for you to insult me. You want me to pull that plug right now, I will."

"I wasn't necessarily referring to you."

Brady spoke up again, guarding the wound in his shoulder with his right hand. "Quit stalling, Crazy Man. We both know who you're talking about." With his left, he pointed at Strom, then Dunning. "Him, and him, along with half the cops in this county. They killed Jack Mackay, and then they killed Baumgarten because he could prove it. Both their names are on the list Mackay gave me for safekeeping." The finger swung around to aim at Padilla. "That list is rightfully mine. If anybody here is going to cut a deal because of what's on it, it's going to be me."

"No deal is going to be cut here," Strom told him.

"Even if there were to be a deal," Kubiak added, "what's on that list would have nothing to do with it." He addressed Padilla and Trejo. "The list of cops working for Jerry Wheeler is meaningless. It always was. I imagine at some point, a long time from tonight, you two and Brady will have a laugh over that fact, if only because you came out of this better than Baumgarten. But if you really wanted the names, all you had to do was ask the company bookkeeper. She was sending out memos to the security staff."

Christine Hughes glared. Kubiak angled himself so he could take in the officers at the desk, along with the others in the room. "I only kept bringing it up to keep everybody dancing," he said. "Baumgarten, on the other hand, took a blind leap in believing that its existence could, in any way, implicate anyone on it in the deliberate murder of Jack Mackay."

"Why couldn't it?" Brady asked. "Because cops are too good to shoot a poor slob in order to cover their tracks? One of them shouts 'gun' and he doesn't even have to be the one unholstering his own. It happens all the time, Crazy Man. Your head is still in the sand at the beach."

"That's how Baumgarten thought I felt. But whatever you imagine happened up at Loon Lake, the one indisputable fact is that Jack Mackay died as a result of the barrel of a gun being put into his mouth, and a bullet being fired through that barrel and up into his skull. That is not the result of a bunch of cops full of adrenaline acting in the heat of the moment. One or two of those officers would have had to climb down into the ditch where Mackay's car was stuck, approach this man who was holding a loaded weapon, take the weapon from him without a shot being fired from anyone's gun, place Mackay's pistol into his mouth, and execute him in cold blood. All while the half dozen or so other officers involved in the slow speed chase stood watching and doing nothing? The idea is ludicrous."

"It's still possible," Brady grumbled.

It was Kubiak's turn to shrug. "Up until tonight, I would have had to agree with you."

"I don't get it," Padilla interjected. "First, you said Baumgarten was killed because he could prove the cops killed Jack Mackay. Now, you're saying it went down just the way the cops told it. Make up your mind. Which is it?"

"Neither."

"What? Now you're mixing it up backwards."

"I said Baumgarten was killed because he was making noise about reopening the investigation. And if that were to happen, it would become plain to all involved that very little that morning went down the way the police reported it."

"So, they're lying, and Jack Mackay was murdered."

"No. He shot himself, all right."

Crawford spoke up. "If that's the case, who put the bullet in that bedroom closet in Brady's house?"

"Whoever shot Jerry and Bernice Wheeler."

"This is nonsense," Dunning said through his teeth. "You finally admit Jack Mackay shot himself. Now you want to confuse the issue by arguing whether or not he shot the Wheeler couple."

"There's nothing confusing about it," Kubiak said. "It's obvious he didn't. In fact, he wasn't even there that morning."

Dunning let slip a curse, turned to Crawford who threw up his hands. It was Brady, however, who drew the room's attention as he half rose from his chair.

"What I want to know," he thundered, pointing that finger again, "is what you two doing in my bedroom closet?"

Before anyone could answer him, Strom strode forward and placed himself in front of Kubiak.

"That's it, I've had enough. Kubiak, you're finished. The rest of you can all go home."

Trejo stood and took a step toward the door.

Chapter Twenty-four

This time, Padilla tried to follow Trejo's lead. They both were shoved back into their chairs immediately. Brady continued to rail, evidently assuming the police had found a bullet in the closet of the house in which he lived on Chicago's west side. Dunning had moved closer to him and was working at convincing him otherwise. Aside from Kubiak, no one noticed Christine Hughes, who had stood and was stiffly moving along the wall to the front of the room. She stopped at the door, chin jutting straight out, purse over her shoulder, and waited for Strom to acknowledge her.

"You said we could go," she stated coldly when he looked her way. "I'm going."

He told her that was fine and that he would get her a car. One of the officers headed out the door, but made the mistake of not taking her with him, which left her standing awkwardly alone. Her eyes landed on Tommy, her boss, and stayed on him, challenging him to join her. He thought it over, stretched, pushed his chair back.

"I could use a drink. What time is it, anyway?"

"I'd think, Tommy," Kubiak said sharply enough to quiet the room, "that, of everyone here, you'd most want to stay."

All eyes now on him, Tommy retreated behind a shy grin. "I don't get you, Mister Kubiak."

"Yesterday you were ready to put me on the payroll if I could come up with anything you thought you ought to know about the circumstances surrounding your parents' deaths. Now, here I am giving it to you free of charge."

"Yesterday you weren't talking crazy. I haven't made sense of a word you've said since you told us all we weren't getting enough sleep."

"It's actually very simple. Sit down. You need to hear it."

Tommy searched the faces in the room. His eyes lingered on the Mackays, landed finally on Andy Shultz, whose expression sent him back into his chair. Kubiak turned to Strom.

"When Baumgarten came to me for help four days ago, I turned him away for the same reasons you've been stonewalling me all weekend. The case was closed, the file was put away, and what I already believed about Mackay's death from the little I knew was enough to keep me from expending any energy in finding out the truth. Baumgarten didn't help his argument any either, if only because the only facts he was interested in were the ones that might show him a profit. But he had one point right, and it's the one that got him killed. How was it that Mackay had to pump three bullets into himself in order to commit suicide? I tried to explain it away just as you did. He was juggling the gun during the police pursuit and accidentally fired the first bullet into his kneecap and the second through his cheek and out the open car window. Like the scenario of your execution of him at the end of that pursuit, it's possible, but not very likely, especially without the existence of that second bullet. How long did you search for it in the weeds along those winding roads up at Loon Lake, Strom? How long before you gave up?"

Kubiak nodded at Christine Hughes. "Your scenario was much more plausible. Jack Mackay wasn't shot juggling with that gun. He was shot struggling for it. But not with Jerry Wheeler, and not in Jerry Wheeler's house. The Wheelers were already dead. Their killer knew Jack had spent the night at Brady's house on Willow and drove there with the gun. Jack managed to wrestle it away, but in the process, took those first two bullets. The one that passed through his cheek I found tonight in the wall of that bedroom, along with Jack Mackay's blood."

"You don't know yet," Strom said, "what gun that bullet came out of, or when it lodged in that wall. Besides, even giving that it did come from Jerry Wheeler's handgun that morning and that is Mackay's blood, you'll never prove he wasn't the one who carried it into the house."

"The proof is Baumgarten not being here in this room with us tonight. Someone was so intent on cleaning up the evidence of that struggle that they went so far as to torch the house when Baumgarten persisted in his inquiries despite the threats against his life. Threats that were carried out only days later. The person who arranged to have Baumgarten killed was covering up more than a couple of flesh wounds to a street punk no Lake County cop cared about, anyway.

"Andy, you were the one who finally explained to me why the Wheelers were murdered. The night before that morning, when Jack came home from work, Jerry

Wheeler planned on telling him not only that he was fired, but that he was no longer welcome in his house. Well, I believe that's exactly what he did and exactly when he did it. Their confrontation took place that night, and when it was over the Wheelers were left very much alive. Jerry had already packed up his things, so Jack wound up spending the night at his hideaway on Willow, but unfortunately for the Wheelers, not before letting at least one other person know the gig was over. And it was that person who visited the Wheelers the next morning.

"I wasn't given access to the reports, but unless the police were deliberately misleading the press, when the first officers arrived on the scene in response to Jerry Wheeler's 911 call, they found the front door of the house wide open. You know the layout of that house, Andy. The side door in the kitchen leads directly to the garage and the driveway. The path out of the front door leads down to the sidewalk. I doubt anyone in that house ever used that front door, and Jack certainly wouldn't have run out through it, only to have to then run across the front lawn, in full view of any neighbors who might be watching, then back around the side of the house to get to the Civic. No, the reason the police on the scene found that garage empty was because Jack stormed off in that Civic the night before and never came back. Whoever killed the Wheelers entered that house as a visitor, through the front door, and left the same way.

"Then, there's the time line. Again, Strom wouldn't share anything with me except the time Jerry Wheeler made his 911 call, seven-oh-seven, but we can approximate how long it was between the time Jerry was shot and the police spotted Mackay in the Civic. First, you have to figure it took the police five or six minutes to arrive. Add another ten, at least, for them to enter the house, find the bodies, then protect and survey the scene. More backups arrive, and they get briefed. Someone thinks to get a license and description of the Wheelers' car because the garage is empty. That's done, and the information is dispatched. Another ten minutes, minimum. Finally, a cruising patrol car spots Jack on Route 83 just outside of town. I'll give that four minutes just to keep the total number round at a half hour."

As Kubiak spoke, he had been moving along the far wall to the back of the room. He stopped at the end of the rear table, leaned in toward Tommy seated four chairs down.

"Tommy, the Legion Hall is only a few blocks from your parents' home. We made that run yesterday in under ten minutes. Where do you think Jack Mackay was during the other twenty?"

"Hell if I know."

Kubiak waited.

Tommy shrugged. "He was in that house on Willow, like you said."

"What was he doing there?"

"Bleeding, obviously." The smile for the audience didn't work. "He went there to hide, after killing my folks, maybe pack some things. But he was bleeding too heavy and went out to find a hospital. I don't know."

"But he wasn't shot by your father. According to the police's theory, he didn't even shoot himself accidentally until after they spotted him on Route 83. I'm talking about the half hour before they spotted him. Where did the blood come from? And what about that bullet?"

Tommy's voice rose. The weak smile was long gone. "I told you, I don't know. I swear to God, I don't. You're the one talking about a bullet, not me."

Andy laid his arm across Tommy's chest.

"You're cold-hearted, Kubiak. I told you things in confidence only hours ago, and all the time you were planning to use them against this boy. He didn't kill his parents, I can promise you that."

"I'm not saying he did. Only that he murdered Paul Baumgarten. If it makes you feel any better, Tommy, you only screwed up twice. The first time was at Legion Hall when I threw Baumgarten's name at you. You tried to play it too safe and said you'd never heard of him. That was impossible, not with the profile he was presenting around here. Even Andy knew who he was. But just to be certain, I gave you a chance to make the same claim again when I walked into this room just now and announced that everyone in it had had contact with Baumgarten. You didn't argue the point.

"The second mistake was that phone call you made to your girlfriend after we had been arrested up at Loon Lake. You panicked, and I can't blame you. Here I came looking for the killer of the man you murdered, and in stringing me along to find out how much I knew, you wound up leaving me in a police interrogation room with the detectives investigating the homicide. Kimberly did the smart thing, phoning Osgood and having me sprung as quickly as possible, but your call to her provided the first connection between the two of you. It could only have been you; no one else knew I was there."

Osgood didn't need to argue the fact, Kimberly refused to turn and look at Kubiak, and Tommy wasn't saying anything—so Andy Shultz, still physically shielding his good neighbors' son, jumped in again.

"You do a fine job of twisting things up," he said. "I

told you, these two kids might have seen each other once, but that ended long ago. Everybody knows that."

"Everybody thinks that. Funny thing about love, Andy. It can die quickly enough on its own, but it seems to thrive when someone else tries to kill it. They did a good job keeping their affair a secret so Jerry Wheeler could believe it was over. They had to, or, as you said, face the possibility of his funding drying up. And once the Wheelers were murdered, one of them had an even better reason to keep it a secret.

"However, these two were, in fact, planning on leaving together tonight. With my coming up here asking questions after Baumgarten, they realized things were getting tight. Tommy just had to finish up arrangements concerning power of attorney on his new properties, and Kimberly was already packed. By breakfast, she was supposed to be in Chicago, but believe me, by this time tomorrow we wouldn't have been able to find either of them. If things up here worked out for them in the long run and my son-in-law was convicted of Baumgarten's murder, they could always come back claiming to have eloped and spent a year-long honeymoon. The money from the sales of the house and business would be waiting for them."

Kimberly Mackay continued staring straight forward at that long chalkboard. Kubiak considered moving up by her, but decided to stay closer to Tommy.

"Poor Kimberly," he said. "You finally shut Baumgarten up by convincing your boyfriend to bash in his skull with a claw hammer, and three days later I'm sitting across from you in Osgood's office asking the same questions he was. That outburst of yours was real; it was the apology later that was phony, but you knew instantly you had made a mistake, that you'd stand out as the prime suspect in the Baumgarten homicide by showing your intent on squelching any further investigation into your brother's death.

"And poor Baumgarten. Living in your mother's house with you. Every time he took a step forward in finding out how your brother died, he confided in the one person who wanted it kept covered up. You couldn't talk him out of his mission; after all, you were Jack's sister. So, you had Tommy call and threaten him, even arranged for him to call once when Baumgarten was out so you could feign fear and maybe get your mother to talk him out of pressing forward. In fact, that's how Tommy knew my son-in-law's name when he called in the threat to him. My son-in-law thought Baumgarten must have blurted it out during one of the threatening phone calls. He didn't. It's just that you knew everything he knew when he knew it.

"But Baumgarten wouldn't be stopped, so you had him meet you Friday night. What line did you give him, Kimberly? Who did you tell him he was going to meet? You promised him something, because he was in a hurry. That was why he borrowed my son-in-law's truck. You took him to that auto salvage yard off Route 176 where Tommy was waiting. And what had you told Tommy? Certainly not that you killed his parents. Was it just that Baumgarten's inquiries were bound to make Jack look like a victim, a martyr even, and his father, along with the police, the villain? Or, did you tell him Baumgarten was getting—how did you phrase it to me this afternoon in your bedroom—creepy with you?"

Tommy spoke again. His eyes were half-lidded, his voice so low and flat Kubiak had to cock his head in order to hear the words. "Jack Mackay killed my parents," he said. "Kimmy had no reason to."

"You're wrong, Tommy," Kubiak told him. "She had the opportunity, and in her mind, every reason in the world. When your father fired Jack, not only did her and her mother's source of income disappear, but so did her plans of leaving this town she'd always loathed if she wanted to stay with you. You were being given back the lumberyard, and if you wanted it, you'd have to stay and run it. I'm going to give her the benefit of the doubt and believe when she went to your parents' house that morning she only wanted to talk your father into hiring Jack back. We'll never know how their confrontation escalated unless she tells us, but at some point, it resulted in your father waving a gun he wasn't willing to use, which is always a mistake, especially if whoever you're waving it at is willing to use theirs.

"Do you think it was because your mother started screaming that Kimberly shot her first? Or did she hate her that much because she saw her as what she might become if she stayed living in this town as your wife, a woman who, as you put it, yearned for nothing more than she already had? I suppose your father was an easier target. After all, she put the second bullet through his eye when she thought the first might not finish him. Then, she ran to tell Jack, thinking maybe he'd understand. He wrestled the gun from her, but not before taking two more of its bullets. I imagine she ran then, and he took off after her. Poor Jack. He barely made it around the corner before he was spotted by the police.

"I don't care, Tommy, what you choose to believe about what went down that morning, but the fact is there was one bullet left in that gun when Jack won that struggle for it in that bedroom in the house on Willow. And he chose not to use it on the person who had just pumped two bullets into him, but instead, used it on himself at the end of that police pursuit. Why would a cocky young man like Jack do such a thing? Because he simply couldn't turn that gun on the girl he'd wrestled it from. And as my wife happened to explain to me three days ago when I first brought the subject up to her, he knew that by putting that bullet into his head on that rural road up at Loon Lake, he could close out the whole mess, and in doing so, protect the one who used that gun on your parents. I count three people in this world for whom he might do that, with Christine Hughes the least likely, with or without her alibi. And of the other two . . . well, it wasn't Mrs. Mackay who talked you into meeting Baumgarten in that salvage yard Friday night."

Kubiak waited for another protest from Round Lake Beach's only surviving Wheeler. Tommy's face had gone white; his lips were pressed bloodless. Kubiak leaned in closer.

"I don't know if you went there meaning to kill him. If you had, you might have brought a weapon more efficient than that hammer. It must have been bloody work, but at least you and Kimberly didn't have to worry about leaving stains in your Civic when you pulled out of there. All you had to do was scrub them pale the next morning and who could distinguish them from Jack's blood? That is, until now. You see, now that I've brought up the possibility, Lake County will have no choice but to do a DNA test on the bloodstains in your car. If there was even one drop of Baumgarten's blood on your pants or the soles of your shoe . . .

"It's finally starting to sink in, isn't it, Tommy? But there's no need to lose any more sleep over it tonight. After all, considering there's a moratorium on the death penalty in this state at the moment, it's likely you'll have every day of the rest of your life to mull over the fact that the only reason you'll never walk free again is because you conspired to cover up the murder of your own parents by killing the one man determined to find out what really happened that morning."

Tommy was not looking at Kubiak, but was staring at the back of Kimberly Mackay's head. Kubiak couldn't blame her for not turning around, as any look she might shoot at Tommy could have been interpreted as an indication of her involvement. And her cold indifference just might have successfully carried her out of that room had not Osgood, at that moment, chosen to lean into his clients, put his arm around them both, and whisper something only they could hear.

A low sound came out of Tommy's throat, a barely perceivable utterance somewhere between a moan and a growl. Then, he was out of his chair and flying forward at the back of his girlfriend's neck.

With two officers flanking him, he didn't even make it over the table at which he was seated, and his face came down flat upon it with a grisly crunch.

Chapter Twenty-five

"Do you think they broke his nose?" Denise asked.

"I don't have a clue."

The counter at which they were sitting was surprisingly crowded for this time of morning. Outside a good half of the cars on the road were still running with lit headlights. The headlights of Maria's car, Hollinger at the wheel, had been behind the Contour since Round Lake Beach. When Kubiak, still hungry, had decided to pull into the diner he had visited Sunday night after being held by Strom, Hollinger continued south, onto the expressway, with a honk and a wave.

Strom had spent nearly an hour alone with Hollinger after the police had picked him up. Denise imagined apologies from the detective. Kubiak knew better.

The counter girl recognized Kubiak. She asked him if he wanted his burger the same way, apologized for the diner's not offering beer at this hour, and made it plain she would have lingered longer if Denise had not been present.

"I've been to a hundred counters in my day, Kubiak," Denise said when the girl moved on. "I can't think of one where the man behind it remembered what temperature I liked my burger."

"Maybe if you ever considered ordering a burger."

She had ordered only toast. But then, she had already spent the first half of her night in Denny's.

"I still can't help but feel sorry for Tommy," she said. "His parents murdered by the girl he loved enough to kill for. He lost everything tonight, even his right to indignation over their deaths."

"Before your heart breaks, close your eyes and picture him caving in Baumgarten's skull with a claw hammer. I'll save my pity for Jack Mackay. Putting that bullet in his head to save his sister was the one honorable thing he did in his life, and I nixed that tonight."

"Well, you did it with your usual flourish. Have you ever considered putting away someone for murder without an audience?"

"You and Crawford seem to think I actually enjoy this sort of thing. I don't, not one bit, but I had no choice. Strom was willing to give me nothing. Kimberly was all set to run, so I had to finish it tonight, and I never would have gotten her into that police station alone. By my insisting Strom gather them all, she couldn't be sure I suspected her of anything. Besides, I had nothing concrete on her. I was counting on breaking Tommy down, and if I had done so without witnesses he might have been able to rationalize his girlfriend's murdering his parents before I could drag him in to make a statement. As it is, I'm not sure a jury will ever convict Kimberly in the Wheeler homicide. We'd all prefer to shrug it off as the work of a type like Jack Mackay. Jack, himself, certainly must have known that much at that moment he took his own life."

"So, the whole thing was more of a gamble than you let on."

"Yes, but it was all I could come up with on such short notice. By the way, you're usually a little more vocal during my performances. I don't remember you saying a word."

"With David's fate in the balance, I thought it better I didn't make any wisecracks."

Kubiak used his straw to poke at the ice in his Coke. The counter girl refilled Denise's coffee, shot Kubiak a grin, disappeared again.

"You mentioned," Denise said, "something Kimberly said to you when you were in her bedroom."

"About Baumgarten's getting creepy? He wasn't."

"I was more curious about what, exactly, you were doing in her bedroom."

"Oh, that. She's a little young and dangerous for my taste, don't you think? It was perfectly innocent. I only followed her in there because I was afraid her mother might try to kiss me again in the kitchen."

"Oh, well, why didn't you say so?"

Denise stirred her coffee.

"That isn't what you wanted to ask me."

She stirred and stirred.

"No," she finally responded. "What you said about the futility of trying to kill love . . ."

"I actually thought that part was pretty good."

"What if David had been more involved in this than he claimed, and your investigating into the matter had uncovered evidence that proved him guilty?"

"Of Baumgarten's murder?"

"Of anything that might have . . ."

"Put him away?"

"Exactly."

"I would, of course, have had no choice but to turn him in."

"Regardless of who Maria chose to side with?"

"Absolutely."

"You don't think she'd . . ."

"Our Maria? No, not for a minute. Though, it might have made for some pretty stressful holidays over the next year or so."

Denise only stared into her coffee, not believing a word he said.

"As it turns out," he continued, "the only tragic outcome of all this, as far as our family is concerned, is that we never celebrated our daughter's birthday."

"Well, we did have this morning at the museum. It wasn't the jolliest party, but I am sorry you missed it."

"I don't suppose you'd want to go back tomorrow. Today, I mean. We could have a real outing, do it up right, however you do a museum up right."

"Sorry, Kubiak. I don't think any of us are up to it quite yet."

"There's always the zoo. It was my original choice. Then, again, Labor Day is coming up in a week or so. Maybe we could spend the weekend in the country. Granted, people tend to do things like breakfast at diner counters and commit murder awfully early up here, but I've heard you haven't lived until you've slept the night with cicadas screaming in your ear, or stood on your front porch in the morning and smelled your neighbors' chimneys. I'll even spring for another pounded fish."

"I think not."

"Well," he asked, after a moment. "Is there anything in particular you'd rather do, then?"

"I'd prefer just to go home."

Home. Kubiak signaled the friendly counter girl and asked that their food be bagged up to go.